But First Maintain the Wall

Emma Batten

Happy reading Emma x

First published in Great Britain by Emma Batten

ISBN 978 1 9995820 0 5

Printed and bound in the UK

A catalogue record of this book can be found in the British library

Edited by Maud Matley & Steve Clifford

Proof read by Rosemary Bartholomew

Cover design by Andjela K

Cover photo by Tony Riddeck

www.emmabattenauthor.com

This book has been inspired by the slogan of Romney Marsh as penned by Russell Thorndyke and used in his series of *Dr Syn* novels:

"Serve God, Honour the King: But First Maintain the Wall."

To my friend, Maud Matley, with love and thanks for your never-ending enthusiasm and support for my journey as an author.

Forward

This novel takes the reader back to 1758 and the village of Dymchurch on Romney Marsh. A place huddled in the shadow of an ancient seawall, protecting both the village and low-lying countryside.

Descriptions of the village and local area are as accurate as possible and many of the properties can be seen today. All characters and events are entirely from the author's imagination.

Information on the maintenance of the seawall and Dymchurch in the 18th century comes from the following resources:

The Dymchurch Heritage Group and their heritage trail

Romney Marsh, Survival on a Frontier by Jill Eddison

www.theromneymarsh.net

With special thanks to Maud Matley for all her help with the scenes set in France and to Peter Brown for his advice on the sailing scene. Thank you to Steve Clifford for his proof reading, advice and interest in my writing. Also thanks to Chris Dann for additional proof reading.

Chapter One
1758

The first he knew of them was the rhythmic drumming of hooves and the pulse which vibrated through the hard clay soil. In those few seconds before they cantered past him, he became aware that it was now fully dark; he must have been sleeping for some time. And, where was he? Of course, he'd been walking since before dawn and had reached the sea... the sea, and that huge expanse of a wall.

It was as he raised his head just a little, to get a sense of where the noise was coming from, that it happened. *Thwack!* A hoof clipped him just above his left ear. Pain seared through his skull and deep within his head before, thankfully, his world descended into darkness.

The hours passed and, despite the thick woollen cape wrapped tight around the young man's slight frame, his body began to chill. If he had been conscious he would have heard the slap of the high tide on the seawall. If he had been aware of the world around him he may have noted the wind had picked up its pace, pressing on the bent willows and hawthorns, and causing the sheep to huddle together for shelter.

Perhaps it was the thunderous roar that woke him as it alerted all of Dymchurch to the danger ahead. Or perhaps his brain had rested enough and his youthful body was not yet ready to succumb to death. He wasn't aware of that almighty rumble, but for whatever reason he stirred and gradually pulled himself up until he sat in the foetal position. With his back arched, arms wrapped around his legs and his head resting on his knees, all he knew was the searing, pain pulsating in his head. Death would have been kinder. It would have been less painful.

Time passed as he sat hunched in his own private pain, trying to form his thoughts into some order. He recalled leaving the place known as home... it had been early, before dawn. Walking all day. Towards the coast... yes, that was it... nearing the coast... seeing it from the cliff tops then walking into the town of Hythe. But Hythe was too close, he had to keep moving. He remembered that much. But where was he now? He had no idea, nor the strength to stand and look about him. And why did his head hurt as if he had been kicked by the devil himself?

Slipping in and out of consciousness, he was aware only of the all-consuming throb, throb, throb on the left side of his head. When he next opened his eyes, an hour had passed and two things had changed: the sky to the east was lightening and where the land had been dry there was now water lapping against his feet.

It was this new development which forced him to think beyond the pain in his head. He believed himself to be sheltering beneath a stunted tree, yet, he dipped his finger in the water and tasted it, – salt-water rippled at his feet. Had he still been lying unconscious, and the water level had risen further, he would have drowned. Clearly the Lord intended him to live.

Easing himself to his feet, with one hand on a

branch of the tree and the other supporting his head, he stood while the world spun around him. Before he'd had time to look about, or even step clear of the puddle, nausea overcame him. He vomited so that now seawater and the contents of his own stomach moved at his feet.

"Damn," he muttered. "By God, what's happening to me?"

He was in no fit state to answer his own question, yet he acknowledged that he felt a little better for all that his shoes were now doubly spoilt. Lifting his damaged head, he saw he was standing at the edge of a grass field and great pools of water covered half the land. They rippled in the brisk wind, making waves that shone as the moon revealed itself from behind clouds which raced across the sky.

There was nothing for him here, no-one to help and no track to walk along. Some reason had brought him to this place before nightfall and at some point he had been badly injured. Standing with his feet in salt-water and vomit was not going to bring back his memory and he sensed that there was a road towards the east, where the sun was about to rise over that long bank or wall. So, just one step at a time; that would do it, no need to think beyond the moment. One step at a time would take him to the road.

How strange that the land was sodden and as he reached a sturdy bridge, four planks wide, he wondered what had led him to cross it the evening before. Grey water reached the very brim of the ditch and licked at the planks. It pressed upon ragged plants and the scrawny heads of last summer's reeds. Its swirling movement caused nausea to rise in his throat as all the world whirled with the water. He clung to the wooden railing – thank God there was something to hold onto. Slowly, he crept onwards until the bridge had been crossed.

People! There were people swarming up the vast bank. They moved backwards and forwards as if they were labouring at something. They were grey, without features, in this pre-dawn world. What was it that brought the men from their beds at this early hour? He started to move slowly... still slowly... towards them. Now all his focus was on these people and, as he neared them, he wasn't aware that a cart approached on the road behind him.

"Get out of the way you fool!" a voice bellowed.

But the clay-mud was slippery and although he lurched to the left, towards the bank, it wasn't enough. The cart eased to a halt, clipping him lightly on his hip and sending him reeling to the ground.

The man who pulled him up wasn't tall but was stocky with bulging muscles. His chest was broad and his neck thickset, with not a trace of fat on him. His hair was a pale orange-brown, thick and wavy on his head and through his sideburns. Wiry, orange hairs sprouted from his ears, nose and limbs. He stood like a bulldog about to attack and barked: "This is no time for foolery. We are up against the tide worse than ever today – there's been enough acres flooded. What do you have to say for yourself?"

"I..."

What *did* he have to say for himself?

But the bulldog was not done with the stranger. "Blazes, a harder man than me would have left you to wallow in the mud for the next cart to roll over, for I doubt you were worth saving." With his piece said, the huge man pushed back his long, matted hair with clay-covered hands and spat at the ground.

"By God, I did nothing wrong."

The young man found the spirit he had lacked since being clipped in the head by the horse.

"And so now you take our Lord's name in vain." And with this, the massive hand clouted the slender figure across the back of his head.

For the second time that night, the world descended into darkness as he slumped onto the ground.

When he next opened his eyes, the sun was glancing over the seawall, casting soft rays across the land. Too much light, he lowered his lashes a little. His head still pounded like hell from the earlier injury. Perhaps if he lay on the ground for a few minutes and played dead he could work out what was going on.

He was at the base of a steep slope – the seawall presumably. The immediate area looked like a battle ground, the earth churned up by recent activity. It wasn't raining but the ground was wet with tufts of rough grass and weeds that had been thoroughly trampled over. The land was strewn with broken twigs and lumps of clay and, if he opened his eyes a little more, there was a donkey pulling a shallow cart away from the scene. And, there were men, swarms of men, labouring like worker ants – carrying bundles, working at something, calling out orders and encouragement.

"High tide an hour before noon," someone shouted. "By God, we're going to make it; we're going to win this battle!"

A huge cheer filled the air. But they didn't stop working, not for a minute. Labouring in teams of five or six, they were gathering branches, tying them into bundles and passing them on to the next team. A section of the bank was open, exposing its structure like an animal with its flesh stripped off by hawks. He

11

lay on the edge of it all, ignored by these workers, yet they must have been aware of him being there.

"There's more carts on the way." The voice belonged to a man standing close to him. He was cutting ragged branches into manageable lengths. "Coming from Burmarsh way."

"That should do us for today," replied another voice, as someone stepped over his prone body.

Through his eyelashes he saw the outline of a man and holding a bundle of thin pieces of string or some form of material. One of the lengths fell and slapped the side of his face, causing him to flinch.

"So you're not dead then." A foot nudged at the young man's shoulder. He opened his eyes a little and waited for the next kick or thump, but this was not the thug who had felled him to the ground. No, this was an older man of slighter build, who bent to kneel beside him. His skin was caked in clay-mud and his greying shoulder-length hair adorned with small clumps of mud that clung on and swung like beads as he moved. His working clothes were filthy, showing that he was no shirker when it came to labouring on the seawall. "Bailey's gone for now; you can stop playing dead." As the stranger spoke he smiled a little, skin creasing in his clean-shaven face. His eyes were a clear blue and showed no malice.

"I don't know what game you were up to earlier, but I suppose you were here to work," the man spoke sternly but not unkindly. "So, get yourself up and just keep your head down. I imagine you've got a damned awful headache from Bailey's fist, but there's nothing to be done about it and we'll be finished here before the sun moves to the west."

"I… I don't know what..."

"I don't want to hear about it now, I've got to hand

out these leathers and then start on the faggots. I'll leave you with John here; he won't cause you bother." He turned to a nearby labourer. "John, keep an eye on this fellow here, will you?" Then back to the newcomer: "What's your name, lad?"

"Harry... it's Harry."

"Well, Harry, there's some hawthorn just come in on the last cart, you stay here with John and bind up these faggots while I pass on the leather." A pile of leather was thrust into Harry's hand and he strode off.

"I'll hold 'em and you tie 'em," ordered John, as he offered a bundle of eight to twelve branches which had already been tied once at the top. "Tie in the middle and then at the bottom. It's not hard – till your hands get sore from the wet and once they start bleeding it's hell – but you'll be all right for a while."

Harry fumbled over the laces. It wasn't difficult, tying a knot, he knew that. He'd been doing it since he was small. The twigs punctured his hands and the leather made his fingertips sore, but that didn't bother him. It was a simple action of placing one end over the other... and what was it that came next? Time after time he faltered, his brain seeming to be unable to grasp this simple task.

Not wanting another punch around the head Harry pulled the leather tight, tied a double knot and then started again. Three ties on each bundle, or faggot as they seemed to be called, then John put them on the ground and a young lad of perhaps eight or ten took them to another group of men.

Once he had mastered the task Harry was able to take a look at his surroundings, dominated by the great bank, or wall, on which the men worked. He could see now that it had been broken down, or breached as the men said, by the sea. It was perhaps

13

twenty feet high, taller than his cottage back home... back in Elham. Solid too – you could take a horse and cart on top of it and probably pass one going the other way. Its framework, which had been exposed by the force of the sea, was almost repaired but still lay open for all to see the upright stakes and bundle after bundle of faggots rammed between them.

Turning to look at the countryside, Harry was puzzled by its flatness. He was used to the rolling hills, neat fields and clusters of woodland that was the Elham Valley. But he had left all that behind and walked to the coast and here were the levels of Romney Marsh: irregular fields, stunted trees, ribbons of reed-lined ditches and water.

The pools of water had come from the sea of course. This land had been drained for centuries and was no longer marshland. In places the salt-water covered half a field and the sheep huddled on the islands that were left. Gulls were swooping and gliding gleefully above pools; dipping into them, then riding on the surface. The sun, rising in the sky to the east, caused the pools to sparkle and dazzle Harry's eyes that were already tender from the headache.

So, this was Romney Marsh... full of demons and witches if legend was to be believed... a place of low-lying mists, riddled with watercourses and plagued by killer mosquitoes. A place to pass through as quickly as possible. He wouldn't be staying here; he'd be gone before the day was out.

"You from around here, lad?" asked the man who had first spoken to him. Harry had heard him called Owen.

"Er, no. Elham, I came from Elham." Harry found his voice for the first time in the last hour. Before he had got by with a nod or grunt.

14

"Looking for work are you, or visiting?"

"Going to see someone... family. Not here, somewhere else," Harry lied.

"Well, you've done your bit on the wall today, even if you aren't from hereabouts." Owen passed Harry more laces and together they tied the branches as John held them.

Another five... ten... fifteen faggots tied and thankfully the wood had run out. The desperation to work tirelessly was easing. Men were constantly climbing the wall and reporting on the height of the incoming sea. The mood was good; the workmen exhausted but hopeful that another tide of water would not be deposited over the Marsh. News had come from elsewhere – the second breach had been filled and the men had let out a roar of a cheer.

"This way, lad. We'll help pack the last bit of clay in." Owen pointed to a great pile of mud and Harry followed his lead.

Together they took handfuls of cool, slippery clay-mud from a flat cart and packed it into gaps, covering all the faggots until none of the wood could be seen. The clay felt good on his raw hands and Harry liked the sensation of pushing it into place. As the last of it was pushed into the bank, one of the lookouts shouted from on top of the wall: "It's turned, the tide has turned!"

There was a roar of approval from the clay-caked workers, followed by back slapping and hand shaking. Despite his aching body and confusion, Harry felt good to be part of this great achievement, to be part of the team that had filled the breach in the great seawall and saved Dymchurch from the incoming tide.

Chapter Two
Phoebe

In the early hours of the morning, the young woman's breathing was deep and regular; her sleep was dreamless. Lying hunched on one side, her body was in the habit of moulding itself around the lumps in the thin mattress; she held the rough sheet and threadbare blanket tight around her.

Her bedroom was at the back of the cottage and so she only heard the rhythm of the tide when it was at its roughest, slamming against the wall and dragging its load of debris and shingle back with it. That night, high tide came when Phoebe's sleep was deep and she had no awareness of the wind gathering force or the waves swelling and throwing themselves at the wall of hawthorn and clay-mud.

The cottage in which she slept was built below sea-level, but Phoebe thought nothing of its being vulnerable to the might of the sea. They were sturdy cottages, those which lined the road through the village. As for the seawall, it had stood there for centuries, solid and impregnable. Impregnable? Well, almost. It had given way in the past, Phoebe knew that, but not in her lifetime.

'*Thank you, Lord, for the wall.*' It was a part of their prayers and the people of Dymchurch trusted He would take care of it. God and the team of men who maintained it six days a week.

So, as the night reached its darkest hour, Phoebe slept soundly. As the spring tide reached new heights, it slapped upon fine cracks which had opened up in the wall during the previous winter's frosts. Easing its way into the core of the structure, it licked upon hawthorn faggots which had lain dry and dormant for decades. As the wood flexed, the salt-water took its chance to penetrate further and deeper into the seawall.

It was as if the wall had its own ancient form of flexing, creaking, groaning communication that travelled along its length. And so it was that as the water entered two areas, at least a mile apart, the message was sent and the agreement made that those places would give up the fight at the very same moment.

Did Phoebe stir? Did she feel the vibration which shook the village as parts of the wall quivered and fell? Clay-clad banks opened up from within, exposing the centuries-old framework of stakes and faggots, and a low rumble echoed throughout the vulnerable village.

Phoebe slept on, unaware that the invading tide took with it broken twigs and as much clay as its waters could carry as it sought to reclaim its right to the former salt marsh. Leaving its spoils across the coast road in the Willop Wall area and in the cottage gardens of the Church Knocke region of the village, the sea flowed through the breaches. Again and again it surged, until the moon dictated its retreat.

"Get up, girl! Don't you go thinking that you can get a full night's sleep, not while the men are out to save the village."

Phoebe's head spun as the words were spat into

her ear and her bed cover was wrenched from her slim body.

"The village?" she repeated, groping for the security of her blanket and pushing wisps of her long, dark hair away from her eyes.

"Did you not hear? Are you deaf as well as born lazy?" Now a great chubby ham of a hand tugged at the young woman's shoulder. "The bleeding wall has breached! They've all gone, those who can, to do their part in saving the village."

Phoebe swung her legs out of the narrow bed and, reaching for her shawl, she repeated, "The wall has breached?"

"That's what I said, didn't I? And your uncle, God bless him, is out there working alongside the others."

"The wall has collapsed?" The wall, the seawall – so wide, so thick, seen from every point in the village and stretching a full three miles? In her mind, Phoebe saw it crumble and the tide pouring over and through it. What hope was there of saving Dymchurch? "All of it?"

"You're as dumb as those chickens what peck around in the yard. All of it? What d'you think them wall-workers do all day if it's not trying to keep us safe? It's broken through in a couple of places, but the sea will soon take hold if repairs aren't made."

In the darkness of the room, Phoebe could barely see the shape of Aunt Peggy. But she knew she stood there, her hands on wide hips, bulbous lips pouting and eyes protruding as she looked upon Phoebe with distaste.

"It's broken through in two places?" Understanding dawned on the young woman who had been forced from her sleep.

"I suppose you think you've reason enough to turn

your back on it, leave the men to their work and go back to sleep? I'll have none of that!" A finger came through the darkness and jabbed at its target.

"What shall I do?" Phoebe's brow furrowed as she tried to grasp what was needed of her. Did Aunt Peggy want her to work out there, amidst the salt-water and stricken wall? What help could she be compared to those men who laboured on the land all day or made the maintenance of the wall their livelihood? But if Uncle Giles had gone – and he was as spindly as a branch of thorny hawthorn – surely Peggy with her stout legs and muscular arms would fare better out there in a night such as this? Phoebe tried not to grin as she imagined her aunt up to her petticoats in seawater and shoving handfuls of clay-mud into the broken wall.

"What are you to do?" A snort of a laugh erupted from Peggy. "Why, you're to wait for your uncle to return with the kettle on the boil and a nice bit of bacon ready to fry in the pan for him."

Phoebe stood, waiting for Peggy to move aside. Only a part of the room was her own space, with its bed and chest of drawers filling one length of the room. The area beneath the small window and all around the fireplace was stacked with crates of supplies for the village shop, which was owned by her Uncle Giles and in which Phoebe laboured long thankless hours. In her daydreams, she aspired to having the room to herself: a comfy chair or a small writing desk beneath the window and a fire in the grate. There had never been a fire lit in the room, not in all the years that Phoebe had begrudgingly been given a portion of it as her own.

Peggy turned her bulk towards the doorway and waddled out to the landing, then looking back she gave her final orders: "An' get that copper nice and hot too. He'll come in good and mucky. Saturday or not, I want them clothes on the line by morning and you can't say anyone will think the less of me for keeping my man clean and respectable."

Walking across the bare floorboards to the top of the stairs, Phoebe placed her hand on the banister and turned to Peggy. "I'll do that and pray the wall is soon repaired."

"There will be no soon about it, girl, but when the repairs are done good and proper your uncle will have you waiting for him." Peggy turned towards her own bedroom at the front of the cottage and before Phoebe had reached the base of the stairs she heard the groan of the bed as her aunt returned to her slumber.

The hallway was nothing more than a small space between the shop at the front of the cottage and the kitchen at the rear. Stepping into the kitchen, Phoebe saw that the remains of last night's fire still smoked. She took a handful of kindling wood and some scraps of paper then knelt before the hearth. Having pushed aside the fire-guard, Phoebe placed the paper and wood-sticks on top of the embers. She then stood and reached for a twisted paper spill from a jug above the fireplace and held it against a lit tallow candle until a flame took hold. Kneeling again, she carefully inserted the spill amongst the fuel, pausing a moment for it to catch light.

As the light strengthened, Phoebe heaved the kettle onto a hook above the fire and, leaving it to warm, she trudged towards the scullery. There was no fire set below the copper but a basket of kindling wood was at hand. Holding her shawl tight about her chest with one hand, Phoebe bent to move the kindling from the basket and stacked it in place under the copper pan. Taking another spill from the kitchen, she lit it from the candle and held it against the kindling wood until the flames claimed it.

It was cold and damp enough in the scullery, but water had to be drawn from the well. There was only a bucketful in the copper and her aunt wouldn't thank her for heating that small amount. As she opened the back door, Phoebe's heart slumped; the wind was brisk and rich with the smells of the sea. The pump was shared by three neighbouring shops and Phoebe slipped into the yard behind the draper's in order to use it. Pressing down on the handle with both hands, she soon had the water flowing and, with the bucket nearly full, staggered back to the scullery.

The journey was repeated four more times before the copper was full enough to satisfy Aunt Peggy. By then the kindling was all aglow and the fire had taken hold of the logs placed beneath the copper pan. Returning to the warmth of the kitchen, Phoebe moved the kettle partly away from the heat. It was about to boil, and who knew when her uncle would return?

What was it like out there on this blustery night? Did the sea flow over or through the wall which had seemed so indestructible for all the years that Phoebe could remember? And did it trickle through and allow its wavelets to curl around the edges of cottages and ease their way under doors? Or did it surge, carrying a load of sand and shingle to abandon on the paths and in sweeping ridges against the gravestones?

Phoebe couldn't see it in her mind's eye or imagine how the Dymchurch men could compete with the strength of the sea. Would they notice? Would they have time to give attention to a small figure well wrapped up against the chill March winds? No,

Phoebe was sure... fairly certain that she would go unnoticed if she were to venture out into the night.

Still in her nightdress, Phoebe pulled a thicker shawl from a hook by the kitchen door and wrapped it tight around her shoulders. She walked through the scullery, pausing to check on the fire, and out into the back yard. The night-sky was thick with clouds racing over the face of the full moon. The south-easterly wind was coming straight off the sea laden with the scents of seaweed and salt. It tugged at the door to the chicken coop and whistled through the old sow's wooden plank home.

Phoebe could walk from one yard to another behind the rows of shops and homes fronting Dymchurch High Street. Picking her way past pieces of old sacking, piles of logs, a discarded broom and a broken shovel, the young woman passed by the back of the low terrace named Dormers before slipping through an alley leading to the street.

The High Street was empty; there was no sign of the rampaging sea. Phoebe hadn't realised that her stomach had been clenched until she felt the wave of relief sweep through her body. It wasn't that bad then – the village had not been enveloped by the incoming tide. But Peggy had said it was at Church Knocke the wall had broken down in some way that she couldn't picture, so Phoebe turned to the east and, keeping snug against the walls of the buildings, set off towards the church.

She walked alone in the night-time world, the thin cotton nightdress billowing around her ankles, stout boots kicking at the pieces of stray thatch. There were loose stones on the road and the occasional branch which had broken free while the wind whipped through Dymchurch. The tide must still be high, Phoebe reflected – the rush and release of sand and shingle-laden water filled the air with a low rhythmic roar. The village at midnight, or whatever hour it was, was alive with the sounds of nature.

Although Phoebe believed herself to be alert to the signs that men were on the road, when she did finally become aware of people nearby, they were almost upon her. Darting to a safe hide and slipping down the side of Well Cottage, Phoebe pressed herself between a tree and the low boundary wall.

"Come on, girl, get them legs moving." The voice was a low drawl and laced with affection. "Come on, lass, they've a need for this hawthorn along at the wall."

An elderly donkey and hunched-up old Marsh-man passed by. Their pace was slow and the cart small, yet they had left their beds to be a part of saving the village.

Then, as Phoebe was about to continue along the road, she heard the wheels of a faster-moving cart as they crunched upon the road. Two men led the sturdy farm-horse and their cart was three times the size of that pulled by the humble donkey.

"Hey, Moses, we'll need that hawthorn before dawn!"

"Aye, and you'll get it soon enough."

"Still got the old girl then? Thought you'd have eaten donkey pie many a year back!"

"Lucky she's deaf or you'd get a kick; she's still got her spirit," the old man replied.

"Good for her and you too, Moses. We'll see you along at Church Knocke."

"You will, she knows her way now, does my old donkey. This is our second trip tonight."

"You're doing Dymchurch proud, you and the old

nag." And with that the second cart was out of sight, leaving Moses and his donkey to trudge on alone.

Phoebe slipped from her hide and darted across the road, then flitted from the shelter of one cottage or store to the next before she reached the foot of the seawall. Here she was looking up to the poorhouse and its adjoining schoolroom, which were built on the seawall itself.

She was lucky not to be living `in the poorhouse. Lucky to have been taken in by her aunt and uncle. That's what they'd told her when she scrubbed their floors, served in the shop and brought in the logs. She had better than she deserved, so they said. How could that be true? Phoebe was even-tempered, in good health and her mind was lively. How could she deserve less than the bed in the corner of a store room and a life of being no better than a serving wench seven days a week? The maids at the New Hall were treated better; she knew they were.

Her pa was a foreigner and worse than that – French. Her ma should have known better and had died in disgrace. To trade with the Frenchies was all good and proper and to do so was to follow the ways of decent law-abiding Marsh folk. But they should stay in their place: them on their side of the channel and us on ours, excepting for when there was trading to be done. Phoebe couldn't be sure of what had happened to her pa. Memories remained of him swinging her high, of his laugh and the gentle songs they shared as she sat upon his knee.

Climbing the bank beside the poorhouse, Phoebe crouched on the summit of the wall and looked to and fro along its length. To the east, there appeared to be some movement and, as the clouds passed by the face of the moon, at least a score of men could be seen working away on the bank of the wall. This was the area of the breach; she was sure of it. The sea had by no means calmed, but the moon had done her duty and pulled it back from the wall for the time being.

Moving back down the slope a little Phoebe crept, in a crab-like scamper, towards the Church Knocke area of the seawall. As she neared the workmen, it was clear that the wall had lost its usual arced form; part of it slumped and had spilled out its innards. The moonlight was strong at that moment and slick clay shone in the silvery light. Water gathered in shallow puddles and streamlets made their way from the wall, taking the easiest path between the cottages and towards the road.

A tenacious little bush clung to the slope of the seaward some thirty yards from the damaged wall and for Phoebe it made a good hide. Hitching her nightdress up to her knees she crouched behind the bush and watched the cycle of work.

First the carts arriving and the hawthorn being pulled off them, then those twisted, thorny branches cut into manageable lengths. Then groups of two or three men pressing the springy branches into bundles and finally, as they were tied with laces, the hawthorn surrendering to the control of the men. Next the hawthorn bundles were crammed between upright stakes that formed the skeleton within the wall. The movement of hawthorn between the men was done without much debate. It was as if this well-ordered system had been planned at the bars of The Ship and The Ocean and everyone knew, in the event of a breach, exactly what their task was.

As more carts arrived, Phoebe shifted her position, suddenly aware of the chill in the air. As she stood, she was exposed to the brisk wind which swept in from the sea. It was time to return to the comfort of the kitchen and to ensure that all Peggy's orders had been completed before Giles returned, exhausted, filthy, but no doubt triumphant, from the part he played in repairing the wall.

The fire under the copper was weak, but a couple of fresh logs would be enough to heat the water and the fire could be relit when her uncle returned. Plunging her hands into a bucket of cold water, Phoebe washed the remains of the seawall mud from her fingers. Then, having kicked off her boots, she entered the kitchen and checked on the kettle. It simmered on the range; her aunt could find no fault in that. Abandoning her shawl as she walked across the kitchen, Phoebe slumped into a comfy chair. Her body relaxed and soon she was fast asleep in the comfort of the chair, with a rug across her body and the warmth from the range a welcome consolation for having been taken from her bed.

Chapter Three
Harry

Harry gave a nod, unable to voice his thanks as the young woman offered the pie. When had he last eaten? Not since sunrise, he was sure of that, so it must have been at some point the day before. No wonder his belly felt so hollow and his thoughts couldn't quite get themselves in any order. He had been thinking of moving on; he'd given enough of his time to these people and this wall that had nothing to do with him. But if there was food on offer he'd spend a little longer working alongside Owen and John.

But for all that Harry's body needed the nourishment, the pie was rich with meat and nausea came in waves through his body. He took a sip of the ale, hoping to calm himself. His skin was covered in a light film of sweat and his head pounded from the clout it had suffered the night before. Harry picked at the pie, while the others crammed theirs into their mouths, with no thought to the amount of mud they consumed with it.

"Not got an appetite, lad?" Owen was wiping his mouth, the pie gone.

"No, I mean I'm hungry... I'm in need of it, but..." Harry turned and staggered a few steps away from Owen and John before expelling the weak ale and pie. He stood for a moment, looking down at the foul mixture, recalling the earlier sickness when it had swum with the seawater at his feet.

"He's not right," John was saying when Harry returned and slumped beside them. "Bailey hit him harder than we thought."

"I don't know if it's more than that...," Owen replied. "He's not got much to say for himself but for all that he looks like a decent young lad." He turned to Harry. "Where were you bound for? I doubt you're fit to walk beyond Dymchurch, not since you had Bailey's fist at your head."

"Sussex, I was going to Sussex," Harry forced the words out. "I'll bed down in a barn tonight and feel better in the morning."

They sat in silence for a moment, before Owen spoke again: "It looks like you have no place to go, so if you'd care to come back for a wash and a bowl of pottage with me and my wife, you'd be welcome."

"Thank you, I would... thank you." Harry imagined a fire to warm himself by and the opportunity to rest his throbbing head. Perhaps his clothes could have a bit of a clean-up and the pottage would be gentle on his stomach.

"We'll be getting back then." Owen stood and watched as Harry forced himself to stand at full height. "You're not right, lad, I can see that, but you'll be safe with me and Bess. You need folk keeping an eye on you."

Harry smiled weakly and willed himself to walk just one step after the other, past the mud-clad strangers to a place where he could rest. A step or two in front, Owen stood about the same height as Harry's own five feet nine inches. The older man's build was slight, his back bowed a little from years of work. Pushing his hand through his own mid-brown hair, Harry realised that it was just as clay-encrusted as Owen's grey locks.

The track to Dymchurch village hugged the base of the wall. It was slippery, all trace of grass and weeds having been scoured from it after a day of heavy boots walking constantly upon it. Owen was forced to slow his pace, which suited Harry, who felt unable to stride out in his usual manner.

"I usually take this little path; I like it snug under the wall and out of the wind, but I've had enough of sliding about so we'll cut across this bit of land and onto the other track." Owen nodded towards a wide track running just a field's breadth from the wall. "We'll be back at the cottage in no time and perhaps in the morning you'll be able to make your way into Sussex, or wherever you need to go."

They walked towards a fine, two-storey building of regular proportions under a red tiled roof. Cottages and barns clustered around it and, as they walked closer, Harry screwed up his eyes and forced his brain to read the battered tavern sign which swung in the breeze, causing trouble for his befuddled mind. 'The Ship' – well, that seemed fitting enough for a place such as Dymchurch with the sea making its presence known beyond the wall.

What was that swinging in the distance? Of course, the rope of the village gallows, thankfully free of a body. The wooden frame stood on a patch of land, with the church to its right and a sprawling red brick and tile house to its left. The church was tiny, with a slender square tower – Dymchurch couldn't be much of a place, if that was its place of worship. Not that it mattered to Harry; this wasn't the place for him – too close.

They left the triangle of church, tavern and house,

with the gallows as its centre point. The track continued, but now houses and cottages lined it, set in no particular order and varying in size. There were a few beautiful red brick buildings on the seawall side of the road. One had orange-red tiles hung on the walls. This house and its neighbours were big and solid, homes of the local gentry no doubt. Did they sit before their fires in their wigs and beribboned clothes while the likes of Owen and John kept them safe from the sea?

In contrast, just opposite, were the more humble cottages – some clad in wooden planks, others of rubble and mud. Most of them were single storey, their roofs thatched with reeds. Extensions were added wherever it suited and their small plots of land were home to chickens, a pig and sometimes a small pony.

It was from these poorer dwellings that people waved and called out to Owen.

"It's done then. The wall's been fixed."

"We'll sleep safe in our beds tonight."

"That was a mighty roar when she broke through!"

Owen smiled and gave a word or two in return, but the two of them kept walking. Harry could do that – put one foot in front of another in a steady rhythm. But, if he had to dodge a cart or slow down while Owen spoke to someone, then he lost his balance and the nausea threatened.

Now the village changed form again as cottages joined to become stone terraces, with shops in their midst. High on the wall was a ramshackle tavern and, just beneath the slope of the wall, low cottages crouched. Who would want to live here, on top of the road which ran alongside the wall or hunkered down within its shadows? Harry had seen how the sea could break through and imagined the damage that would be done if the breach were here, in the centre of the village.

It was now that Owen tapped on Harry's arm and gestured for him to follow him down a path to a small cottage made of wood, with a roof of tightly-bound reeds. It huddled beneath the seawall, surrounded by a modest plot of land. Now Harry would learn about the people who lived below the wall.

Owen pressed the latch and the wooden front door swung open. Harry followed the older man, stepping straight into the main living room.

"Home at last and a young visitor with me," Owen announced.

"Oh, love, what a day you've all had! I've been that worried and went up on the wall to see the tide turn. Did you fix the breach? Is it sound? They say it is, that's the word in the village."

As she spoke, the woman got up from the table, leaving her darning under the light of the window, ready to fuss over her husband and the young stranger. She was a small woman with gentle curves and grey-brown hair pulled back into a bun. A beige dress in a coarse material fell in loose folds right down to her ankles and was topped with a white apron. Without waiting for Owen's reply, she continued, "There, look at the two of you, you're that dirty I'll be at the copper all tomorrow morning and I don't suppose this young man has a change of clothes with him."

Horror twisted Harry's stomach. His bag… it didn't have much in it, just a fresh set of clothes, his pen and notebook, a Bible and some food. But it was all he had… The field, with the willow trees… of course, it would be where he had slept the night before, perhaps under the tree. Please God, let it be out of the reach of the water. He would have to return for it later, as soon as he felt able to search for it.

"I did have clothes... a bag..." Harry began to stutter his explanation. "I'll have to go back for it."

"Not yet, son. You need to rest," Owen turned towards Harry, "Now, Bess, this is Harry, he's had a bit of an accident and is all of a muddle, but he's harmless, you can see that. Harry, this is my wife, Bess, she'll look after you good and proper, you can be sure of that."

Harry managed a faint smile. Bess looked like everything a mother should be, not like his own poor faded ma with those deep furrows in her thin face, her eyes lacklustre and her shoulders sagging under the burdens of hard times. Sorrow for her difficult life lay heavy in his stomach, but it was over now – at only forty years old she had been given her release.

The cottage was lovely and warm; it smelt of wood ash and fresh bread. The brick fireplace was massive, covering most of the wall to the left as he entered the room. There was just enough space for a door on either side. There was an open fire, with metal poles hanging over it and a pot hanging over the flames. Hooks driven into the bricks had metal tools hanging from them and in the wall there was a little metal door for the bread oven.

The centre of the room was dominated by a solid pine table, with a bench and chairs. Colourful rag rugs were strewn over the brick floor and a couple of comfortable chairs sat either side of the fireplace. To his right a huge dresser reached up to the low, beamed ceiling. Through the two small windows in the far wall, Harry could see the grassy bank of the seawall rising up. It was beneath one of these that Bess' worktable stood, with the pile of neatly darned socks upon it and a basket of material on the floor.

The room was no better or worse than the living area in his own home, but there was a difference – here was a room where happy memories had been made, a place one could feel safe and welcome.

Harry became aware that Owen was talking, telling his story.

"...So there he was and you know what a temper Bailey has, he knocked him out no sooner than the boy opened his mouth."

"Anyone can see he's nice enough; that Joss Bailey is nothing but a bully." Bess took a step towards Harry. "You're safe here, lad. But what were you up to? New to working on the wall, are you? Perhaps you came from one of the villages – Burmarsh or Eastbridge way?"

"No, I was just passing through... I'm not staying."

"He says he's from Elham, but with that knock to the head he's all in a muddle." Owen bent down to unlace his boots.

"Owen, go along to the cupboard and take out one of your old nightshirts, I can't think what else to dress him in." Bess began to fuss over Harry. Her brow was lined as she touched his filthy jacket. "There's some hot water by the fire, I'll do a bowl for him first and you after. He all right, perhaps a little simple, but maybe he'll find his wits when his belly is full. So, you're not from The Marsh then? Elham – what sort of place is that? Still down on the levels or up on the hills?"

"It's up high," Harry spoke quietly. "A day's walk from here."

"And what led you to come all this way and get yourself mixed up with Joss Bailey?"

"Leave the lad alone, Bess." Owen had removed his boots and jacket. He had a kettle of water in his hand and the nightshirt in the other. "He'll tell us when

33

he feels good and ready. Now, come along into our room and you can have a wash in private."

"I don't know how I came to be by the wall." Harry forced the words; just to put them in some order was an effort beyond what was comfortable.

"Never mind, lad." Bess gave Harry a reassuring pat on his arm. "Perhaps it will all come a bit clearer in the morning."

Harry followed Owen through the doorway and into a small bedroom, dominated by a sturdy wooden bed with a patterned quilt upon it. Standing before the washstand, he removed his jacket and then his linen shirt, revealing a slim but strong body. As he washed the clay-mud from his arms, the marks of his trade showed on his arms – burn-marks from the sparks which flew as he beat metal at the forge.

A smattering of freckles was revealed as Harry washed his face. He then ran damp hands through his brown hair, pushing the waves into order, tentatively working around the egg-shaped bulge on the side of his head. This wasn't the work of that thug on the seawall, no, this was the result of something else – but what? Harry scowled as he pulled dried blood from his hair.

Finally, Harry slipped off his breeches and swiftly wiped over his legs. He was tiring fast. After pulling Owen's nightshirt over his head, he walked barefoot through to the living room, the bundle of his own clothes in his arms.

"There you are, you might feel a bit silly in a nightshirt but it's only the three of us here and at least you're clean now," Bess reached out for the dirty clothes and put them in a basket. "Sit down there, Harry, in the chair by the fire and we'll eat once Owen has cleaned himself up."

Harry gave a weak smile. "Thanks." He slumped in the chair, the nightshirt covering his knees and his feet nestling into the rag rug. A relentless ache still radiated through his head and he was so tired. It would do no harm to close his eyes for a moment.

When he woke, Harry's first thought was that his head still hurt and he reached to prod at the swelling above his left ear. The room had darkened and was now lit by candles and firelight. But where was he? Of course, the man from the wall, Owen, had taken him home, which had been very good of him.

"He's awake." It was Bess.

Harry opened his eyes a little more. "I'm sorry, I didn't mean to..."

"Now don't you go worrying about having a sleep. You're not well, we can see that."

"It's my head... I don't know what happened to it."

"You were thumped by that bully, Joss Bailey," Owen reminded him. "When you arrived at the wall."

"I know," Harry screwed up his forehead in an effort to remember. "But I'd already hurt my head and I don't... I don't remember."

"You must be hungry." Bess stood, went to the dresser and, picking up three plates, continued, "You missed the bread and bacon earlier, and slept around to dinner."

"I am," Harry admitted, his stomach was hollow, but he had eaten with the others by the wall and... "But I was sick last time, I don't want too..."

"Just a little then, and eat it slowly. It's that knock to the head that's done it, lad." Owen gestured for Harry to seat himself at the table. "Sit up here, but if you're not feeling right then go back to the chair, don't worry about seeming rude."

Harry shot a smile in Owen's direction. He'd be on his way tomorrow, but was grateful for their care and the comfort of the cottage. His head spun after the effort of walking those few steps to the table and he propped it up with his hand.

Bess began to ladle a thick mixture of vegetables and beans into wooden bowls. "I'll just give you a couple of spoonfuls, but if you can keep it down then there's more in the pot."

There was a jug of mild ale on the table and Owen filled three tankards with it. Then he cut chunks of bread and pushed one in Harry's direction. Harry stared down at the food; it looked good but his head swam so much that he wondered if he could raise his spoon to his lips. Please God, let him be able to eat the meal that these good people had provided for him, and let him not make a fool of himself.

Owen was speaking. Harry forced himself to concentrate on the words.

"We thank the Lord for this tasty meal which has been provided for us and for keeping us safe today. May He today and all days help us maintain the wall. Amen."

"Amen," repeated Bess.

"Amen," muttered Harry.

Chapter Four
Phoebe

Easing herself onto Peggy's stool behind the shop counter, Phoebe was sure that she could rest for a while – perhaps even lean upon her arms and close her eyes. It was always quiet after dinner on a Saturday with the villagers choosing to rest in front of the fire or do chores within their homes.

Aunt Peggy's eyes would be drooping at this very moment and Uncle Giles would enjoy his pipe before he spent an hour in the vegetable plot beyond the yard. Having been driven from the armchair at five in the morning in order to tend to her uncle's needs, Phoebe was weary and her spirits low. She allowed her dark lashes to lower over deep brown eyes and her long plait of glossy brown hair to fall over her shoulder as she slumped.

Phoebe's thoughts moved without reason from the open wound on the face of the seawall, to the poor old donkey playing her part in the team of workers. Then to the lone horseman she saw galloping through the village when she returned home. What was he doing? Did he race like this for his own reasons or did he carry a message for those labouring on the breached wall? Her breathing slowed and her body relaxed further before, realising it was doing wrong, jerking her awake.

Half an hour or more passed with Phoebe resting the best she could on the stool and counter top. Her thoughts meandered and eyelids to drooped before the scrape of the shop door on the stone floor forced her senses to be alert.

"Here you are, Phoebe my sweetness, sitting here as I knew you would be. What would my dear old ma do if you weren't here with a jar of honey and a pound of flour for her baking?"

Phoebe forced a smile. Why did her heart slump and stomach lie heavy within her slender frame?

"Honey and flour – I can do that for your mother, Aaron." She reached for a square of brown paper and, having pushed the stool back, slipped around the counter to where the flour was stored in large wooden barrels.

"And a kiss for your love?"

Her back was turned to him and the outline of a pert bottom displayed; the green cotton of her dress pulled tight as Phoebe reached low into the barrel for the scoop. Before she could give her reply, Aaron's hand had clasped the tempting curve and she received a firm squeeze. Turning in annoyance, although well-versed in the routines of courtship between herself and Aaron, she lifted her face to his. The hand on her rear pulled her in, while the other took her chin – ensuring that the kiss would last as long as he chose it to.

His tongue, which licked around her own, tasted of tobacco and brandy. Brandy – so there had been a celebration of some kind, despite the fact that the village had been under threat the previous night. His kiss was demanding, as his hand roamed up the arch of her back, slipping under her apron and towards her small breasts. Then it was over and Aaron stood back.

"No more of that, Phoebe, you'll have to wait until we're somewhere a bit more private. That aunt of yours could be here any moment and there'd be trouble for you behaving like a girl of easy virtue."

He gave her a grin and grey eyes met brown. Aaron wasn't tall, but his body was lean and always poised for activity. Easily bored – if there was not a tavern wench on his knee, a game of cards to win or a wager to be made – then he became restless, strumming his fingers or pacing up and down. The air of arrogance, coupled with the position of importance held by his family within the village, had female hearts fluttering within Dymchurch. But try as she might, Phoebe's heart did not sing when she spotted him in the distance or dutifully lifted her face to his.

"Were you out there working on the wall, Aaron?" Phoebe eased herself away from him as she wrapped the flour within the paper. "Uncle Giles was there and Aunt Peggy had me up in the night to be ready for him with fried bacon and tea whenever he came home."

"I was out there in the night and I'm telling you, Phoebe, it was a rough one."

"It would have to be to breach the wall like that and in two places."

"I like it that you were up waiting for Giles. Your aunt is showing you how to care for a man and I'm looking for a girl who can see how it's done. My ma would like that too, for all that you've got that Frenchie blood running through your veins."

"I'm Dymchurch too, as well you know." Phoebe's words were sharp... sharper than intended.

"I know that, my love, and I hope that sour tongue hasn't been learned from Peggy."

"I'm tired, Aaron. She woke me in the early hours and has had me working at the copper all morning,

39

then here in the shop while she's sleeping in the chair."

"She could do with hiring a wench to do a bit of the labouring – shall I tell her so?" He made a move as if to slip behind the counter and through into the living quarters.

Phoebe blocked his way. "You don't want to go spoiling her sleep or it will be hell for me once you're gone."

"I suppose you're wanting another cuddle before I'm on my way," Aaron rolled his eyes. "You're a lucky girl, Phoebe, there's plenty of comely wenches out there, but I've taken a fancy to you though perhaps I could do better for myself. And my ma too, she has a nice word or two to say about you. She can see you're a hard worker."

Reaching out to place a hand on her waist, Aaron pulled her close as they stood in the small space behind the counter.

"You're welcome to go looking for someone more suitable," Phoebe retorted. "There's plenty of pretty Marsh girls out there who may suit you well."

"No, I like your spirit, girl. Just be sure to watch that you don't turn too mealy-mouthed with it. And I like this too..." With his hand on the back of her neck, he demonstrated his claim on her again.

The kiss was swift but savage, his lips pressing hard on Phoebe's and, as he released them, he gave a sharp nip with his teeth on her lower lip. Her eyes flashed a blaze of disgust as Aaron turned away; already her lip felt swollen as the tender flesh reacted against the unexpected assault upon them.

"Ma said it would be nice to see you when you're done in the shop. She likes a bit of company now Ruth and Grace are married, and Ruth being all the way over in Hythe makes her feel a bit lonely."

"I'll be there at half past four, same as usual." Was she not allowed a moment to herself as she moved through life as a skivvy to her family, shop assistant at the general store, and companion to a lonely old woman? Visualising the red brick workhouse which sat on the seawall itself, Phoebe gave a sigh of acceptance. How tired and unreasonable she felt today. Half the girls in the village shared a mattress with siblings before moving into their marital bed. And to spend the afternoon in the shop, talking with the housewives and looking out on Dymchurch life – well, if she couldn't sit stitching and sipping tea with the ladies of the New Hall, then at least she didn't have to gut fish, spend her days at the copper with her face all red and perspiring, or at the bar of The Ship with beer slops running down her apron.

The afternoon passed quietly and Phoebe was able to carefully unfold a large sheet of thin paper which she kept hidden away with the stores of food wrapping paper. Spreading it out upon the counter she took time to smooth out the creases before refolding it in half so as to make it a more manageable size to handle. Finally, she took a moment just to look at the pattern of the lines on the paper, marvelling at the intricate lines of the Gothic print and the details of the small illustrations. Then, with her forefinger slowly following the words, she settled to read one of the five ballads which were displayed on this one sheet.

The first told the tale of unrequited love between a milkmaid and a farm labourer. Phoebe's lips moved and her brow furrowed as all her concentration went into sounding out the rhythmic lines. She smiled on reading the final syllables of the second and fourth lines of each stanza, marvelling at the writer's ability to find so many ways to rhyme.

How coy this milkmaid pretended to be as she fluttered her eyelashes and found numerous ways to lure the labourer. How unfeeling the man was as he ignored her natural beauty and trim figure, preferring the company of the men as they stacked hay upon the rick or tended the animals in the fields. In these verses the sun always shone and work was not arduous. The broadsheet was well read, but Phoebe never failed to smile at the verse when the labourer finally noticed the beauty and good temper of the milkmaid, only for her attentions to have moved on to another.

Phoebe was lucky that her uncle supported her desire to improve her reading, although his preferred material was the Bible. She often spent an hour in the evening struggling over the tightly printed lines of her Bible, the words dancing beneath the weak flame of a candle. While understanding the good messages to be learned within these pages, it was the ballads on the broadsheet which fired her imagination and made her smile.

Movement from the room behind the shop caused Phoebe to hurriedly fold the precious sheet without completing the story of Robin Hood and Maid Marion in verse.

"Time to count up the money," Giles slipped through the doorway and stretched his scrawny arm to the wooden box of coins.

"It's been quiet," Phoebe began to apologise.

"They were all in this morning, keeping your aunt busy with their chatter about the breach. We took coins aplenty then." His thin lips extended into a crooked smile as the money was poured over the shop counter. Then he picked out a couple of shillings and a few pennies, and pushed them in Phoebe's direction. "Something to spend on some ribbon or suchlike."

"Thanks." Phoebe turned and stepped into the inner hallway, then ran up the stairs and into the space known as her bedroom.

Kneeling down, she lifted a loose floorboard and pulled out a small leather pouch. Easing the pull-string opening apart, Phoebe pushed two shillings into the pouch to join a small collection of pennies and shillings. The other coins she placed in an old patterned dish sitting on her chest of drawers.

Then she ran back downstairs and, stepping into the kitchen, she spoke to Peggy. "I'm just going out for an hour or so, to see Aaron's ma as usual."

Turning her head in Phoebe's direction, Peggy pouted her disapproval, "Get yourself back upstairs, girl, and into your Sunday dress. You don't go visiting the likes of them in that old rag. You've got opportunities there that none of us would have expected."

Phoebe retreated up the stairs and took her dress of blue cotton from a hook on the wall. It was a finer weave than her workday dresses and looked well with her pretty lace trimmed shawl. But there was a chill in the air and the sea-breeze was still brisk, so Phoebe risked Peggy's disapproval and wrapped her thick woollen shawl around her shoulders. Skipping down the stairs she called out goodbye, without giving her aunt the chance to voice any words of advice, and left through the shop door.

Turning right, Phoebe walked past the neighbouring shop, her tiredness lifting as she turned the corner, past cottages fronting the road, and took the lane which led to St Mary in the Marsh.

A wide plank bridge spanned one of the many sewers feeding the sea with the water they gathered from the land. Standing for a moment on the bridge, Phoebe looked down at the bare mud banks and sluggish water. It must be low tide and the water would be pouring out through the gut in the seawall, then trailing down the sands. The lower banks had only the stubby ends of last year's reeds while, higher up, the banks were fringed with the faded, weathered remains still rustling in the breeze. It wouldn't be long before the strong spikes of fresh reeds pushed their way through and the cycle of new growth began.

Phoebe watched a pair of ducks make their way along the centre of the channel before turning and stepping off the bridge. Here, the Dymchurch houses were more spread out along the roadside, each in its own strip of land. Some slumped at the roadside, single storey and topped in reed thatch. Others were brick, two storeys high, with roofs of soft orange tiles.

Just before the straggle of houses ended and the lane strode out through open countryside, Phoebe reached Aaron's home. It was a flat-fronted house, with brick walls and windows spaced evenly, one either side of the door and a matching pair above. In the gable end, a smaller window gave light to the attic room belonging to Dinah, the maid. The single storey extension to the back, housing the scullery and various store rooms, was her domain from before dawn until after supper had been eaten and cleared away.

It was Dinah who opened the front door to Phoebe's rap on the knocker. She didn't speak but merely inclined her head in Phoebe's direction. Not to be deterred, Phoebe forced a bright smile and spoke.

"Good afternoon, Dinah. I've come along to see Mrs Chapman."

The maid stood aside, allowing Phoebe to pass into the hallway, before closing the front door. Phoebe knew she was expected as this had been the pattern of her Saturday afternoons for the last couple of months. So, without waiting for Dinah, Phoebe walked through into the sitting room.

"Good afternoon, Mrs Chapman. I do hope you're well after all the trouble last night?"

"I knew nothing of it, dear, nothing at all." Caroline Chapman rose from her chair beside the fire and took Phoebe's hands in her own as a gesture of welcome. "Come by the fire; there's such a chill setting over the Marsh."

Phoebe settled down in a chair opposite the older woman and held her hands out towards the heat. "You weren't disturbed by the men when they got the call that help was needed?"

"I'm not sure that there was a call... now I do hope Dinah has made something tasty for us. A call, you said? No, they were out on business anyway – Mr Chapman, Aaron and Daniel. There was something that had to be done and they have no fear of the Phantoms. Just look the other way, that's what Aaron says, and they'll give you no bother."

"Look the other way," Phoebe reflected. "It sounds a little foolish, but it's the way of the Marsh. I know that."

There was something very comfortable about the hour Phoebe spent in the company of Mrs Chapman. The room was very elegant of course, with long drapes at the two windows facing the road. The lower walls were panelled and painted cream; the upper walls had delicately flowered wallpaper in soft greens and yellows. There were bookcases either side of the fireplace and Phoebe was hoping that one day, she might gain the courage to ask to look at the books and maybe borrow one. The settee and chairs were upholstered in a green velvet and at the window was a dear little writing desk.

Then there was Mrs Chapman herself – a little chirpy, like a small bird, but always very pleased to see Phoebe and interested in her opinion. She wasn't an elderly woman but, with four grown-up children, she wasn't young either. She appeared to be in good health and busied herself with various good deeds throughout the village. With two daughters now busy with their own families, it seemed that Phoebe's visits were not only welcome but had become necessary to ease the lonely times.

"Ah, now here's Dinah," Mrs Chapman announced unnecessarily. She stretched her neck to see the contents of the tray before it was lowered onto the table before her. "Apple cake, splendid." Then she brushed the sullen maid away with a wave of her hand. "I'll pour, thank you, Dinah."

"My uncle was out in the night, helping to repair the wall at Church Knocke," Phoebe told her. "Peggy woke me to have tea and fried bacon ready for him when he returned. He was gone for hours."

"We all have to do our bit or the sea would be upon us in no time." Mrs Chapman put a generous spoonful of sugar in Phoebe's teacup.

"He was cutting hawthorn into lengths. That's what he told us, working in a team and enjoying it, for all that the wind was harsh and they worked through the night." Phoebe frowned as she remembered her uncle's exuberance when he returned from the village. How unlike his usual sour manner.

"Teamwork is good for men," Mrs Chapman nodded knowingly. "And my own men, whatever they were up to, didn't return until dawn and then they had the horses to rub down."

"If the horses were out then they must have been carting clay," Phoebe informed, giving her limited knowledge an airing.

"I'm not sure Mr Chapman would like his Raven to be referred to as a carthorse, dear." Mrs Chapman gave a slight smile.

How strange that, in her world of tending to her grown-up family, the older woman had no interest in the wall and the protection it gave to both Dymchurch and the flat lands beyond. Conversation moved to Mrs Chapman's daughters and then to the tapestry lying loosely folded in a basket beside the chair. When the hour ended and the sun was low over the Marsh, Phoebe left with a thin volume of poetry clutched within the folds of her shawl. Eager to open the pages under the light of a candle in her bedroom, there was a skip in her step as she walked home.

Chapter Five
Harry

Despite his determination to be free of Dymchurch, Harry felt uneasy about leaving the comfort of Owen and Bess' cottage. At nineteen years of age, it was a long time since he had needed the security of a mother's love or a father's guidance. Yet, having lived without these for too many years, he had willingly succumbed to Bess' gentle fussing and Owen's words of advice.

Standing at the cottage door, Harry attempted a smile. "Thank you. For everything. The food and the bed... and the clothes." He looked down at Owen's breeches, which had been adjusted to fit him. "I'll be back with my own clothes when I find my bag. It will be near the wall – where the sea broke through – that's where I must have left it."

"Take care, lad. You've had a wallop to that head of yours and you don't want to get yourself into any more trouble," Owen cautioned.

"I'll take it easy and be back for my own breeches – thanks for washing them, Bess. Then I'll be on my way."

"You'll stay for some lunch first?" Bess reached out to touch Harry's arm.

"I... I've got a long way to go."

"You'll need some food in your belly," Owen

reminded him.

"I will," Harry smiled. "Thank you."

What was it that slowed Harry's pace when he should have been eager to find his bag and leave Dymchurch behind him? His head still felt as if an iron band was wrapped firmly around it and his step was a little unsteady, preventing him from striding out at his usual rate. Was it a reluctance to retrace his footsteps towards the east, when his destination was the west? Or was it a child-like need to be nurtured by these good people in their cottage beneath the wall? The bag must be found though; a spare set of clothes was not to be left as if it were nothing to him. Not when it had been his own dear mother who had patched his breeches and darned his socks.

Having wandered across the road Harry peered into a shop window, curious to see what Dymchurch had to offer. Tools, nails, hinges – an ironmonger's. Looking up at the sign he read *W. Nailer and Sons* – a family business which had, no doubt, been there for decades.

The next window revealed rolls of materials, a table with a measuring stick, scissors and spools of ribbons strewn upon it. Then there was the butcher's shop with hooks outside and bits of meat and dried blood on the counters, along with predatory flies. Harry screwed up his nose and moved on, past a terrace of low cottages with windows projecting from the tiled roofs.

He paused again and wiped a clear circle on the dirty glass window of the next shop. Through the gloom Harry could see the shapes of barrels and measuring scoops on the floor, and shelves from floor to ceiling full of packets and jars. He had the urge to have something sweet upon his tongue and gave the door a push; it swung open easily. Harry stepped into the shop, a room no bigger than his living room at home. The floor was stone and the back wall was shelved in dark wood. There was a shop counter with pieces of paper on it for wrapping the food. The barrels were under the counter and all around the edge of the room.

Lifting the lid on a barrel, Harry saw it was half full of oats. The next had a finer brownish powder, flour. He picked up some jars from a shelf and looked at dried fruits of all types. There were some open baskets with nuts in them. Harry picked one and gave it a shake, hearing the nut rattle in its shell. Then something more tempting caught his interest.

The jar was filled with glossy honey-brown coloured twists. Reaching across the counter, Harry pulled it forward. As he untwisted the lid and bent down to inhale their sugary sweetness, he didn't notice an inner door open.

"Hell and damnation, what brings you sneaking about my shop on a Sunday?"

Harry jumped and took a step back, dropping the opaque glass lid that clattered down beside the jar. A tall, scrawny man stood over him. His shaggy hair was a dull brown, sideburns curling almost down to thin lips turned up in a snarl, and a hooked nose upon his slim face. He wore breeches and a tunic with a white shirt of a rough cotton or linen. His socks were thick and long; on his feet were leather shoes fastened with a buckle.

"Have the rats eaten your tongue?" The man spat the words out, causing Harry to recoil from the shower of spittle. His grey eyes were filled with disdain and upper lip continued to be held in a twist of disgust.

"No, I... I just came in to buy some sweets."

"So, you take me as someone who would sell you a barley sugar on the day that the good Lord declared to be a day of rest?" A long bony finger came out and prodded at Harry's chest, causing him to flinch.

"I didn't...." A Sunday, was it a Sunday? The cogs within Harry's brain struggled to recall what day it was. "I've got money." Heart pounding, and with the sensation of that gnarled fingertip tattooed on his chest, Harry's hand pushed deep into the pocket of his breeches. He withdrew the money and held it out in the palm of his hand.

"Money? What kind of coins are they?" The shopkeeper flicked at Harry's hand, causing the coins to fall on the floor where he kicked them into a dusty corner between the barrels. "Coins that a thief and a trickster uses no doubt."

"No, it's real money. Why wouldn't it be?" Harry defended himself. "Cast by the blacksmith in our village.

"I'll take coins minted by the farrier or the grocer and those with the King's head on them. That's the currency of Dymchurch, not your pretty pennies."

"I just came in for some sweets, that's all." Harry shrugged and turned to the door, but a scraggy hand clamped on his arm and stopped the retreat.

"I'll say it again, I take a dislike to anyone who thinks that I would disrespect the Lord's day. To anyone who thinks that they can come in my shop and buy a few sweets on a Sunday, even if they came with a bag of real money." Then, with venom in his eyes, he uttered, "And I especially take offence from you, by God I do."

Still clutching Harry's forearm, the shopkeeper turned towards the inner doorway, from where he had just appeared. "Peggy, we have a young thief here! A lowly scallywag if ever I saw one. Keep an eye on him whilst I fetch the bailiff."

His wife appeared so quickly that she must have been listening from the next room. She was a small, dumpy woman with little piggy eyes that surveyed Harry from between folds of fleshy skin. "But Giles," she whimpered, "he's a tall lad and if he should attack me and escape, you'll be none too pleased."

"You set yourself here by the doorway, wench, and take this in your sweaty palm." She was handed a stout wooden pole that had been tucked away behind the counter. "Look at him and stop your fretting. There's not a jurat on the Marsh that would worry if you were forced to wallop him. He's bad through and through, you can see it in his eyes."

Piggy eyes looked up at clear blue and without saying any more about it she set her voluptuous backside on a sturdy little stool. The pole remained clutched in one hand, whilst the other sought for a handkerchief within the pocket of her apron. She patted her moist brow and settled down to keep her watch, plump lips in a dissatisfied pout.

"I'll be off to the New Hall and you can be certain this one will be getting all he deserves. You can be sure of it." With that the shopkeeper closed the door behind him and stepped out onto the street.

Harry waited, slouched against the wooden barrels. He would have happily slumped on the floor and given in to the exhaustion which lay heavily upon him. Putting his fingers to the side of his head, he knew that the swelling must be the cause of this tiredness he suffered. Both the chair and, later, the straw mattress on the cottage floor had been comfortable and sleep had come easily. Yet Harry had woken with his head still throbbing, albeit with less of a vengeance, and he was still unable to explain the cause of the gently rounded lump above his left ear.

Allowing his eyes to close a little, Harry could sense that Piggy's own eyes were upon him. He wouldn't look at her though – the floor, the barrels, even the jar of barley twists – he would look at anything but her pouting lips and sweaty folds of flesh.

The sound of wood catching and rubbing on the stone floor caused Harry to jump a little. He turned to see the shopkeeper enter with a look of self-satisfied pleasure on his bony face, thin lips now twisted into a smirk. His companion was a man dressed in plain but clean clothes, with neatly brushed hair and a pleasant face.

"Here he is," announced the shopkeeper, looking Harry up and down with renewed disgust. "Didn't I tell you he looks as sly as a fox?"

Straightening himself and pulling at the creases in his jacket, Harry looked at the new arrival before letting his gaze fall to the floor.

"I'll leave that for my master to decide if you don't mind," replied his companion. "We'll leave for the New Hall immediately and Sir Rupert Bannerman, Leveller of the Marsh Scotts, will send for your account in the morning."

"Oh, I'll be ready and waiting. I can't abide his type."

"Come on, lad." The man, presumably a servant, gestured for Harry to follow.

Even though he walked towards the unknown, Harry's spirits lifted as he stepped out of reach from the shopkeeper's vicious tongue. Turning left they walked along the village street. The servant walked swiftly and Harry found himself scampering behind him, past shops, cottages and the Rose Inn. The ground was uneven and his breeches became loose at the waist. The road swung to the right and upwards until it was almost level with the height of the seawall, and they stayed on this raised track until it parted with the seawall and led them towards The Ship.

From the seawall road the view of the coast should have been outstanding, but Harry kept his eyes firmly averted from the gentle sway of the sea. It would only cause him to feel dizzy and his step to waiver. It seemed that everyone on the road was heading in the same direction. Family groups striding out and elderly couples ambling along – all swept along by an invisible current, which no one moved against. Of course, it was a Sunday and the bell was calling the people of Dymchurch to the tiny church with its slim tower.

The man who had come for Harry was clearly a servant from the main house – the New Hall was it? Someone there would want to speak with Harry. Not the Lord of the Manor, but the Leveller of the Marsh Scotts. Frowning, the young man considered the unfamiliar title. The Leveller... it was no good, his brain was just too slow to think of what that could mean.

If only this man would slow down, Harry could ask him what was happening. It was all a mistake, he hadn't meant to buy anything... not if it was a Sunday... he just hadn't thought, not with his head hurting like blazes. It might be worth speaking to this servant; he might let him go on his way. Lurching forwards, attempting a few longer strides, Harry's head spun and he lost balance, tripping but not quite falling over a loose stone on the road. The servant turned and looked back, slowing his pace for a moment.

Harry took his chance to speak: "I didn't steal anything... I was... I was just looking. The door was open; I thought the shop was open."

"That's no business of mine." The servant turned away, picking up his speed again.

"I forgot it was a Sunday." Harry blurted out his final appeal.

"That was foolish. You'll have me late for church now and Sir Rupert won't be pleased. I'm telling you – I won't take the blame."

"So, can I go now?" Harry had to try.

"That's not for me to say. I just follow orders."

"Where are we going?"

"To the New Hall, of course. You'll spend the night in gaol and stand before the Leveller of the Marsh Scotts and the other magistrates in the morning."

"Gaol?" Harry's throat tightened as they rounded a corner and saw the rope on the gallows swaying lightly in the breeze. "But I only..."

Harry let his words fade away. They believed him to be a thief and so gaol was the place for him until he could prove them wrong. And if, in the morning, the magistrates believed him to be a thief then it may not be the gallows for him – more than likely he would lose a hand.

As they walked along the track between the church and New Hall, Harry already felt the shame of being seen as a felon. Churchgoers lowered their voices and slowed their pace, turning to wonder at who the stranger was and what crime had been committed. Were they eager to enjoy the sport of having someone to taunt in the stocks? Did they relish the thought of seeing a body swing at the gallows? What other sport was there for the people of Dymchurch?

Now Harry had his arm taken as he was led over

the shingle area in front of the New Hall. The building stood at a right-angle to the roadside, a traditional red brick and tile-hung house with irregular square windows and a central doorway. Before his presence could contaminate the grandeur of the place, Harry was marched swiftly across the forecourt of the property, away from the front and to a side door.

The doorway was low and the door made of planks. How different from the freshly painted and evenly panelled front door, Harry reflected. This side door was for servants and criminals; those unworthy of using the front entrance. Harry was led, in silence, down a few steps and to a studded door leading to his lowly quarters. As the door was opened, he noted the dark metal bolt on the outside, worn smooth from decades of use. Inwardly recoiling at the horror of being imprisoned, Harry was given a gentle push into the cell. With no further words from his gaoler, the door closed behind him, followed by the slide and clunk of the bolt being drawn across.

The room was small and square, with a bare stone floor. The walls were clad in roughly-hewn planks and the grey-white ceiling was supported by wooden beams. With no movement of air, a musty stench filled his nostrils and settled as a layer on his tongue. Harry screwed up his nose in disgust.

A wooden bench stretched the length of one wall. Stepping up, Harry stood on the bench and was able to look out of the small barred window set in the thick stone wall. It was dirty, with trails of spiders' webs both inside and out. Using the tip of a finger, Harry rubbed the dirt from one section of glass, as many others had done before him. Now, he could see the shingle to the front of the New Hall and a corner of the churchyard.

He jumped down from the bench and gingerly

picked up a blanket in a pincer grip that allowed the folds to fall freely. It looked clean enough and he was cold, so Harry wrapped the blanket tight around him and lay down on the bench, hunched on his side and using his jacket as a pillow.

He might have dozed a bit, he wasn't sure, but after lying there for some time, Harry was aware of footsteps coming towards the cell. As the door ground against the stone floor, Harry swung his legs around and sat himself up. The movement was too quick for him and the room swayed erratically for a moment, while sickness threatened. Harry allowed his head to be supported by both hands.

"Some food for you." The manservant put a plate of bread and cheese down on the bench alongside a mug of something to drink and an apple.

"Thanks," said Harry, and the servant left.

Picking at the bread, Harry forced a few pieces into his mouth. Pushing it aside, he lay down again. He must eat, Harry knew that, but later... he would eat it in a while.

How much time had passed while he slept? It was hard to tell, with nothing to mark the passing of time, other than the movement of the sun and the darkening in the sky, as night fell. But the sun could not be seen through Harry's tiny window to the outside world, and the cloud-laden sky was no darker than it had been when he had last looked. Kneeling on the bench, the blanket still around his shoulders, he looked out upon the churchyard and forecourt of the New Hall.

After a while, Harry became aware of a hollow feeling in his stomach and reached across for the bread and cheese. The bread was now very dry, but it was all he had and a sip of the weak ale eased its way down his throat. Nibbling at the cheese, Harry realised that the feelings of nausea had passed, and so the much needed food could enjoy a peaceful passage to his stomach.

With his brow furrowed and head propped up in his hands, Harry sat on the edge of the bench. How could he make sense of events since his arrival in Dymchurch, when he couldn't explain the swelling on the side of his head? He recalled the early morning trek along the Elham Valley and, late morning, the views of the sea and the approach to Hythe. Then he had wandered along the shingle beach, tired and less sure of his plans. But what had led him to be lying under the willow tree in a field? Massaging his brow, as if to stimulate the thoughts, Harry was forced to conclude that probing into forgotten memories would only hurt his head more by.

He found himself sitting, as if in a stupor, blue eyes following the ragged lines of the stones set into the floor, or watching the progress of the black spider in the far corner. Picking up the apple, Harry gnawed at it without tasting. An occasional scrape, perhaps of a door, or a flurry of quick footsteps came from the room above. These and the spider were the only forms of life he was aware of.

Time passed – one hour, two hours? The church bells began to ring. Harry could imagine them swinging backwards and forwards, high up in the slim tower. From outside muffled voices could be heard and the crunching sound of movement on the shingle. Harry turned and knelt on the bench, positioning himself so he could peer out of the window.

A tall man, with a grey wig and a bow at the nape of his neck, was stepping into the churchyard. His coat was dark green, probably velvet, and tailored to fit his stocky frame. With her arm resting gently on the man's, a woman walked beside him, her soft brown hair a mass of carefully crafted ringlets on a head held high on a slender neck. Balanced upon her curls was a small hat with a huge arching feather upon it. Her dress was a golden colour, nipped in at the waist and then splayed out from the hips with layers of materials. Her sleeves became wide at the elbows, with layer upon layer of white lace at her wrists. Harry couldn't see their faces as they were turned towards the church. What were the characters of these people who lived in the New Hall and no doubt ruled the whole of Dymchurch? Were they haughty and uncaring or kindly and supportive?

Crowding behind the gentleman and lady of the house, on the narrow path, were the members of their family. Five of them – two boys and three girls. The eldest boy and girl didn't look to be beyond twelve years of age, yet they carried themselves as if they were every bit as grand as their parents. The younger ones were still little adults with their frills and curls, but were less formal in their manner as they skipped up the path. The little boy was the smallest of them all, still being at an age to wear a dress, and being fussed over by his siblings.

Knowing their place, the servants came next. The nursemaid was only a step behind the children. Then the butler and the other staff, all dressed in their smartest breeches and jackets or long dresses. The path to the church porch was short and they were soon inside, along with the other villagers. Soft light glowed through the windows, making Harry yearn to be a part of something that brought people together as one large family.

The bell no longer rang out and Harry had nothing else to do but turn and slump back upon the bench.

Later, when he heard the sound of footsteps on the shingle again, he hadn't the energy to get up and look.

As darkness fell, the servant returned with an oil lamp which gave a nice warm glow to a corner of the room. Harry grunted his thanks but didn't bother to speak. A blanket of depression had settled on him. What was the point of asking about how long he would be kept there or what his punishment might be, when he would be told nothing good?

Not long after that, supper came in the form of bread and soup. The soup was barely warm with lumps of fat forming on the surface. He dunked the bread into the thick liquid and ate it quickly. It was tasty enough and even the fat sat happily in his stomach.

Harry lifted the lamp onto the bench and held his hands up to the heat. He must have spent a long time, hunched up, the blanket around his shoulders, just staring into the flickering light. After a while the light became weak and the prisoner curled up again on the bench to prepare for sleep disturbed by nightmares and long periods of wakefulness.

Chapter Six
Phoebe

"What was that? Do you hear it, Peg?" Uncle Giles straightened, his chin tilted in the direction of the shop.

"It will be them bleeding rats at the grain again. Phoebe, find that idle cat and show her where the work is." Aunt Peggy took a long sip of the cider she enjoyed after a Sunday dinner and closed her eyes.

Her belly was full and work was done for the day. She might do a little cross-stitch later, if she could find the energy, but a nap in front of the range was the usual routine.

With a pile of plates in her hands, Phoebe placed them in the scullery sink. "She'll be out in the wood shed." It was a favourite hide for the cat; Phoebe envied her ability to conceal herself from Peggy and Giles.

"Shush your chatter; it ain't no rat." Giles stood and, taking a step towards the doorway to the inner hallway, he continued, "There's someone or something in there and they'll be sorry if they're out to cause trouble."

Phoebe and Peggy watched in silence and heard the slight movement of wood against plastered wall; it was the sound of a wooden pole being picked up and they knew that, as he entered the shop, Giles carried his trusty wooden club. Then came the sudden snap of his voice: "Hell and damnation, what brings you sneaking about my shop on a Sunday?"

After that, Peggy lifted her huge body with a greater ease than Phoebe had seen in a long time, and her pale blue eyes glittered in anticipation as there came a clatter of something being dropped. Peggy darted towards the doorway.

"Have the rats eaten your tongue?" Giles snarled at the intruder.

There came a low reply, something muttered. Phoebe couldn't hear the words but whoever this person was, she willed him to get the better of Giles. A frisson of excitement, mingled with fear, shot through her slender body as Phoebe followed her aunt into the hallway.

"So, you take me as someone who would sell you a barley sugar on the day that the good Lord declared to be a day of rest?"

Phoebe could imagine him, her uncle, standing over some poor young lad. He must be young if he'd taken a chance at snatching a sweet or two. He'd be enjoying this, Giles would; he was born a bully of weak people. But put him in front of anyone with an aura of confidence and her uncle simpered and grovelled like a serving wench in front of the handsome sons of the New Hall.

In the hallway, Phoebe stood still and alert, but heard no response from the intruder. Peggy was pressed up against the door to the shop, enjoying the best entertainment of the day. The next words came from Giles – laced with venom, his lips would be curled and eyes casting daggers.

Her uncle was saying something about not selling sweets on the Lord's Day and taking offence to anyone who suggested he would. How pious he sounded. How unfeeling to this poor boy who probably only tasted a barley sugar on Christmas Day and then had to share it with his brothers and sisters. Phoebe could imagine the lad standing there, stick thin and in rags, in fear of the beating which was sure to come. Then Peggy was being called for and was slipping through the doorway as fast as an eel in a Marsh ditch.

"Peggy, we have a young thief here. A lowly scallywag if ever I saw one. Keep an eye on him while I fetch the bailiff."

Aunt Peggy made a show of being frightened, fussing about the thief being tall and how he might harm her. Phoebe smiled to herself; there were not many people who would take on the bulk of her aunt! But tall? Her aunt must be joking, for it must be a boy, and to call the bailiff, well, he wouldn't take kindly to having his time wasted on such minor business. She heard Peggy being handed the wooden club and then the shop door was slammed and Giles set off to the New Hall.

Now Phoebe took her chance to peep through the doorway and see the stranger for herself. He wasn't a child, like one of the lads from the cottages beneath the wall, standing there. This was a young man – tall, slim and well kempt. Not someone she recognised. A good-looking lad of about her own age. Phoebe would have remembered if she had seen him around the village. There was something about him though – he looked so confused and dejected. Not a hint of defiance that you would expect from a would-be thief.

Peggy was sitting on the stool, her voluptuous bottom spilling out on either side. He, the stranger, stood slumped against some barrels, his head propped up by a hand. Phoebe peeped, taking in his light-brown hair, smattering of freckles and clean-shaven face. He didn't look like a thief. His eyes rested, just for a moment, on the crack in the open doorway. Phoebe stepped backwards, knowing that he couldn't see her, but still wary of drawing attention to herself. She had best return to the scullery and would hear her uncle's version of the event later.

"Lord, we thank you for saving our homes and people from the force of the tide. We understand that although the sea is mighty, You are mightier still. You challenged the good folk of Dymchurch but thought to spare us and the Marsh."

The vicar spoke with passion and all the reverence his position commanded. Sitting between her aunt and uncle, Phoebe listened and relived those night-time scenes on the seawall. They went, as a family, to church twice on a Sunday. Uncle Giles was a man who set great store by honouring the Lord with his presence and thought this, coupled with regular prayers, ensured his safe passage to heaven. Any unchristian actions he partook between church services and his prayers were irrelevant.

For Phoebe, church services were a time of peaceful reflection in the small church of St Peter and St Paul, with its plain, narrow tower. It was a time to pray for the soul of her mother, who had lain in the churchyard these past five years. And as for her father, who had narrowly missed swinging from the nearby gallows, she prayed for his good fortune and that one day they could be together again.

After the service, the talk was all about the previous night as experiences were shared and relived.

"What of that lad who bore the brunt of Bailey's

fist?"

Phoebe paused, her interest aroused as she walked out of the church and was about to turn to her mother's grave.

"Harry – he left us this morning," Owen, the village carpenter, replied. "We'd have liked him to rest awhile and expected him back once he'd found his bag somewhere along by the Willop, but he must have decided not to stop off."

"I thought he'd have come in to say farewell, if that's what was planned," John Waller mused.

"That's what we hoped. He was to fetch the bag and fill his stomach before walking on. He wasn't right; his head was hurting something bad, but he was set on heading into Sussex."

"A bit simple, but decent enough," John reflected. "He did his part in helping to save the wall and worked hard."

"A bit unsure of himself, but perhaps it was just Bailey's punch that had him all of a muddle."

"You won't hear from him again," John said.

"We won't, but I know Bess will be worrying and fretting for a while." Owen paused before continuing, "Not just Bess; I'll be thinking of him too. He was a decent young man for all that he had his troubles."

Harry – could that be his name? The name of the stranger who now languished in the New Hall? Phoebe looked across the track to the home of the most influential man in Dymchurch. What was Harry – if that's who he was – doing in that tiny cell? How did he feel, trapped in a damp room, half sunk below ground level? Could he see anyone from that tiny window which looked to the front, but probably gave little more than a view of the ground?

Phoebe stepped off the path to allow the ladies of

the New Hall to sweep by.

"Mother, do tell Catherine to give me a little of her gold thread."

"I won't. She never replaces it and I need it for my own needlework."

"You don't. Your frock could be any colour, but I need it for the gold crown."

They barely noticed the slight figure who moved aside for them. Did any of them take a moment to consider their unexpected house guest? Did they care if he walked free or swung for placing his hand on a jar of barley sugar?

Kneeling before her mother's headstone, Phoebe was distracted. She usually took this time to whisper her thoughts fancyed that she was enfolded in the comfort of her mother's arms. For those moments she felt brave and loved, able to face her aunt and uncle for another week.

Today she tried to tell of the breach in the wall, asking her mother what her memories were. Surely the wall had broken within her lifetime? But soon her thoughts had drifted to the young man who had been caught in her uncle's shop on a Sunday and then to the conversation between Owen and John. It gave her the first hint of who he was... who Harry was.

As she suspected, Harry was not a Dymchurch man but a stranger travelling through. Yet he had *not* travelled through; he had remained here in the village. Owen was worried; he cared about this Harry and thought he had bade farewell to him. If Owen knew that Harry was just yards away from the church then he and Bess would want to help him. Phoebe was certain of it.

Was there anything Owen could do to help Harry? Phoebe wasn't sure. But he should be told, should be given the chance to know and perhaps there was something...? Muttering her apologies to her mother, Phoebe stood and turned from the grave, then ran over the grass to join Peggy and Giles at the church gate.

Dusk had fallen upon the village winding its way along the length of the seawall. Dark shadows gathered in the crevices of the church, the New Hall, the red-brick vicarage and The Ship Inn. Darkness wrapped itself amongst the crooked cottages slumped under the wall and the sturdy cottages lining the road to New Romney.

Some folk didn't care to venture out after nightfall. They scared themselves and others with tales of strange happenings after the sun sunk beneath the flat land. Dymchurch was known for its witches riding their brooms along the length of the wall and the hobgoblins skulking within its shadows, causing mischief for the hard-working villagers.

By day the people of the village went about their business in an honest and God-fearing way, abiding by the rules of the Cinque Ports. By night, they stayed at their own firesides or used the well-worn paths between The Ship and The Ocean. It just wasn't the way of the villagers to go out and about at night and, as tankards of ale were cradled in their hands, they muttered about the strange goings-on that happened when night fell on this remote village.

Phoebe thought nothing much of these tales. Not that she had reason to go out at night, and why would she want to? The short step to the log store was bad enough when the air was thick with drizzle or the wind strong as it whipped its way through the alleys between the cottages. Her father was a Frenchman who had regularly braved the English Channel in his business taking him between Wissant in Normandy and the shallow shores of Dymchurch. He travelled at night, across the inky sea and felt no fear. So, if he could do all this in order to trade with Marsh folk, then his daughter would think nothing of these tales. Witches, demons and hobgoblins – they would cause her no trouble.

"I'm going to walk to the wall and see the moonlight on the sea," Phoebe informed Peggy as they neared the family home.

"Funny sort of thing to do." Peggy's thoughts were on the comfort of the chair by the range and a small glass of brandy. "There's no moon showing anyhow."

"But when it breaks through the clouds, it will be magical."

"Hmm, I suppose it's that Frenchie blood that makes you all romantic about these things... you're not meeting a young man, are you? I won't be having any of that; you've been looking a bit secretive and I saw all that with your ma, God rest her soul."

"No, I just want to see that the wall is keeping us safe after all the troubles last night."

"You go along then, girl." Peggy turned to follow Giles through the door to the shop. "Don't get taken by them witches, I'll need you tomorrow to see to all the laundry."

Phoebe hurried across the road and took the path leading to Owen and Bess' cottage. The shape of it, low and irregular, could barely be seen as the bulk of the seawall rose directly behind it. But wisps of smoke rose from the chimney and a faint light showed at the windows, guiding Phoebe to the central front door. She rapped upon the solid oak panels and heard the exclamations of surprise from within. It was Owen who opened the door a crack.

"It's me, Phoebe, from across the road."

"Come on in, lass." Turning back to the room, Owen repeated, "It's Phoebe, from across the road."

"Come on in, love." Bess ushered her to a chair. "Now, what brings you here? Is everything all right with your aunt and uncle?"

"Oh, they're just the same as ever," Phoebe grinned. "It's something else. Something I thought you needed to know about. You might be able to help someone in trouble... I don't know how, but maybe...?"

"Who's this then, Phoebe?" Bess frowned and then the words rushed from her: "Not that young lad, Harry, him who got into trouble on the wall?"

"Yes, Harry. He came into the shop and... well, you know what my uncle is like and, before he knew it, Harry was being taken off to gaol at the New Hall."

"Gaol?" Owen and Bess repeated in unison.

"I don't think he did anything wrong. He didn't steal." Phoebe's voice rose as she recalled the confused figure, slumped a little against the barrels. "It was because it was a Sunday, you see. You can't buy from the shop on a Sunday and so Uncle Giles..."

"He assumed he was there to help himself." Owen shook his head slowly as he imagined the scene. "No, that wasn't it at all. There was something wrong – he'd had a knock to the head and wasn't himself."

"The poor love." Bess stood as if to snatch at her shawl and make off to rescue him herself. "He wouldn't do wrong; he was off to Sussex, or so he said, and didn't even leave the village."

"Well, it answers our questions as to why he didn't return," Owen replied. "He'd left his bag over Willop way and needed to go back before going on to Sussex."

"He didn't get a chance," Phoebe added. "Now he's in gaol and will have to speak for himself before the court. That's what Giles says. Owen, I thought you'd want to know. You helped him out yesterday and maybe… maybe there's something you can do?"

"He needs someone to speak for him." Owen frowned as he pondered on Harry's fate. "There's no one else he can call on to say a good word for him."

"He does need someone, or who knows what will happen with that Giles Woods out to make trouble. Sorry, Phoebe, I know he's your uncle but…" Words tumbled from Bess as she tried to do right by Harry. "You'll go along to the New Hall right away, won't you, Owen? See if you can get the young lad out of gaol and back here. Say that you'll vouch for him. Make sure he doesn't run off."

"No, I won't go now, much as I'd like to." Owen spoke slowly, deliberating on his words. "Sir Rupert Bannerman wouldn't be best pleased to have me show up. I'll go in the morning and speak for the lad."

Chapter Seven
Harry

When dawn came, Harry moved from lying to sitting. There was nothing else to do. Gingerly, he probed the swelling above his left ear; perhaps it had subsided a little during the night? He rubbed the back of his head where he had suffered the clout from Bailey. The servant came along and took the chamber pot. His eyes slid towards Harry as he made his brief progress across the room, but neither spoke. On his return he brought both the clean pot and an earthenware bowl of grey porridge. Lifting the spoon from the bowl, Harry watched the thick substance drip back. He let it sink back into the mixture and ate some.

It must have been mid-morning when the bolt was next slid back, and the cell door opened. The servant stood in the doorway and spoke: "They are ready to see you now."

"What for?" Slumped on the bench, Harry barely raised his eyes.

"You've to go to court. Settle this dispute."

"Court? Where is it? Here in Dymchurch?" Harry swung his legs to the floor and stood up, swaying gently as his head caught up with the sudden movement.

"Upstairs." The servant looked Harry up and down and added, "Smarten yourself up, lad. You've not got much going for you so tidy your breeches and shirt. Make yourself look a bit respectable."

Harry stood a little taller and straightened out his clothes, brushing his hands over the linen shirt, adjusting his jacket collar and pulling his socks straight. He ran his hands through his nut-brown hair and looked towards the servant. Trying to put a smile on his lightly freckled face, Harry noticed that the servant didn't have much to say, but he seemed all right.

Moving away from the cell, Harry was led up a few steps to ground level and towards the back of the house. Then more stairs – a steep, wooden staircase. In a house like this, it couldn't be the main staircase. No, this must be for servants... servants and criminals. Harry followed his short, stocky companion along a corridor. Finally, they stopped at a doorway.

"Wait here." The servant tapped on the door and opened it. Then drawing himself up a little taller, he announced Harry's arrival. "He's here, Sir."

Harry was given a nudge. With his heart pounding and stomach clenched he stepped though the doorway. The room was large and square. The walls and furniture were all a mid-brown wood, plain and sturdy. The windows were neither large nor small, but it was the vast white-painted ceiling that gave the room a sense of space and light. It reached up high into the eaves of the house and was only interrupted by thin wooden beams.

Harry found himself standing in this room, not noticing any of the details afore-mentioned, but finding himself transfixed by the Leveller of the Marsh Scotts, Sir Rupert Bannerman, whom he had seen the evening before. He sat with his consorts – the magistrates of The Marsh or whoever they were. The three of them were within a raised, boxed-in seating area, not unlike a box-pew in a church, but this stretched along the whole of one wall. The central figure stood and Harry could see the splendour of his fitted coat – a rich blue material with thick gold braiding at the cuffs and an opening at the front. At the neckline, layers of frothy white shirt splayed out. His wig was grey and lay in carefully groomed waves which were pulled to the nape of his neck and tied in a neat ribbon.

Sitting either side of Sir Rupert were two shadows of the great man himself. They were still bewigged, their coats decorated and shirts frilled, but with less extravagance in their dress. Pens were poised for action, their eyes were upon Harry and their faces showed a mixture of pity and distaste.

"Sit there." The man who commanded everyone's attention, in all his blue and gold magnificence, was speaking to Harry. His voice rang out, clear and confident as he gestured to a high-backed seat in the centre of the room, directly opposite the raised, boxed-in seats.

Harry lowered his eyes to the polished wooden floor and somehow forced his legs to move across the room, just those few steps to the seat. He sat down then raised his eyes to the man. Had he done the right thing in sitting? Had he been meant to sit? The great man nodded his approval and lowered himself into his own chair.

There were four other people in the room, sitting on wooden benches, at right angles to the man in blue and gold. Harry recognised one as being the local vicar, a pleasant-looking man of no great age, his brown hair tied back neatly and wearing a black suit with a plain white cravat. He looked to be a steady character, not suffering from pride or excessive piety. If Harry's opinion was correct, he could feel at ease that the vicar's judgement would be fair.

Beside the vicar was a very different character; Harry's stomach lurched as he recognised that great hulk of a man who had first pulled him up from the foot of the seawall and thumped him without hesitation. He lounged on his chair, burly arms folded and legs splayed outwards, wearing the clothes of a working man. Pale eyes, fringed with ginger lashes, were fixed on Harry and the bully's lips were twisted midway between a snarl and a sneer.

The third was someone Harry did not recognise. Dressed in a smart jacket and breeches, with a frilled neck-tie, he was clearly someone of importance, yet not of the same rank as those who sat within the boxed bench. With a leer of contempt upon his face, the fourth man was the shopkeeper, clearly eager to see Harry swing for his crime.

Waves of nausea streamed through Harry's throat and his skin became clammy. Averting his eyes from those who were keen to see him suffer, he fixed them on the wooden panelling of the boxed-in seating. There they remained, even when the great man before him began to speak.

"We are here in court to discuss the matter of theft from a shop in Dymchurch yesterday. I have before me the young man who was accused of this unlawful act and will be hearing about the events leading up to this incident as well as the theft in question. It is a matter to be taken seriously and, as Leveller of the Marsh Scotts, I will, with my fellow bailiffs, decide on the punishment.

"With us today are Giles Woods, shopkeeper, along with Reverend Green, Doctor Robbins and local landowner Joss Bailey." Sir Rupert Bannerman waved his hand in the direction of the men on the bench and then, raising his voice a little, he asked, "And who are you, young man?"

Raising his head, Harry's eyes met those of the man he now knew as the Leveller of the Marsh Scotts. His mouth was dry, yet somehow he managed to form the words, "Harry... Harry Farrers."

"And where do you live, Harry Farrers?"

"Elham, I've lived there all my life."

"It is not a place I am familiar with. A village in the direction of Folkestone I believe. Is that correct?" With a frown on his face the Leveller of the Marsh Scotts looked intently at Harry.

Thinking of the low cottages and flat-fronted Georgian houses bordering the village street, the sturdy Norman church and the valley in which the whole place nestled, Harry nodded his head.

"Elham is your home, yet we find you here in Dymchurch. What of your family?"

His family – the soil on his mother's grave would still be fresh, while his father's had five years of grass and weeds weaving their roots through it. Two young brothers, dead before the age of five, were the gentlest of rises in the ground covered with clover and buttercups. His sister was in service in the big house, due to marry the head stable-hand; she had survived and escaped.

"I don't know," he muttered, looking down at the dark wooden floor.

"He doesn't know," repeated Sir Rupert. "Do you have any family in Elham?"

"Not any more." He didn't count his stepfather; he wouldn't slur the memory of his soft-hearted mother by allowing a connection to remain between her and that

75

man.

"You have no family or home?" Sir Rupert persisted, "You seem disinclined to help me or yourself, Harry Farrers."

"Just my sister, Sir, and she's in service. And as for a home, I... I had a room... a bit of loft space above the farrier's. It was warm enough and I had food for the work I did."

It was true enough – a few boards set amongst the roof beams, with nothing more between him and the open sky than a few rafters and clay tiles. His bed had been a meagre layer of straw, within a hessian sack. The luxury of having the heat from the farrier's fire settling around him in wintertime became hell in the summer as it rose and stifled him when he rested in his space within the eaves.

It had been a year before his stepfather had removed him from the house. A year in which he had seen his mother become a thin, nervous character, fussing around a man who was never satisfied. It had been after the baby was lost, it was decided Harry was to blame. If his mother hadn't been hurrying to buy yarn to darn the elbows in his jacket, she wouldn't have slipped on the ice... That night his belongings were removed to the area of loose planks and from then onwards he spent day and night with the sweet smell of iron laced with pungent woodsmoke.

"A farrier's assistant – a worthy trade. Now, we learn a little about Harry Farrers – he has some skill but no family to speak of." Sir Rupert repeated the little he had learned. "Yet this young man of prospects finds himself in a Dymchurch shop. I am keen to learn how this came about before I saddle my horse and ride to New Romney to partake of a glass of brandy with the bailiffs of that town. Let us take little time over this case; my throat is in need of a fiery tonic. Harry Farrers, tell us what brought you from Elham to Dymchurch?"

"I was passing through." Harry raised his eyes a little and, looking at Sir Rupert, he continued, "I was passing through on my way to Sussex. I've got family there."

"Family in Sussex," Sir Rupert repeated. "So now, my friends, we have learned a little about this stranger who sits before us. But we are here to discuss the matter of theft from Mr Woods' shop. The court will now hear Mr Woods' version of the event."

"Thank you, Sir, much obliged, Sir," snivelled the shopkeeper. "I heard a noise from my shop, Sir, and walked in to find this young man with his hand on my jar of barley sugar. I asked him, Sir... I asked him what he was up to and, would you believe, he told me he wanted to buy some sweets! On a Sunday – would I sell sweets on a Sunday?" He turned towards the vicar for support, "I would never take money on a Sunday. He offered me money, but it was foreign money or something of that type. It wasn't the King's coins or Dymchurch tokens. I'm telling you – it wasn't what you or I would recognise. I tell you, he is nothing but a dammed thief."

"That was an interesting account," summed up Sir Rupert. "May I ask, Mr Woods, did the young man you see before me today have the sweets in his hand or in his pocket?"

"No, he didn't, Sir. I was that quick in hearing him in the shop that he hadn't the time to pocket them. But, it was as clear as day what his intention was."

"I see," replied Sir Rupert. Then, looking to the side benches, he asked, "Does anyone else know of this Harry Farrers?"

77

"He was caught messing around by the seawall," snarled Bailey, fists clenched as he remembered his fury when he found the boy. "By God, we worked hard that day to fill the breach in the wall. Since daybreak every man and boy who had the strength was there to save our village and the farmland beyond. And, what did we find? That young fool ambling along without a care in the world, slipping on the clay and getting in the way of my cart. Drunk no doubt, for he had no wits about him, and I'd be surprised if he had even noticed that the wall had breached, for all that there was water everywhere!"

The bailiffs sniggered, trying to hold their laughter between pinched lips. The Leveller of the Marsh Scotts looked at Harry, his face a mixture of amusement and disgust. "Did you know that the seawall had breached?"

Questions. Too many questions. Harry's head pounded and again he felt like he could vomit at any moment on those polished planks at his feet.

"There was a lot of water," he muttered. "I... I don't know."

"He saw a lot of water, but he doesn't know. He thought nothing of the ragged hole and the tides threatening the good people of Dymchurch." Sir Rupert shook his head apparently in disbelief that anyone could be so ignorant of the ways of Dymchurch and the importance of the great wall.

"I don't remember," Harry offered all he could, "my head..."

"So we have this young man of... how many years are you?"

"Twenty-one."

"A young man of twenty-one years who claims to be from Elham. He has no belongings and no one to

78

vouch for his good name. He has no family to speak of but appears to have a trade. He was found, possibly drunk, by the seawall, hindering the movement of a cart. The next day he was caught attempting to steal barley twists from the shop, although he did offer money... foreign money or some form of coins not accepted within Dymchurch. Did you forget the day? What possessed you to enter a shop on God's day of rest?"

"I didn't think of the day," murmured Harry. "The door wasn't locked."

"You thought nothing of the day! Are the people of Elham not decent God-fearing folk?" Sir Rupert shook his head. "And let this be a lesson to you, Giles Woods, to lock the door when your shop is closed."

The shopkeeper briefly bowed his head in acknowledgement. The bailiffs, who flanked the head magistrate, raised their eyebrows and leaned across to whisper to one another. Joss Bailey sat back, legs outstretched, looking pleased with himself. The shopkeeper turned his gaze to Harry and sneered, hard grey eyes not leaving the boy for a moment.

Harry just sat hunched up, head throbbing, as he continued to fix his attention on the floor. Afterwards, he could not have described one feature of the windows, the walls or the furniture. He only knew of the wide, wooden floorboards, worn through the centuries and polished to a deep, glossy brown. He twisted at the sleeve on his tunic and yawned.

"Doctor, do you have an opinion on this case?" asked Sir Rupert.

"It seems that the lad may have suffered some trauma which left him confused. Or perhaps he was born a simpleton. He is clearly in want of wisdom and may I suggest that he did not set out to steal but has not the wit to know what he is doing from one minute to the next."

"Not a thief?" raged the shopkeeper, jumping to his feet. "He deserves to have a hand cut off and then he will learn not to be a thief!"

"I would like to remind you that it is the bailiffs and I who will decide his fate," Sir Rupert spoke coolly. "Vicar, do you have an opinion?"

"I do not know him but I am inclined to agree with our doctor. I see the young man as simple and he could probably be trained up to do a useful job within the community. In fact he tells us that he worked in the farrier's at Elham and was obviously well-thought of to be provided with a home, regardless of how humble it was. He could be found something that requires no skill and where he will harm neither himself nor others. He speaks of family in Sussex and could be released to be on his way in that direction, but I doubt he would have left Dymchurch before he got himself in more trouble. However, I do have another solution that may be of benefit to this young man, whom we have established is of low intelligence and unfit to care for himself."

"I would be interested to hear of your solution, Vicar. He is still young and I feel that if we could set him on the path of righteousness then perhaps he could learn to keep out of trouble." Sir Rupert looked upon Harry in a kindly manner, and Harry felt that perhaps he might leave today with both hands intact.

"The offer comes from Owen Bates," the vicar told the court. "I saw the lad with him yesterday and took it upon myself to see Owen and Bess this morning and tell them of his fate. Owen is a decent, law-abiding and God-fearing man who takes seriously his duty to help maintain the wall. He and his wife are childless and are happy to take Harry as their own, to feed and clothe him and ensure he is able to do a day's work."

"Thank you, Vicar. Owen Bates is indeed a good citizen of this village and although the young man before us has passed his childhood years, there is no doubt that he is in much need of parenting." Sir Rupert nodded thoughtfully. "Now, I will discuss this with my fellow magistrates and we'll tell you of our decision."

The three men spoke in whispers and when Harry dared to raise his head to glance at them, he saw that their faces looked serious, yet kindly. He looked towards the other men. Joss Bailey slouched, a look of contempt on his face. Giles Woods, still with his eyes narrowed and thin lips curled, was looking less certain of the outcome and his own moment of success.

Looking down, Harry saw a tiny spider surface from a gap between the floorboards and his gaze followed its journey until it was out of sight. The knot in his stomach was tightening and his mouth was dry. Follow the spider. Think of the spider. It appeared again, trundling back towards him, and the knot loosened.

It took only a few minutes for the Leveller of the Marsh Scotts to discuss the matter with his bailiffs and soon he was standing again in all his blue and gold splendour.

"I hear that you, Harry Farrers, entered a shop on a Sunday, apparently with the intention to buy barley sugar. Yet you had no money that was of any use within Dymchurch. The bailiffs and I cannot determine if it was your intention to steal, but we believe it was not your plan. We have heard of the way that you entered our community and your lack of respect for the maintenance of the seawall. I am inclined to agree with our doctor who suggests that you have suffered some form of injury or distress, leaving you unfit to act responsibly."

He then turned to address the men on the benches. "Gentlemen, it seems like a fine idea and a good opportunity to give a person who lacks our intelligence, the care and support he needs. I recommend that Harry works for the good of our community and spends the spring and summer labouring on the seawall. He is to do six months' service to our village and during that time he will live with Owen and Bess Bates. Later, if Owen sees fit, he could set him up in some other trade."

There were murmurs of approval from both the vicar and the doctor, coupled with snarls of discontent from the two who had set themselves against Harry. However, it was not for them to question the wisdom of the Leveller of the Marsh Scotts, Sir Rupert Bannerman.

"Harry Farrers, do you understand what is expected of you?" Sir Rupert addressed the young man before him.

"I do."

"I expect you to show respect to Owen and Bess Bates. If I ever see you in this courtroom again you will be treated with less lenience. I will be making it my business to check on your progress."

"Thank you, Sir." Harry forced the words from his dry throat.

"Sir, if I may, then I shall take Harry to Owen Bates so we can all be sure that he arrives safely." The vicar looked towards Harry with a kindly smile.

"You may, Vicar."

As the knot in Harry's stomach unravelled, he felt the tension ease in his limbs. Pausing at the corner by the gallows, he glanced up and took a deep breath of air. Thick with the smells of salt and seaweed, it felt good to let it fill his lungs. The wind was brisk, straight off the sea, and the sky was dull. Small pieces of debris – a piece of reed thatch, a gull's feather, crisp leaves from the previous autumn – sped along the road, catching on a rut or stone, pausing, then lifting again on the next gust.

For now, he would think nothing of his enforced time in Dymchurch. His body would not swing from the gallows and his hands remained securely on his wrists. When this damned headache had passed, Harry would have his wits about him and watch out for the likes of Giles Woods and Joss Bailey. They were a danger to him and he knew it.

"Ready then, lad?" The vicar gave a gentle pull on Harry's arm.

"Yes… sorry. Yes, I'm ready."

Chapter Eight
Phoebe

"Blazes! Where's that aunt of yours?" Uncle Giles snarled as the shop door swung open, crashing against a barrel of oats. "And, move that barrel, girl, before the damned door gets broken by someone coming in and thinking nothing of smashing it against my stock."

Phoebe's heart soared. Never in the long and difficult years of living with Giles and Peggy had her uncle's temper caused a flicker of a smile on her face. But now she was forced to turn away… to make a show of tidying the packets on the shelf behind her, for the smile was sure to break free at any moment. Giles pushed his way past her and through the doorway to the hall. Now Phoebe allowed the grin to emerge as, just for a moment, she silently savoured Harry's victory.

"Peg, you won't believe it. It was the vicar himself that made sure he walked free. Spoke up for him he did, thinking nothing of my good name and God-fearing nature…" The words erupted from Giles' mouth as he passed through the hallway, and the door into the kitchen was slammed behind him. Phoebe was forced to scurry in his wake, so as not to miss out on the news.

"I'm telling you, Peggy, I never saw a lowlier

scallywag in my life. Sitting there, his head in his hands, looking at the floor. You saw him, Peg. You saw him. What did you think of him? Blazes, you saw him for what he is – some foreigner passing through and taking a chance at stealing from my shop on a Sunday. On a Sunday of all days! And me already been to church that morning and back there in the evening – with no thought at all that our very own vicar would turn against me."

Phoebe's teeth dug into her lips as she tried to hold back the joy that was clear to see in the spread of them. If her uncle was to turn about and head back to the shop, she would be forced to share in his outrage. And if her aunt had anything to say on the matter, Phoebe could not hear it. She would be nodding and murmuring her agreement, while all the time knowing that this would give an extra dimension to the gossip to be shared from behind the shop counter.

"I said he was too young, didn't I? Didn't I say when he came here to Dymchurch that he was too young to be a vicar? Didn't I say that we needed someone... someone more knowing to guide the men of Dymchurch? There's all sorts of things that go on here... things that a good wife like yourself should know nothing of. But a vicar – well, he needs to know about his flock and we're a tricky lot to understand, us Dymchurch folk. Now if he were in somewhere civilised like Hythe or Canterbury, I'd say nothing about it, but this just goes to show..."

Peggy must have taken her chance to utter a few words, as Giles' next words had Phoebe fleeing to the shop. "I'll tell the girl then."

It was with some trepidation that Phoebe moved through to the kitchen for the midday meal. But it seemed that her uncle's anger had subsided to a simmering sulk. He jabbed at Monday's cold meat, pulled off pieces of dry bread and moved the fried vegetables around the plate before finally pushing them between thin lips. Peggy's eyes were still aglow, but she knew better than to speak any more of it. Besides, there was enjoyment to be found in the plate of crisply-fried vegetables and cold mutton.

Monday afternoon was always spent amidst the lines of washing in the yard. Straightening the sheets and pegging them back in place, turning the breeches and dresses to allow the wind to blow through, shaking out the creases. If the wind was brisk and the air dry, the clothes would go on the airer and be taken down to be folded the next morning. If a sea-mist hung in the air, or the day was rainy, the kitchen would be filled with soapy condensation for days. Then the irons would be placed upon the hotplate and Phoebe would spend an evening smoothing, pressing and folding the clothes and sheets.

It was the same as far as Phoebe could see between the woodsheds, privies and storerooms of the High Street cottages. Washing lines stretched out from the corners of buildings or sheds to sturdy poles. The results of a morning's plunge in the copper and squeeze through the mangle were stretched out as banners in the breeze.

That Monday was good for drying clothes, despite the sky being dulled with cloud. The wind was brisk, whipping the sheets into knots, but welcome nonetheless. Phoebe was pulling a large sheet off the line, battling to fold it, when she jumped to feel a pair of hands clasp her waist from behind.

"Aaron!" Her voice was irritable; must he come bothering her? "You'll have me in a muddle and I don't suppose you've come to help."

"I'm no washerwoman," Aaron laughed, as his eyes appraised her slim figure and glossy dark hair loosely knotted at the nape of her neck. "And if I decide to wed you, then there'll be no need for you to be fretting about washday."

"I'm not sure that I want to marry, Aaron. You know that." Phoebe's words were bold, for what chance did she have of a good match within the village? There were many young women who wouldn't think twice before walking down the aisle to marry this young man. But her stomach clenched as she doubted that there could be any happiness from their union.

"Lucky for me that it's your uncle who will give his approval." Aaron spun her round and pressed a quick kiss on her lips. "I'll bring him a nice bottle of French brandy and he'll be as happy as can be. Perhaps next time I come by some of the liquor… perhaps that will be the time."

"Set your eyes on another girl, Aaron." Phoebe pulled away and scowled at him. "Your mother would be just as happy with any companion, and I'll make do here with Giles and Peggy. It could be worse; look at those folk at the poorhouse up on the wall."

"But I've a fancy for you, Phoebe. You know that."

Phoebe shrugged her shoulders, "Well, I've told you enough times, Aaron, that I'm flattered, of course I am, but I'm not the girl for you."

"How old are you now, Phoebe?" the young man asked.

"Nineteen, as you well know." Her tone was sharp with him and it didn't come readily to her. She didn't want to be that person with a sour tongue and sharp retorts. Life with Aaron would be a battle of their wits until she became weary of their life together.

This was not the love she wanted. An easy companionship and respect for each other was the relationship Phoebe yearned for. And if her man wasn't as wealthy as Aaron then what did it matter, as long as he didn't drink his earnings away in the tavern and treated her with regard?

"Nineteen, so you are," he grinned at her. "Almost an old maid. I'll ask your uncle for your hand at Whitsun and, until then, there's many a wench that will be a little more forthcoming with their kisses than you, my love."

The sheet had been a barrier against Aaron all this time and now Phoebe placed it in the basket. She tried to change the subject. "Where have you been this morning?"

"I've ridden to Lympne and back. Now the horse is with the farrier, just opposite The Ocean here. Her shoe has been loose since we passed the Willop and picked up this sack." Aaron inclined his head towards a strong sack with carrying handles at his feet.

"You found this over at the Willop?" Phoebe frowned.

Bending down, Aaron loosened the buckles on the sack. "I don't know who would be leaving all their belongings lying around; I don't even know why I bothered to pick it up."

"It should be handed in to the vicar," Phoebe suggested. "Perhaps he'll have an idea as to what to do with it. There will be someone who needs it, although goodness knows what it was doing left all the way out towards Willop."

"You're right of course." Aaron flashed a grin at her. "But I've just passed by the vicarage and have news to pass on to my pa. We've secured some land at Lympne and are to grow hawthorn and brushwood there. Doing our bit for the seawall, you see."

"Land at Lympne? I didn't know your family wanted land." Phoebe frowned, uncertain of exactly what Aaron's family did. Yes, they were hardworking, always busy at something. But exactly what that 'something' was, she couldn't be sure.

"If a patch of land at Lympne helps Dymchurch, then it's something that interests Pa," Aaron stated. "And there's a few empty buildings up there. Nice and private. Useful for storage no doubt."

He was doing it again, drawing her in, getting her interested. But Aaron's business and that of his family were nothing to her. Phoebe knew that. So, although her curiosity was aroused, she chose not to ask any more. Instead she looked back down to the bag. It was of a decent quality, with a nicely-crafted buckle and no wear at the seams. Not the sort of bag that someone would leave around and think nothing of it.

Phoebe had heard talk of a bag and now it came to her: the conversation overheard in the churchyard. This bag must belong to Harry, who had set off to find it when he had been caught in her uncle's shop. It was a mystery as to why Harry had left the bag in the first place, but Owen had spoken of a knock to the head and perhaps the poor lad was confused. He hadn't looked at all well when she had seen him slumped against the barrels in the shop, waiting to be taken off to gaol.

"I'll take the bag for you, Aaron," Phoebe offered. "You need to get home and I can slip over to the vicarage; it would be no bother to me."

"You're a good girl." Aaron pushed the bag towards her with the toe of his boot.

"Like I said, it's no trouble." It irritated Phoebe to see him push the bag through the dirt and picking it up she brushed it clean with her hand.

"I'll be off then." Grasping roughly at her apron, Aaron pulled her towards him. His kiss was lingering, his tongue flicking into her mouth.

Phoebe held the bag as an obstruction between them and submitted without protest. What was to be done about Aaron? For the hundredth – no, the thousandth – time over the last few months, Phoebe despaired of how to escape his interest in her. She had never encouraged it, well... perhaps at the beginning when it had come and caught her unaware and she had been flattered. Of course she had been flattered; it had been so unexpected and he had a certain appeal. But his manner was rough and although he seemed to like her well enough, Phoebe could not help noting that he expected her to be grateful for his attention.

It was Peggy who came as an unlikely saviour when, unbeknown to the entangled pair, she crept up behind them and jerked Phoebe away from Aaron's grasp.

"Off with you!" Peggy roared at Aaron, her body quivering. "You keep your mucky paws off, unless you've come by to have a word with her uncle about a wedding."

"Not yet, Peg," Aaron winked. "See you later, Phoebe."

"There'll be no 'see you later' unless you come all respectable to the front door and ask properly if you can come and sit with Phoebe in our kitchen, or take her for a nice walk along the seawall," Peggy screeched at Aaron's departing back.

Turning to face the fury of Peggy, Phoebe bent to pick up the basket containing the sheet. It would iron well with a little dampness still within it.

"I didn't want him to come bothering me; he's become a nuisance." Phoebe began her defence.

"I know what young women are like, I was one myself once," Peggy cackled. "I gave him a lashing with my tongue, but it's nothing that hasn't been going on for centuries. You just watch yourself, my girl. You'll have everyone from Dormers nosing out at you.

Peggy inclined her head in the direction of the terrace of low cottages, the next along the road beside their own taller, squarer terrace of shops and homes. These cottages had small windows peeping out from orange tiled roofs.

"I don't like him much at all," Phoebe tried again. "And I don't want to wed him if he comes asking."

"You'd be lucky and that's a fact. There's some that wouldn't care for that French blood of yours."

"I'm Dymchurch too, as I told him only yesterday," Phoebe scowled. "And I'm not ashamed of my pa, I wish he'd come back for me and tell that Aaron to chase after some other girl."

Turning towards the house, Phoebe kicked at the ground as she walked, scattering loose bits of shingle. She could hear Peggy's next words before they came from her podgy mouth; she'd be blaming Phoebe's temper on her foreign blood. It wasn't right. Pa was the gentlest, kindest man and yet he could do no right – neither when he was here as a loving husband and father, nor afterwards when he was chased out of Dymchurch.

"Watch that Frenchie temper, my girl!" Peggy yelled.

Phoebe flung the bag into the scullery, tucked the ironing board under her arm and stamped into the kitchen. The washing basket was tossed into Peggy's armchair and the ironing board set up. As her temper cooled, Phoebe placed two irons on the metal rack beside the fire, then placed the sheet out on the board, brushing away the worst of the creases with her hands. Having wrapped a piece of rag around the handle of the first iron, Phoebe lifted it and placed it upon the cloth, then began the arduous task of smoothing out the bedding.

Peggy always stayed in the shop on a Monday afternoon, happy to leave the laundry to Phoebe. She might waddle out and check on her niece occasionally, but Phoebe knew she had plenty of opportunities to slip away and return the bag to its owner. That is, if Harry *was* the owner.

Crouching down in the scullery, Phoebe undid the soft leather buckle. Guilt gnawed at her stomach as she prepared to pull back the material and gaze at someone else's possessions. Perhaps this was all he owned in the world and it seemed wrong to look through all that was precious to him. But maybe this sack contained an old woman's stitching or a travelling salesman's samples. How foolish she would look to present it to this stranger… this Harry… and for him to be there with Owen and Bess, his own bag already with him.

The folds of material opened to reveal a set of clothes neatly rolled up, and a bundle of socks. There was a Bible, a slim box to hold a pen and what was this? Phoebe was drawn to a narrow book, her fingers curling round the binding and caressing the worn cover. She drew it from the bag and allowed it to fall open, revealing a collection of poems. A connection was made with this young man who was, in her heart, no longer a stranger but someone who shared a love for the written word.

Her eyes were fixed upon the cover, in some parts shiny and others dull, in the way that the patina of age varies as it takes its toll on leather. Inside, the pages held lines of neat print, with the occasional handwritten note in the margins. How she longed to take this book to the light and read the spider-like scribblings, to see into the mind of whoever had read these poems and felt the need to express their own thoughts. The cherished book must be replaced, but not before Phoebe raised it to her lips and planted the softest of kisses upon the worn leather.

Clutching the bag against her body with both hands wrapped around it, Phoebe ran lightly from the scullery and through the back yard. She darted down the alleyway between the cottages and paused to look up and down the High Street. Then she crossed the road and went down the track leading to the cottage under the wall.

There was no need to rap on the front door as Owen was working to the side of the house, gathering logs and stacking them in a lean-to store. Wiping his hands on a leather apron, he paused as he stood amongst the wood chips.

"Good to see you, lass. We got him home and let's hope that's the end of any bother for the lad."

"I'm so pleased," Phoebe grinned. "I'd heard of course and Uncle Giles was in a right temper over it all."

"What brings you here then?"

"It's this bag; it was found out at Willop and I heard that Harry had left his somewhere in that direction."

"That's right." Owen took a step forwards as if to take the bundle from Phoebe's arms. "He's in no fit state to go searching for it; I was about to go looking myself."

Phoebe offered the bag. "I had a quick look... just to be sure."

"Well, come on in and meet him and we'll know for certain then." Owen walked towards the front door. "But you'll have to excuse him if he's not quite right. It's rather a knock to the head he's had and, last I saw, he'd fallen asleep across the table!"

Chapter Nine
Harry

When the vicar delivered Harry back to the cottage hunkered down below the wall, they found Owen working on the land to the side.

"You've come back then?" was Owen's only comment as he swung an axe at a log. "I'll chop and you put these logs in the store over there. We'll be needing them for the fire; the winter store has run low."

Harry set to work carrying logs to the wood store. The rhythm of the chore soothed his mind as he tried to empty it of all thought and, for that moment, concentrate on the task. The store, leaning against the side of the cottage, had that comforting smell of seasoned wood. Tension eased with the cycle of lifting, moving and stacking. Owen passed the occasional comment, but allowed Harry this time to his own thoughts, and the young man appreciated it.

It was Bess, coming through the doorway with a tray of weak cider and slabs of fruit cake, who broke the contemplative silence.

"Here you are, lad, time for a rest after the morning you've had."

Harry looked down at her and gave a weak smile.

"I'm glad you came back to us," Bess said. "I was worried about you setting off on your own, with that bump on your head."

"You got yourself in some trouble then?" Owen sat down on the bench outside the front door of the cottage and leaned back against the rough cob walls.

Harry looked down at the muddy ground strewn with wood chippings. "Sorry... I didn't mean to... I wasn't stealing... I've got money, of course I have. I did have, but that shopkeeper pushed it out of my hand."

"Of course you did." Owen looked Harry directly in the eye. "You don't set off for Sussex without a penny in your pocket; I know that and you're a decent lad. I know that too." He gestured for Harry to sit down beside him. "You've a bit to learn about Dymchurch now that you're settling here for a while and you've already learned to keep away from Giles Wood for the time being. Bess and I will make sure he causes you no bother. You keep out of trouble, work hard, and all this will be forgotten." Owen finished his drink and stood up. "Now, talking of hard work, we've more wood to chop before Bess has dinner on the table"

They laboured for a while longer until the sun, although mostly obscured by the blanket of cloud, had reached the peak of its journey that day. Its feeble rays shone down upon the slate-grey sea, the village hugging the wall, and the acres of flat lands beyond. When Bess called them in for lunch, Harry was grateful – he needed to sit, or preferably slump, in a chair. His world was beginning to spin, and the side of his head was aching again.

"Thank you, Lord, for what we are about to eat. We welcome Harry into our home and may You guide us as we teach him to live respectably. Give us strength to maintain the wall and keep Romney Marsh safe."

Listening to Owen's words, Harry felt his head swaying as it bowed towards the table. But he was hungry too, so the cold meat, chunk of bread and pickled vegetables were welcome. His last meal had been taken while sitting on the edge of the wooden-plank bed in the Dymchurch gaol. Forcing himself to sit upright, Harry regretted not being able to enjoy the food as much as it deserved.

He nodded and smiled occasionally but for the most part any conversation washed over him; he sensed that these new people in his life understood. There was a gentleness about them that he hadn't experienced in a long time. Although he was many years past being a child, Harry still needed to feel safe and nurtured. He knew that Owen would never raise his fist to Bess, nor swing a piece of iron in his direction. He knew that Bess would not cower at the sound of her husband's footsteps and that he, the young son, would not look on, powerless to help the victim. And so, with good food in his stomach, the warmth coming from the open fire and, most importantly, the blanket of safety that wrapped itself around him, Harry allowed his aching head to rest on his hands and he closed his eyes... just for a moment.

When he woke, Harry saw that the table had been cleared and it seemed that the room was empty of other people. A noise came from outside, the rhythmic *thwack* of an axe on wood. But from inside the cottage there was only the comforting sound of wood crackling and the occasional shifting of a log as it settled deeper within the fire. Harry pushed his chair back, just a little, and, using his folded arms as a pillow, he laid his head back down upon the table top.

He was on the seawall, but it wasn't the seawall. It was the churchyard wall back at Elham, back home. He was pressing clay into gaps between the stones and could feel the cool sensation of it in his hands.

The clay kept coming and holes remained unfilled. What was the urgency? What was he trying to hold back?

Harry stirred and an awareness came that he had been in a deep sleep. A much needed sleep, but something had changed and it was time to wake. Before he saw her standing there, Harry was aware that there had been a shift in the balance of people within the home. Someone else had entered the family unit and, for this moment, it was not the three of them.

When Harry opened his eyes, the table was flanked by three others. There was Owen in his leather apron, and Bess now encased in a white apron with damp patches of soapsuds on the front. And then there was the newcomer, but not a stranger, as although he was seeing her for the first time Harry knew that she came as a friend.

Standing there she looked a little uncertain, the beginning of a smile playing around the edge of her lips. Her eyes were on his own: dark brown fixed on his grey. But after a moment she lowered her gaze to her hands clasped in front of her. Her skin was the colour of the underside of a fawn or a baby rabbit, smooth and unblemished. Tied in a loose knot at the nape of her neck, her hair was straight and a glossy brown; the colour of the much-loved and well-polished oak cabinet his mother had kept her treasures in. How old was she, he wondered? Perhaps about his own age, which was twenty, or thereabouts. She wasn't tall and would probably reach his shoulder or a little higher. If he were to place his arms around her slender waist, her head would rest nicely on his chest. This young woman looked like a truly beautiful person in body and soul.

Harry worked his lips into a smile; his mind was

still befuddled from sleep and this beauty before him caused his heart to flip in an unaccustomed manner. With his hands on the edge of the table, he pushed the chair back and attempted to speak:

"Hello, I'm sorry... I was... I've had a bump to the head and..."

"Of course. I understand." Her voice was soft, gentle, inviting confidences.

She looked down at the floor and Harry's gaze followed hers. Frowning, he saw his bag at her feet.

"You've got my bag," he said. It sounded rude but he didn't mean it to. He tried again. "I mean, thank you. You've brought my bag here."

"A friend found it, some distance away, near Willop." She looked into his eyes again, just for a moment before lowering her lashes. Was she shy of him as he was of her? "I was going to take it to the vicar; it seemed like the best thing to do. But then I heard... I heard that you were here, staying with Bess and Owen, and that you had left a bag somewhere over that way."

"I was helping with the breach," Harry explained. "Then we came back here and it was too late to go back for the bag." He stood and reached down, pulling the bag towards him. "I was travelling through and all my belongings are in here, so I'm grateful that you thought of me."

"You've had a rough time since arriving in Dymchurch." Bess laid her hand on his shoulder. "But there's good folk here as well as the wrong-uns you've come across."

"I know that. I've met three of them," Harry smiled.

"Come and sit down, Phoebe, love. Have a cup of tea with us." Bess took a step towards the fire and the kettle with water simmering within it.

"I've got to get back." Phoebe glanced to the door. "They'll be wondering where I've got to, especially on wash day."

"Of course you have," Owen walked to the door with her. "Thank you for coming as soon as you could."

Then she was gone and Harry hadn't quite managed to say 'goodbye' and 'thank you' again. He looked towards the door, which had closed behind Phoebe's back.

"Nice girl," Owen commented. "Shame she's the niece of that miserly Giles Woods. Not a lot of fun in that household for a lovely young woman like her."

Harry, who had already pictured himself exchanging a word or two with Phoebe after church or in the High Street, felt his heart slump.

That night, Harry slept well on the mattress placed on the floor of the living room. And when he woke in the night he listened for a while to the gentle slap of the sea on the wall and the pull of the shingle as each wave retreated. When morning came he felt more refreshed than he had done since arriving in Dymchurch. His fingers, searching out the two bumps on his head, sensed that both injuries were a little less swollen. The headache remained above his left ear, but had receded to a dull ache.

They had spoken the evening before about Harry's enforced stay within the village and his six months labour on the seawall. "You're lucky, they've put you in John Waller's team and he's as fair a man as you could find," Owen had said. "He knows you've had an injury and he saw for himself that you worked despite it. You'll have no trouble from him."

John Waller himself came rapping on the door just

after Harry had spooned the last mouthful of porridge.

"Ready to work on the wall?" John's face was thin and etched with deep lines, yet his smile was wide and eyes shone with warmth. "It's hard toil, but I've got a good team of workers. We'll get you up there and you'll soon learn what's to be done."

"I'm ready." Harry shrugged his arms into his jacket sleeves. "Ready to do my best for you."

They scrambled up the steep bank behind the cottage and stood on the wall. John allowed Harry a moment to take in the length and breadth of the structure, to understand the importance of the seawall and survey the land it protected.

It was the vastness of the gently sloping, pale gold sands that first claimed Harry's attention. The tide was low, moving to and fro with none of the malice shown on the night that the wall gave way. Waves did not break upon the beach with a crescendo of white froth; they merely rippled upon the sand and slid back again. The sea was a dull blue, highlighted with a spread of silver sparkles as the early morning sun began its journey and cast its rays upon the water.

The bay was wide, without any features to engage Harry's attention. No rock pools, cliffs or jetties for ships. Merely the sands, the sea and the bold line of the seawall. To the east, tree-topped hills rose beyond its furthest point and to the west the bay merely ended in a haze of early morning mists. It seemed that Dymchurch was the central area; it would be a morning's walk or more to reach one end or the other.

Sturdy wooden structures stretched from the top of the seawall and across the sands. Looking down upon one of these, Harry saw that it was filled with rock, this in turn had a liberal coating of barnacles dressed in seaweed. These were clearly needed to keep the sand

101

and shingle in place. It seemed, due to the swathes of shingle to one side, that the sea carried its load from west to east.

That morning, the vastness of the sea, the sands and the pale-blue sky above, brought a feeling of peace to Harry. Tension eased from his limbs, and he took some deep breaths of air carrying a slight tang of salt and seaweed.

"Knockes, they're called." John Waller broke the silence.

"Knockes?" Harry turned, his brow furrowed."

"Them bits of wood. Stretching down the beach, keeping the sand and suchlike in place."

"Oh, I see. Knockes," Harry replied.

"This one here is Spittleman's Knocke, marking the end of our bit o' wall. And to the west, over there is High Knocke. That's the other end of our patch."

The seawall, this gently curving rampart, appeared to be the main route through the village. Standing upon it, Harry could see why travellers and locals alike would appreciate being in this position of height. It gave the best view of village, countryside and sea. For mile after mile, anyone who walked or rode here would have nothing to catch them unawares.

The top of the wall must be twenty feet wide, Harry calculated. Two carts could pass side by side with no fear of toppling off. Channels formed by the movement of carts had clearly been filled and, even as they stood there, a pair of horses could be seen approaching from the east. On a fair day such as this, it made the ideal road, Harry reflected. But when the wind gathered force and blew from the sea, to be on this high road would be grim and dangerous. Certainly the low road through the village had its place and, where it hugged the wall, the sheltered track would be welcomed.

Harry looked to the west, towards the area known as High Knocke. The fields beyond the wall were pasture, with a wide cutting of water slicing through and running parallel to the wall. The seawall itself became less distinctive beyond High Knock. Did it extend the whole length of the bay, Harry wondered? For surely all the land was low-lying. Or did it end, only to be replaced with a natural boundary of shingle or slightly higher land?

"So, this is our area, from right here at this knocke to over there," Harry stated. "We keep it in good repair. How many of us working in this place and on the whole wall?"

"Well, lad, that depends on the season because in high summer there's that many of us, you'll wonder how this old Marsh could provide so many strong men to cart clay to and fro all day so as to keep the wall fixed. And in November, when the sea does her best to beat us, we're busy making repairs, keeping the villagers safe. But from here to Everden Groyne there can be over two hundred men working."

"Two hundred men!" Harry frowned.

He looked beyond the ribbon of cottages and outbuildings crowding the High Street and the scattered homes in the shadow of the seawall. Narrow lanes wove their way into the flat landscape. There was a cottage or a farm here and there. And was that a church spire in the distance, to the west? Where did these men come from – these two hundred men, strong enough and young enough to labour all day? His head hurt to think of it. He would learn soon enough.

"How did it breach then?" Harry asked in wonder. "With all those men, working so hard?"

"It just takes a crack when the clay's all hard and brittle from the frosts, and the sea... she finds her way in. And sometimes we don't see what damage is being done inside from just a small opening on the seaward side." To John, the sea and the wall were living, breathing things with emotions of their own. "Before you know it, there's a whole great area giving way and opening up, and the sea, well, she's found her way and forced through with all her might."

"Is that what we do then, look for cracks?" Harry asked.

"We do, but that's been done by those who started just after dawn. There's other damage to repair today; she's scoured away the sand and shingle from the base of the wall and cast it against these knockes. There's shovelling to be done today, lad, and I'm not sorry to have a strong one like you on my team."

John turned from facing the sea and set a brisk pace towards High Knocke. They passed a great outlet where water flowed onto the sands.

"Clobsden Gut." John gave a brief nod in the direction of the water funnelled through the seawall then contained by stone walls until it was expelled midway down the beach. "Taking water from the land and putting it out there, out of harm's way. We keeps it in during high tide and out she goes when the tide is at mid-point. We've got Mark, him who works the sluice gates, on our team. Off he goes every now and then to move the gates."

Now they were past the water outlet and Harry could clearly see a donkey and cart standing on the wall above where High Knocke extended. On reaching the knocke, Harry saw the team of men who had previously been obscured by the wooden structure.

"Hey, lads, give yourselves a breather," John

called, as he and Harry descended wooden steps and stood on the scattering of shingle, shells and driftwood at the high tide mark. "I've got Harry here with me; he'll be on the team until the autumn, helping look after this old wall."

About twelve faces all turned to look at Harry. The men varied in age, some of them barely men – boys of perhaps fourteen or fifteen. Then several around Harry's age, young men of about twenty years old. There were a couple who were of the age to have young families to support and a few more who, like John Waller, had lines etched in their faces showing that their youth was long past. These men all leaned upon shovels with wide, shallow heads; marks on the sand showed where they had been labouring.

Forcing a smile, Harry said, "That's right. Good to meet you all."

One of the older men nodded in the direction of a shovel leaning against the knocke. Harry took a couple of steps and clasped the tool in his hands. Now he stood below the seawall it was clear that the inner framework had been exposed from beneath, as the sea had worked at the very sand and shingle the wall stood upon. Tendrils of twigs and clumps of dry clay swayed, unused to this sudden freedom of movement and now released into the daylight.

"Fill her up and press it in; that's all there is to it. Sand first to fill the space." John picked up a shovel for himself and the team spread out along the knocke. Harry pushed the shovel into a pile of sand. His first day of work on the wall had begun.

Chapter Ten
Phoebe

"Go on, girl, you can manage another pack of sugar." Peggy pushed a brown bag amongst the others in the basket. It perched precariously beside neighbouring packets, threatening to topple out.

Wrapping her arms around the wicker basket, Phoebe sighed. It was all very well filling the basket to the brim and beyond, but it made an awkward load, and if any were to spill there would be a month's worth of reproaches to come. Her aunt opened the door and Phoebe stepped out onto the street, the bulk of the basket obscuring her view of any potential obstacles.

Nervous of stepping in anything unsavoury or tripping over a dog or small child, Phoebe walked slowly, feeling her way with her boots. She passed the neighbouring shops and cottages, then crossed the High Street before resting the basket on a low wall. Scanning the road leading up to Seawall Road, Phoebe noted that it seemed clear enough, picked up the basket and trudged up the slope.

It was a month since the seawall had breached; Easter had passed and the days were becoming longer. Although the sea breeze had less of a chill to it, the sky was grey and clouds raced as if chased by demons. The sun had little chance of warming the vast sands with its golden light. They looked uninviting with their grey-brown mudflats and shallow puddles of water. A couple of men were out in the mud, their backs bent and coat-tails flapping as they dug for lug-worms.

With the basket securely clasped against her apron, Phoebe turned to the east and walked slowly along the road beside the seawall, keeping her sights firmly on the track ahead. On hearing a cart closing in on her, she moved slightly to the left, stepping into a rut caused by the frequent traffic upon the road. She staggered a little and, fearing that the cart was almost on top of her, frantically tried to side-step further towards the edge of the track. Her boots slipped on wet clay and Phoebe came down heavily on her knees. With no hands free to break her fall, the basket came down hard in front of her and her lower ribs took the force of the fall.

Afterwards she couldn't have said which caused her more pain – the searing hurt taking a grip of her stomach or the anguish on seeing several of the packets topple and the base of the basket rammed into the clay-mud. Or was it that the embarrassment was greater than any pain or damage when she became aware that the cart had stopped and it was the newcomer, Harry, who was leaning over her, his hand patting her shoulder and asking if she was hurt?

"Oh, it's you." Phoebe felt a blush rise on her cheeks. How foolish; she had never blushed before, not when Aaron kissed her or even when that handsome doorman from the New Hall glanced in her direction.

"Phoebe?" His voice was gentle as he questioned, "Are you hurt? Can you stand?"

"I… it's just where the basket… where I fell onto it." She moved back, squatting on her heels, arms

107

outstretched and balancing with her hands on the basket. "Just a few bruises and... and some dirty clothes."

Harry placed his hand under her elbow. "Let's get you up."

Phoebe stood with both hands wrapped around her midriff. The hem of her skirt and the bottom of her apron were caked in clay. What would he think of her, this Harry who was new to the village? She looked as if she'd stepped straight out of the poorhouse. No, worse, for although their clothes were ragged they kept them clean. It was all some of them did all day: launder clothes for themselves and the wealthier people of the village.

Why was she thinking about those poor wretches? He had stopped to help her, asked if she was all right and all she could think of was the clay on her skirt. She hadn't looked at him directly, but she must. Lifting her face, Phoebe allowed her eyes to meet his and she saw no mockery or distaste. There was compassion in those grey eyes.

"Thank you." Phoebe spoke quietly. "I'll be fine now. You must have work to do."

"It's high tide," Harry replied. "I'm taking the donkey back to Slodden Farm and then going home for a meal with Owen and Bess." He reached down for the basket and placed it on the low cart. "Now can you imagine what Bess would have to say if she heard I'd left you here with all this mess about you and not stopped to help?"

"Oh, but you did stop." Phoebe's eyes widened in dismay. "You helped me up."

"And now, should I leave you feeling wretched about your muddy apron and spilled food?"

"That's the worst of it," Phoebe confided. "The

food, those packets spoiled. I'll have to return and Aunt Peggy will be furious."

"Aunt Peggy. Would she be the large woman with lips that pout her disapproval?"

Phoebe grinned. "You remember her then?"

"Remember her? How could I forget her standing there with a club in her hand, just waiting to use it? And there was I, just passing by and my head already thumping from some injury I'd suffered the day before."

"Your head? Is it better now?" Phoebe recalled that day, a month ago, when she had first seen Harry slumped against a barrel in the shop, pale and seemingly confused.

"It took a while for the bruising to go down and longer for the ache to fade." Harry rubbed the side of his head. "I don't know what happened. I'd fallen asleep you see; I'd been walking all day. Then when I woke, something had happened to my head and the water was coming in through the wall. I can't remember much more." He paused and looked at the packets strewn about the wet clay-mud. "Let's pick these up and take a look at them. We can wipe them with your apron – it's suffered enough and there's no hope of hiding it from your aunt."

They picked up the sugar and the flour, the oats and the spices. Harry brushed some of the mud away with his hands and Phoebe wiped packets with her apron. They worked in companionable silence; within minutes six packets stood in a row on the flat bed of the cart.

"There you see, not so bad and only six spoiled packets. There must be another ten in the basket as clean as when they left the shop."

"It's still six packets for Aunt Peggy to fuss about."

Phoebe's face fell.

"Now, let's think about this." Harry persisted on looking for a way to help. "Where were you going?"

"Cluny House. Just here along the road." Phoebe pointed in the direction of a low two-storey house facing the sea.

"Well then, there's nothing to worry about!" Harry grinned.

"Muddy packets and a late delivery."

"Not at all. The housekeeper is Bess' sister and one of the nicest women you could hope to meet."

"She is," Phoebe admitted.

"I'll come along to the back door with you and explain what happened. In fact I'll take the blame. I'll say that I knocked into you, that I was careless."

"Oh, you can't do that."

"Well, I'll come with you and show her the packets and she'll put the oats and flour, and whatever else you have, in her storage jars and the paper wrapping on the fire. What will a bit of mud matter then?"

"Thank you." Phoebe felt rather foolish not to have seen it in this way. "I see what you mean. Then it's just my apron spoiled."

"Of course, you'll have to explain it. But it's not as if your aunt would have to clean it and she needn't know that you had your fall before the delivery was made."

"No… no, of course not."

Harry took hold of the donkey's halter and his shirt sleeve fell back. Looking sideways, Phoebe noted his forearm: strong but lean and lightly freckled. She had an irrational need to reach out and run her fingers over his flexed muscles. His hands were a little rough and his fingernails were dirty. But, there was nothing wrong with the signs that Harry had done a fair day's work. His nails were neatly rounded and his clothes fitted nicely, showing that he took good care of himself.

In the evenings, when the dirt had been scrubbed away from beneath his fingernails and any sand or dried clay brushed off his clothes, did Harry read his book of poetry, Phoebe wondered? Did he sit under a lamp and run his fingers under the lines, carefully sounding out the words? And did those verses make him think of other places, different times and the people who figured in the pages of his book?

He was speaking to her and Phoebe tore her thoughts away from the volume of poetry with the worn leather cover and pencil notes in the margins. What was it he had said? Of course, they were at Cluny House and he would come to the kitchen door with her to speak with the housekeeper.

"Thank you. It's very kind of you," Phoebe smiled up at him. She wanted to say more... ask him if he liked to read; if the slim volume of poems was his own. Her words would sound foolish. What an odd thing to speak of.

Cluny House sat almost on the seawall itself, at a point where the wall grew wide enough to accommodate both a broad track and several good brick houses. Cluny was, with its neighbours, on the land side of the wall and now sat just a little lower than the seawall which had been regularly topped up with rubble and clay. With the donkey tethered to a post and the basket in Harry's arms, they walked down a path to the right of the property.

"There's been a small accident," Harry explained, as they were ushered into the kitchen by the housekeeper.

"I can see that." Her hand reached out to the ruined apron. Phoebe looked down at the muddy stains, fearful of ever cleaning away all the evidence of her fall.

"I gave Phoebe here a fright, coming upon her too quickly and you know how slippery the clay can be... she stepped aside and slipped in a rut." Harry smiled and showed the spoiled packets. "A few of these are a bit muddy and she was going to replace them, but there would be no end of trouble..."

The housekeeper, sister to Bess and just as motherly, soon understood the trouble that Phoebe could be in with her aunt. More than that, she saw Harry's need to impress and comfort. The packets were laid out upon the kitchen table, but it was Phoebe's apron claiming the attention.

"You won't sneak that into the wash, not without Peggy noticing." The housekeeper lifted the hem and frowned at the scuffs of mud. Then she turned and opened a cupboard to reveal piles of neatly laundered kitchen cloths and towels, alongside embroidered table cloths in pristine linen.

"This one isn't so very different from your own," She held up an apron, allowing the folds to open as she shook it free. "The girl who comes in on a washday wears these and she's about your size."

Phoebe's spirits lifted as she understood the plan. "Do you think I could... and I'll return it next week?"

"Of course, but you leave the muddy one here and I'll put it into soak now. No cause to have that Peggy fussing over something that need not bother her."

They left Cluny House, reluctantly refusing the offer of a drink and freshly-baked biscuits. Harry still had to take the donkey along the wall to Slodden Farm and Phoebe was of course nervous about the time already wasted.

Walking back to the donkey, Harry put his hand on the halter and looked at Phoebe. She gazed back at him and gave a tentative smile. It was time for them to part and she felt unwilling to step away from him. It must have been a month since they last met; at that time Harry could barely lift his head from his hands. There had been some form of injury; he'd had a knock to the head and had seemed confused.

He was different now; a very different Harry from that lost young man who had mistakenly picked up a jar of barley sugar on the Lord's day of rest. He held his head high and had grown confident through his role as a labourer on the wall and the security of a home given by Owen and Bess. Phoebe didn't know what had led Harry to come to Dymchurch, but she felt that his life before had been unhappy and now he was discovering a place where he could find contentment.

"I'd best get the donkey back, and there's a meal waiting for me."

Did he feel the same reluctance as she did? Would it be another month before they could speak again? Now the fall and the consequences, the ruined packets and the spoiled apron, had lost its blanket of embarrassment. That had been lifted and replaced with the memory of a look, the kind words and his gentle guidance.

"Yes, of course you must and thank you... thank you for everything you did. I..."

Neither Phoebe nor Harry heard the approach of a horse cantering along the wall. For those moments before they parted, their world didn't go beyond the space holding only the two of them, with the donkey and the cart on its periphery. It was only as the horse stopped within that special space that they became aware and, as her stomach clenched, Phoebe took a step away from Harry.

"Now here's my girl!" Aaron swung from his horse

with ease and placed himself before Phoebe with his back to Harry. Placing a hand on her waist, his claim was made. "You're looking a bit ruffled; not being bothered I hope?"

"Of course not, Aaron." Phoebe scowled and stepped away from his clasp. Why did he have to come along now, at this very moment? A minute before and she would have still been in Cluny House and Aaron would not have known about this time with Harry, or the fall, or any of it.

"I stopped because Phoebe tripped; she slipped and..." Harry tightened his grip on the donkey's halter, "I wanted to check that she wasn't hurt."

Aaron turned and for the first time he looked at Harry. "Well, I'm here now and I'll be the one checking that my woman is all right."

Phoebe felt the heat rise in her face and she looked down at her feet. She didn't want to look towards Harry, to see the hurt that he must feel or to read the confusion in his eyes. But despite her embarrassment, Phoebe knew Harry had been kind to her and she would not allow Aaron to speak to him in this way. So she raised her face and said, "I'm thankful to Harry for stopping and if it wasn't for him, I'd be in big trouble with Aunt Peggy. Now we're keeping him from taking the donkey back and for all I've got out of one spot of trouble there'll be more if I'm not back at the shop soon."

Then she turned to Harry. "I hope you've not lost too much time and thank you so much for everything you've done."

"I think that's covered everything." Aaron's eyes narrowed and he looked at Harry with distaste. "It looks like she's fine now, Wall Boy."

"I'm glad I could help," Harry addressed Phoebe,

114

his clenched hands the only sign that he was having to keep his temper in check. With a tug on the halter, the donkey stirred and prepared to move on; his field of spring grass beckoned.

"I don't like what I saw there," Aaron commented, as they both watched Harry walk away.

"You're being foolish," Phoebe retorted. Embarrassment filled and lurched within her stomach, but she was determined to speak her mind to Aaron. "Someone stopped to help me and you didn't think to thank him. You have shamed us both."

"He had taken a fancy to you. And what is he, nothing better than a wall-worker?"

"Nothing better than a wall-worker?" Rage rose within Phoebe. "What's wrong with doing an honest day's work on the wall? If it wasn't for the likes of him, we'd none of us be lying at peace in our beds at night or any other time. You need to show a bit of respect for those that keep us safe here in Dymchurch."

"What's he to you, that you defend him like this?" Aaron's eyes mocked her as he took her chin between his thumb and index finger. "I'm not liking this, Phoebe. Now give me a kiss and we'll both be on our way."

Phoebe jerked her face away and flashed fury from her brown eyes. "I'm done with this, Aaron, I'll not have it. I'll not have you coming along and treating me like this. When did I ever give you any encouragement?"

Aaron rolled his eyes in mock despair. "I like a bit of banter, but this is enough. I suppose you're wanting a ring on your finger and I said I'd ask your uncle on your birthday but I'm not averse to speaking with him before. I'll bring him a bottle of brandy after morning church on Sunday and we can drink to our future happiness – that's mine and yours, Phoebe." He made as if to turn away; as if there was nothing else to say.

Phoebe was forced to raise her voice to say what needed to be said. "No, Aaron, don't bother with the brandy. I won't marry you and you'd be wasting your time if you thought otherwise. I'm sorry if I gave you cause to think different, but we'd not be happy, you and I. Tell your mother that I'll return the book but it's best that I don't visit anymore."

Aaron didn't turn back to look at her again. He grasped the saddle of his horse, put a foot in the stirrup and swung himself up. Then, turning the horse's head to the west, he gave a savage kick beneath its ribs and cantered away.

Chapter Eleven
Harry

"That will be the last of it for today," John called, as he laid his wooden beetle on the ground.

As the team stopped hammering the heavy-headed mallets into the top of the seawall, the call went up: "Harry! Harry! Harry!"

Somewhere along the wall the expenditor had placed his hat on a stake and so, as the wall-workers spotted it, the cry snaked from central Dymchurch outwards to the Willop in the east and High Knocke in the west.

"Harry! Harry! Harry!"

It still made Harry grimace, even though he had been hearing it for a month now. Not that it had anything to do with him; it was the custom of the wall-workers. Long ago, back in the thirteenth century Henry of Bath had drawn up the Laws and Customs of the Marsh. Centuries later he was remembered at the end of each day.

The spades used to dig the clay had already been placed on the cart. Now the beetles were slung in bedside them. The men had been shovelling, moving and packing in clay all day. Taking it from the base of the wall where it slid over the course of time, then filling in the ruts on the top of the wall with more clay and bits of rubble.

Now one of the other young lads would return the donkey and cart, but first they would walk together until they reached the expenditor, who would hand out a shilling and sixpence for the day's labour. Not for Harry though. He served on the wall as a punishment so he took only a shilling for his work. It took twenty minutes or so to reach the expenditor, who was waiting near Church Knocke. As they approached, the other teams could be seen moving along the wall. It was a swarm of about eighty workers who congregated for their money. Harry took his coins with a nod of thanks and turned back to retrace his steps to the centre of the village.

With aching limbs, Harry walked the short distance from Church Knocke to the cottage that had become his home. Stepping down from Seawall Road to the High Street, he passed shops and terraced cottages before turning once more towards the wall. If he had approached from the seawall, rather than the High Street, he would have looked down upon the wooden plank extension to Bates' Cottage. With its new roof of reed thatch and small window to the rear it was a modest space.

The length of seawall behind the cottage was part of John Waller's area, and Harry walked the wall from High Knocke to Spittleman's Knocke on a regular basis. Over the last weeks, looking down at the progress of the new extension his heart brimmed with love and respect for the couple who had taken him into their home. They cared for him as if he were a part of their own family and, in return, Harry was determined to do nothing to bring shame to them.

In the evenings, he had helped Owen bind the reeds into tight, waterproof bundles and, when the

118

rafters were in position, together they had tucked and pressed the thatch into place. For her part, Bess hemmed curtains for the window and threaded rag and string in order to produce a colourful rug for the floor.

An old trunk came from the attic of a nearby cottage. It arrived with decades of dust, broken hinges and a split in the side. Owen had replaced the cracked plank of wood and Harry bought hinges from the hardware shop in the High Street; Bess had given it a thorough clean and a polish with beeswax. Now the trunk was placed at the end of the low bed-frame crafted by Owen. Also made by Owen, but sanded by Harry in the evenings, was a row of sturdy wooden pegs where he slung his jacket and his decent clothes. The much-patched work clothes were stored in the trunk, when they weren't soaking in the copper or airing by the fire.

The room was small, only twice the width of his bed and just a little longer than the bed and trunk. But it was Harry's own space and, more important than that, it was created for him with love. He had enjoyed watching Owen at work repairing the trunk. The smoothing of the wooden pegs was good for the soul after a long day at work on the wall and Harry enjoyed seeing the grain of the wood coming to life as polish was applied. For now Owen had worked enough on Harry's behalf, but the young man was planning to ask if he could make his own piece of furniture under Owen's guidance.

He had a bookcase in mind. Nothing large of course because he only possessed his Bible and his mother's book of poetry. The Bible had been given to him as a child and he enjoyed, on occasion, letting it fall open and then reading a story or two. The print was small and the pages thin, but it bought back memories of a happy childhood and he knew that his sister had her own matching copy. Just to hold it in his hands, when the light was too weak for him to read by, brought him closer to her.

The slim book of poetry with its worn leather cover was infinitely more precious. It was a gift from his father to his mother, and she often sat by the light of the lamp or the window with the book open, her eyebrows furrowed and her lips moving as she formed the words. She could read a letter or a pamphlet with ease; as for poetry, well that was a different matter. The words were not always familiar to her, but she wanted to understand them and to pronounce those as yet unknown in the correct way. She had taken to writing comments in the wide margins of the thick paper and these scribblings were cherished by Harry and strengthened the invisible bond between mother and son.

Like his mother, Harry also sought to understand the words and phrases. He too would study the book and enjoy the rhythm of the verse. He noted the varied styles: short verses and long verses, some rhyming and some not. And he chose his favourites among them.

His bookcase, that is the bookcase he imagined he would have, would sit beside his bed and hold more books he would collect over time. Perhaps he would enjoy some Shakespeare or a modern novel? He would be interested in accounts of British history and nature. The book of poetry would, of course, always be the most precious but the others would gain memories attached to them. Memories which, for now, had not been formed.

Today his room could only be seen in his mind as

Harry approached the cottage from the front. He opened the door to a familiar scene: Bess was moving between the fire and the sturdy, well-scrubbed pine table; she was always determined to have a meal on the table for Harry not long after he returned from work. As always, she greeted him with a wide smile, while her eyes ran over his clothing, assessing whether any patches of dirt needed scrubbing off or soaking overnight.

"You've had a visitor," Bess announced. "Not that she would stay and wait for you, too shy for that! But she brought you something and hoped you wouldn't be offended."

"Offended?" Harry queried. But a visitor – this was a new experience. She… could it be?

"It's on the table," Bess pointed towards a twist of brown paper. "A gift to say thank you."

"It was Phoebe then; she got herself into trouble today."

"You didn't mention it at lunchtime."

"I didn't want to embarrass her." Harry grinned at the memories of the spoiled apron and damaged packets. Then he stepped towards the table. "What's in the packet that might offend me?"

He picked it up and carefully unravelled the paper twists. Inside a dozen honey-coloured barley sugars nestled together. Harry lifted the packet to his nose and inhaled their sugary sweetness. Of course, barley sugar, the very reason for his confinement in Dymchurch and his labour upon the seawall. He could see why he might be offended, but here was a gift from the beautiful, gentle Phoebe, and it made him smile.

"She told me how you helped her," Bess informed. "A lovely girl, she is. Don't you think?"

"I do. But how can I thank her? I can't knock at her door or go in the shop, and I met her suitor today... he wasn't exactly friendly."

"Just give her a smile and a nod at church on Sunday and she'll know you appreciated the gift. Phoebe knows you can't do more than that. But as for that Aaron, he's nothing but a braggart and a bully. Phoebe has a miserable time with those two in the shop, but she won't go off with Aaron to escape them. Sensible girl, she is. I can see that."

"It seemed he had some claim on her." Harry held the sweets to his nose once more, then refolded the bag.

"She told me that she's put him straight. But it might take a while for him to accept that; she's got trouble ahead I'm sure of it." Bess started slicing chunks of fresh bread. "Now get yourself tidied up and call Owen in, will you? No need to worry about girls. You need to keep yourself to yourself and show everyone what a decent young man you are, especially after your difficult start here."

A week passed and Harry started his sixth week of work upon the seawall. Now the sea breeze was welcomed by the labourers, who threw their jackets aside and worked in just their shirts as the temperature rose.

Harry noticed John was spending more time inspecting the slopes with a couple of the more experienced wall-workers. They would often be seen pointing, frowning and moving close to inspect the smallest of cracks on both the seaward and land sides of the great wall.

"It's never an easy choice; sometimes one part wears quicker than another and I'll not be popular if the wall breaches," John stated one day, as the three of them returned to the rest of the team. "Let's just stop for a quick break, lads. Take a swig of your cider and my wife, bless her, did a bit of baking yesterday, so there's fruit pies all round!"

The workers sat on the edge of the wall, feet dangling down towards the sands. The tide was on the rise and would reach them in less than an hour. It was in no rush today, with very little wind to hurry it along. Shining down upon the water, the sun emphasised every ripple with a ribbon of light.

"We've been looking, me, Ben and David, and talking about which stretch is going to have the full rebuild this summer. I've got to get this right: there'll be hell to pay if I make the wrong choice and the wall breaches again. We were lucky last March. Very lucky. And them who tend the areas that breached, well, they were lucky no-one was killed and no homes lost. They still had to answer to the Leveller of the Marsh Scotts, nonetheless."

"So where's it to be?" one of the workers asked.

"The far end, from Wall End to Clobsden Gut. We'll take the labourers who come from St Mary in the Marsh and along the lane leading that way. They'll be thankful they don't have to trek into the village."

"We're to have more labourers?" Harry asked in surprise.

"I forget, with you being new and not used to the ways of the wall..." John began.

"It's the same every summer," David joined in. "Each team chooses a part to be taken apart and rebuilt. There will be two hundred or more able-bodied men working on the wall during July and August. They come in from the Marsh, Romney and Hythe. Those that need work know where to head if they're fit enough."

"I'll be at the General Lathe on the Thursday of Whitsun to tell them all what the plan is," John continued. "Then it's up to the bailiff and expenditor to ensure we've got the hawthorn claimed and the clay allocated."

"They'll not be happy carting the clay to Wall End," Ben commented.

"Well, they'll be less happy if the wall breaches, and the soil is no good here. We need it from Burmarsh way." John put the last piece of pie in his mouth and took a swig of cider. "Another hour 'til lunch. Let's get on with it, lads."

The team had been working on the knocke that morning. The western side had taken a battering from the shingle thrown by the tide and the great wooden uprights were showing wear at the wall end of the knocke. They were going to remove the first four uprights, two at a time, and replace them. The morning had been spent removing the boulders from the gap between the wooden supports. Damp and rotten, the layer of brushwood once forming a cushion between sand and rock would be taken away by the tide.

Already weary from carrying boulders from the beach to the top of the wall, Harry had then started on digging the sand away from the base of the thick upright. The wood had worn to half its original width and would break away easily if assaulted by the blade of an axe. But it needed to be taken clean out of the sand in order for a new one to be placed there. He feared that unless the upright could be shifted soon, the tide would fill the hole with a fresh load of sodden sand.

"Sometimes it works like that, and sometimes the sea comes in and helps us with the job – working

124

away at the base of the post and helping it come out all the more easier," David informed.

"We'll know in a couple of hours," Harry said, as the sea crept further in. It would soon pour down into the hole and work its way further into the foundations of the knocke, exploring new territories as it seeped within the cracks of the worn wood and shifted the sands into new positions.

"Down tools," John called.

Even before the last of the labourers had climbed up the wooden steps with their spades, the sea was swirling around the previously unexplored areas at the base of the uprights. Usually Harry found himself drawn to watching the waters come in, but movement on the wall in the direction of the village caused him to frown with the effort of understanding who or what was approaching them at speed.

The usual traffic upon the wall was a pony and cart trundling along, accompanied by no more than two or three men, or a horse and rider moving at a trot as if in a hurry to be at some place. Women moved with shopping baskets from one area of the village to another; children played on the slopes of the seawall or raced along its top with balls. Fishermen crossed the divide between land and sea. And amongst these moved the wall-workers, a constant amongst the other characters who came and went.

When the winds raged and the sea vented its fury upon the structure of hawthorn and clay, the figures who used the seawall track were bent and scurried along looking neither to sea nor land. Often they used the track through the village or hurried at the very base of the wall, darting through cottage gardens.

In his month of studying Dymchurch life and, in particular, the rhythm of the seawall, Harry had never seen people travelling in great volume along the wall. It was not a place to herd animals and people moved individually or in small groups upon it. As he studied the movement, it became clear he was watching packhorses and an occasional cart. Harry became aware that no-one else seemed to have so much as glanced towards the tide of traffic taking up the whole width of the wall. It was only he who stood watching and trying to make sense of it, while the others cleaned their tools and spoke of the afternoon's work. Yet, there was an awareness, for the donkey and cart were moved until they stood lopsided on the grassy slope of the wall, with two of the wall-workers supporting the cart in case it should topple. And the other men put down their tools then sat, as they had earlier in the day, on the edge of the wall and studied the incoming tide.

When Harry found that he stood alone watching the procession nearing them, he too shifted his position, choosing to go to the landward slope and help support the listing cart. From there he could keep a better eye on whoever was approaching. It was from behind the cart, where he hoped to be partially obscured, that he viewed them passing.

There must have been twenty men. But almost twice as many horses, as many of the riders also led a packhorse. There were three carts, all stacked with barrels. The horses carried bundles of something slung each side of the saddle and the ones with no riders had additional sacks upon their backs.

The day was warm and had led to the wall-workers throwing off their jackets. Even now, having finished work, they had slung them over their shoulders. But these other men had poorly-fitted cloaks fashioned out of hessian sacking or some other rough material, with

126

hoods falling low over their faces. And the horses, who had no need of the blankets they sometimes wore in the coldest weather, had pieces of cloth hung about them, as if to hide a blaze of white or some other feature.

They passed at speed and, like animals appearing from burrows, John Waller's team moved back onto the top of the seawall. No comment was made about the passers-by and so Harry said nothing. He was kept busy with the difficulties of bringing the cart back onto the wall and, when he next glanced back, the procession had moved off the wall and appeared to be heading inland along the lane towards St Mary in the Marsh.

As the men headed to central Dymchurch, John said to Harry, "That reminds me, I was in The Ship last night and that Aaron Chapman was asking after you. Wondering what sort of lad you were and if you were a good worker or the type that was likely to get himself into trouble."

"I came across him just this week," Harry replied, his head all of a muddle trying to work out the connection.

"I said you were as nice a lad as I could hope to have on the team and a hard worker too," John continued. "He didn't seem too happy about that. I'd watch out for him if he's taken a dislike to you. Powerful family they are."

Chapter Twelve
Phoebe

With her heart lighter than it had been for months, Phoebe walked along the base of the wall. Her step was buoyant as she picked her way around clumps of weeds and skipped over patches of mud. The basket, swinging by her side, was now empty of packets and she was returning home for her lunch. Life with Peggy and Giles could be miserable, but there was always a tasty meal on the table.

It had suited Phoebe well enough to dash down the slope of the wall when she saw dozens of men approaching at a fair pace. They came from the east of the village: many of them on horseback, taking up the whole width of the track upon the seawall. She had a call to make at one of the cottages and would have stayed on the wall, but it was no trouble to move down beforehand. The weather had been fair, the grass was dry and besides she was nimble enough to negotiate the steep slope.

Nodding or calling out a brief greeting to villagers as she passed, Phoebe turned inland from the wall and followed a path to the High Street. It was as she passed the coaching inn that a pair of horses trotted by; sitting upright on their backs were a couple of riding officers. They had just passed her when, having come to an abrupt halt, one of them leaned down and grabbed an urchin by the collar.

"Seen anything you should be telling us about?" the law enforcer barked.

"Seen anything?" the boy repeated, his eyes wide and body squirming.

"Seen any of these good Dymchurch folk passing by with packhorses and carts?"

"Yeah, I seen 'em." The boy's eyes lit up. "But it will take a penny for me to remember, seeing that I ain't had a good meal in me belly since Easter."

"You can have a halfpenny." The second officer pulled a coin from his money belt and tossed it at the ground.

The urchin eyed it speculatively, but with the firm grip on his collar he was powerless to make a grab for the precious coin.

"What did you see and which direction were they travelling?" the first man persisted.

"It were two carts laden with hawthorn, travelling towards the east. I'd say they were going to the Willop cos I heard them talkin' about it."

"Farmhands!" the riding officer bellowed as he shook the urchin, who struggled to keep his balance. "Did I speak of farmhands? By the devil's horns, I'm talking about those bleeding smugglers with their packets of tea and bundles of lace, and the brandy that warms many a Marsh-man's throat!"

"I didn't see them, honest I didn't." The boy spoke quietly now, "I weren't lookin'."

"I've got my eye on you, lad," the second officer snarled as he flung the boy to the ground. "I never forget a face and I don't want to come across your ugly one again."

"Then you'll 'ave no trouble in recognising them smugglers what you see in taverns or passing by in the street," the urchin called as he scrambled to his feet and sidled into the doorway of the inn. "For you don't go an hour without seeing one, not 'ere you don't."

Phoebe watched as the nearest riding officer made a swipe at the boy. His whip only flicked at the door-frame of the inn. The boy had pushed his way into the bar and was, no doubt, ducking and diving between the legs of the men. He would leave by one of the back doors leading to the seawall, perhaps having supplemented his meagre earnings with a leather pouch of cash lifted from someone's pocket.

Stepping out into the road, Phoebe attempted to walk around the officers, intending to give their lively horses a wide berth. But they were not done with the people of Dymchurch and noticed the young woman.

"Good afternoon, Miss." It was as if his temper was forgotten as the senior riding officer shot a smile in Phoebe's direction.

Sitting himself a little taller in his saddle and straightening his crimson riding jacket, he tightened his reins and took control of the dancing horse. Phoebe, although irritated at being stopped by the officer, couldn't help wondering if they were to ride around in less conspicuous jackets then perhaps he would have more success in his job.

"Lovely day to be out. Making deliveries, were you?"

Phoebe merely nodded.

"Perhaps to the cottages along the wall, for I saw you just stepping along that track?" The officer inclined his head in the direction of the path Phoebe had taken.

"I've been in the cottages, stopping off for a chat and making deliveries as you said."

"Well, we won't tell that aunt and uncle of yours that you were gossiping rather than getting on with the work." He gave a wink and leaned down over the horse's withers. "Now my pretty, while you were in between cottages, did you happen to see them? Men and horses with all types of packages? I'm on the King's business, as well you know, and it wouldn't be right for a young woman to be keeping secrets from His Majesty."

"Of course not; God bless King George." Phoebe smiled sweetly and looked at the officer directly, meeting his cool blue eyes with her own deep brown. "I've seen no men other than the labourers on the wall and, as for horses, just the old pony and cart or even a donkey and cart. Were you interested in donkeys too, sir?"

"No, not donkeys."

"If I was to see anything, then I'd perhaps tell the vicar or the Leveller of the Marsh Scotts if I didn't happen to see you," Phoebe took a step away from the officers.

"No need for that, my love, you'll see us passing through most days and no cause to bother those good men. The Leveller of the Marsh Scotts may hold some sway over Dymchurch and hereabouts but we work for the King himself – don't you forget that."

"I won't," Phoebe's voice was grave as she took another step away from them.

It seemed as if they were prepared to let her go as, with a bow in her direction, they wheeled the horses away and set them in the direction of the steep track leading to the top of the wall.

After their midday meal, it was Giles who took his place behind the shop counter while Peggy and

131

Phoebe set about doing the washing up at the scullery sink. Perhaps it was the glasses of cider Peggy had supped during the meal, or perhaps she remembered her own years as a young woman, but her manner towards her niece was gentler than Phoebe recalled.

"You didn't go along to see Mrs Chapman last Saturday?" Peggy commented, while plunging her arms into warm soapy water.

"I thought I shouldn't; that it was encouraging Aaron to have false expectations."

"I was sure you'd taken a fancy to him," Peggy turned, her lips pouting at Phoebe.

"Perhaps I had for a time." Phoebe took a plate from the wooden drainer and rubbed it dry with a soft cloth. The action gave her time to reflect before saying more. "He's very popular in the village; I was flattered that he liked me... but then I wasn't so sure."

"It's fair enough if you change your mind," Peggy advised. "And he'd give you the run around; you could be sure of that. Now, some girls wouldn't mind if they were sittin' up in that big house with a maid and a cook and an odd-job boy. So that's for you to think about because they've books on them shelves that I can imagine you'd take a fancy to. But you're a hard worker, for all I say that you're not, and I don't think you'd marry to sit with a book or a bit o' stitching on your lap all day."

"No. No I wouldn't." Phoebe agreed. "I can't see that at all."

"I won't say I'm that fond of the lad. He's polite enough and I can't say otherwise, but there's something about him... he's all full up with pride in himself. That's what it is; he thinks he's someone important and he wants us all to know it. I like a bit of modesty, I do."

132

Unsure of how to respond and unused to her aunt speaking in this confiding manner, Phoebe continued with wiping the crockery and cooking pans, then walking through to the kitchen and placing them on the table. She was aware of Peggy casting glances in her direction and knew the conversation was not over.

"And do you think Aaron has thoughts of the two of you getting wed?" Peggy probed.

"I've told him I won't," Phoebe snapped. "I've had enough of his pushy ways and I hope that's the end of it."

"He's not one to have the decision made for him," Peggy reflected. "And he weren't a bad choice for a girl like you. Nothing worse than not being wed at all – and you're twenty or near enough."

They moved through to the kitchen now and were stacking the crockery and pans in the pine dresser.

"Oh, I'll happily stay unmarried," Phoebe said, with a confidence that she did not feel. "It's nothing to me unless... well, if a decent young man should come along then that would be fine. But if he doesn't... if he doesn't then I'll just have to stay as I am."

Now her stomach lay heavy. Was she to live with her aunt and uncle, growing old beside them, caring for them as they became more demanding in old age? Would she, in turn, have a young girl to order around? Someone to scrub and run errands for her? Would her own private space always be that half of the back bedroom doubling up as a storeroom? Depression placed a cloak upon her. Had she been too hasty in dismissing the bookshelves and dear little writing desk in the Chapman home?

"Brave words. Sometimes I wish I'd been as spirited as you, or taken my time to see if there was someone else about for me." Peggy gave a nod towards the shop, "He always were a difficult man and I wasn't bad looking twenty years back. Not pretty, not like your ma, but I had good skin and glossy hair."

Uncertain of how to react, Phoebe thought of all Peggy had gained from her marriage to Giles: "You have a solid home right here on the High Street, and the shop too; it's just the place to watch all that happens in Dymchurch."

"It is, in some ways." Peggy reflected on the gossip to be heard and the passers-by who could be seen through the open door or dusty window. "Yet Dymchurch has its secrets and sometimes I think that I know nothing at all." Then, taking the kettle from its hook above the fire, Peggy continued in her usual tone. "Fetch the teapot then, girl, I've a fancy for a brew and don't think that uncle of yours will be so understanding. He's got used to the brandy Aaron's been giving him these past few months and I can't say I don't enjoy a glass of it every now and again."

Phoebe lifted the pot from the dresser and put a generous spoonful of leaves into its dark bowl. They didn't sell much tea in the shop – not from the packets behind the counter anyway. The taxes had made the popular drink far too expensive for most of the Dymchurch people. Sir Rupert and Lady Bannerman living at the New Hall were known to drink it regularly and so did the vicar and the family living at the Manor House. They were the wealthy people of the village, those who lived around the church. But even they didn't buy it from the shop. It wasn't often that anyone asked for the bag of tea to be lifted down from the top shelf and for a small portion to be weighed.

The tea they drank, tipped into a pot with no thought to the luxury of those fragrant dark leaves, came from another sack kept under the counter. This sack was, in turn, stored in the base of a barrel with a false bottom. It was one of several sacks stored in this manner; the others were in the store area of Phoebe's bedroom. It was delivered in the night usually and Giles never made any comment; he took the sacks from the log store and hid them away. They never spoke of it, but drank the tea with pleasure, knowing it was an indulgence.

"Take it through then." Peggy pushed a delicate cup and saucer towards Phoebe. The cup looked out of place in the kitchen, but that was how they drank tea: in fine crockery, just like the wealthy people of the village.

The following Saturday afternoon, Phoebe walked through the alleyway between the High Street terraces and onto the main road. Passing the clusters of houses and cottages which faced onto the road, she turned into the Eastbridge Road and then to the road leading to St Mary in the Marsh. The air was warm and the sky a clear blue with the merest wisps of clouds. With an afternoon free of chores, she should have been filled with anticipation of what this time could bring, but Phoebe's task was one that carried a mixture of regret and relief.

In her hand was the slim book so joyously selected from Mrs Chapman's shelves. Now it was wrapped in a sheet of brown paper from the shop, secured with string. Within the packaging was a short note of thanks for the loan of the book and regret that Phoebe could no longer visit on a Saturday. Finding it impossible to give a reason why she could no longer enjoy the tea and company of the older woman, Phoebe left this unsaid. No doubt Aaron had already muttered some excuse when his mother had bemoaned Phoebe's absence the week before.

When she reached the proud house belonging to the Chapmans, Phoebe's rap on the door was tentative. Dinah appeared nonetheless and seemed to look the young visitor up and down with a relish Phoebe had not seen before.

"Coming in are you?" the maid asked.

"No thank you, Dinah," Phoebe spoke slowly and kept her voice steady. "If you could give this to Mrs Chapman with my best wishes, that will be all today."

"Very well." Dinah gave a little nod and the hint of a smirk before the door was closed and Phoebe turned away.

Not wanting to pass by her uncle's critical eye, Phoebe again slipped along the alleyway to the rear of the cottages. She was not going home, but instead turned to the right and passed the woodsheds and outside stores of the middle Dormers' cottage before tapping on the back door and pushing it open.

"Hello, Phoebe, visiting Ellen are you?" A slim woman, engulfed in a large apron looked up from her mixing bowl.

"If she's here."

"Up in her room – you know where to go."

Phoebe walked towards the front of the house and turned to the staircase tucked in beside the fireplace. Calling out to let her friend know she was coming, Phoebe walked to the rear bedroom of the cottage and pushed open the wooden plank door to Ellen's room.

The bedroom was snug into the eaves of the cottage with a small dormer window looking out towards the vegetable plots and chicken coops belonging to the High Street's terraced homes. Ellen lay sprawled upon one of two beds, a crocheted blanket around her shoulders and ballad sheets strewn across the rumpled bedcovers. She was as fair as Phoebe was dark, with a pretty oval face, delicate nose and blonde hair hanging in a thin plait down her back.

"Not seeing Mrs Chapman this afternoon?" Ellen pulled herself up and swung her legs so she now sat on the side of the bed.

"No, I'm done with all that," Phoebe replied. "Not with Mrs Chapman, she was very kind to me. But Aaron... I've had enough of him. I think I knew all along he wouldn't suit me, nor me suit him, but..."

"It's nice to have some attention," Ellen finished.

"And I thought that maybe it would be my chance to get away from Giles and Peggy."

The young women, close friends since Phoebe's mother had died five years before, sat side by side on the bed. They spoke of Aaron: his attraction for the village girls, his arrogance, and the reasons why Phoebe knew that a closer relationship with him would only bring misery. Then, as Ellen's young brother and sister jostled to pass through the narrow door-frame and burst into the room, the friends went downstairs. They left the cottage through the front door and stepped onto the village High Street.

In unspoken agreement, Phoebe and Ellen turned towards the east. Their usual Saturday stroll took them towards the church and The Ship before they turned back. If the weather was fair they would walk along the beach or wall on their return. It was no great distance but they often paused to talk with other girls they knew, so it made a pleasant interlude after a week of working. The afternoon was much the same as any other Phoebe and Ellen had shared over the last few years.

137

"Been to see Mrs Chapman?" Giles looked up from his news-sheet as Phoebe stepped into the kitchen. His eyes were speculative and eyebrows raised.

"Just to return a book," Phoebe replied. "Then I went to see Ellen."

"You'll be taking a walk with Aaron on Sunday though," Giles stated. "Of course you will and no doubt he'll have a bottle of brandy for me. I know he wants to show his appreciation for the lovely young woman you've become. He'll be here for a talk with me before long."

Peggy said nothing, but her piggy eyes followed Phoebe's movements across the room.

"No, I won't be seeing Aaron for a walk," Phoebe edged towards the dresser and took the bread from the earthenware pot. It would need slicing for supper. "I'm finding him a bit of a bother, Uncle Giles. We're not suited, him and I."

"Not suited? You couldn't do much better, my girl." He shook his head and reached for the cider at his side. "I'll be having to make do with this stuff then; he'll not be bothered with the likes of me and Peg now. I'm disappointed. Very disappointed – and can only hope that he'll forgive you when you see differently."

Chapter Thirteen
Harry

Harry was well-versed in the traditions of May Day. Although his experience was limited mainly to the customs of Elham, it was the same in most small towns and villages as far as he knew. There had been the one time, when his sister was courting a young man from Lyminge, that the family had visited the nearby village. His sister had made an extra effort to adorn her hair and dress, but the maypole, the music and the dancing had been much the same as in Elham.

This year May Day fell on a Monday, giving the people of Dymchurch a day of celebration as summer began. It gave some extra time free of labouring on the seawall and Harry was grateful. Even putting on his good Sunday clothes rather than the well-patched grimy trousers and jacket he wore every day, lifted Harry's spirits.

The three of them, Owen, Bess and Harry, left the cottage before the sun was at its highest point in the sky. They walked along the village track, rather than Seawall Road, passing cottages and shop. It was as they approached the open land opposite the Manor House, and the maypole came into full view, that Harry voiced his concerns: "I don't know that I'm welcome here today."

"Why ever not?" Bess tucked her arm through his. "It's a day of enjoyment for the whole village. You like a bit of music and a dance, don't you?"

"Let the lad speak," Owen stopped her words. "He's been to church regular on a Sunday, but this is different. What is it, Harry?"

"Yes, I've been to church and that's the right thing to do. But for all that you make me welcome in your home, I don't forget that I'm here because I was forced to stay. I'm here because they said I did wrong and ended up in court for it." Harry tried to voice the thoughts that had rattled around in his head for weeks. "I work on the wall and I'm part of the team; there's not one man who doesn't treat me as well as the next one. But at the end of the day's labour, I only pocket a shilling and the others get another sixpence. I get the wage of a criminal... well, perhaps not a criminal, but every day I get a reminder that I was forced to work there. Not that I mind. They've been good to me, John and the others. I spent a night in the gaol and I didn't know what was going to happen... It could have been worse, I know that. But perhaps it's best if you enjoy the time together and I'm happy in the workshop or beside the fire with a book."

"Is that why you don't go along to The Ocean with them in an evening?" Owen asked.

"I feel I shouldn't," Harry confirmed. "I don't want to be the cause of any trouble."

They had slowed their pace now, not wanting to be at the gathering before Harry had decided.

"You're no troublemaker," Owen said.

"Harry, you're as nice a lad as any you'd find hereabouts," Bess' tone was vehement.

"You know I mean well," Harry replied. "I'd had a hell of a thump to the head and we'll never know what

140

happened, but it had me so confused that I made a mistake and people thought badly of me. I don't want to be around those men: Joss Bailey, who took a dislike to me on the seawall that first day, and Giles Woods, who sees me as a thief. No, I'll stay in with you two of an evening and keep out of their way."

"I see how you feel," Owen spoke slowly, as if thinking through his response. "But these people have other things to concern them. Those two are nothing but bullies. The ones who count are John Waller, who knows you as a good worker, and Bess and myself. Come along with us for a short time. It will be all eyes on them from the Manor and the New Hall, then slip away if you like and I'll think none the worse of you for it. Or stay on for a bite of hog roast or a meat pie and you'll see you have friends in Dymchurch."

"I'll do that," Harry agreed. "And if I fit in well enough then I'll stay a bit longer."

As they stood, there was the merest tinkle of music in the distance. The villagers, who wandered about exchanging news and discussing the day ahead, quietened and waited for the entertainment to begin. Some of the people gathered moved to the road, awaiting the procession. The sound of the flute, fiddle and drum became louder and Jack-in-the-Green strolled down the road, decked from head to toe in greenery and hawthorn blossom. His rolling gait suggested that he had already enjoyed several pints of ale or cider that morning. As he proceeded, Jack bashed upon a tambourine and if he kept to rhythm it was due to luck rather than skill.

Following behind were the landlords and landladies of the local taverns; dressed in finery, they paraded as if they were the lords and ladies of the village. The women's hair was extravagantly dressed, while the men wore wigs. Dresses and jackets were embellished with layer upon layer of frothy lace. From a distance, they looked very fine. Harry, watching it all, suspected that a closer inspection would reveal tatty costumes, grubby from having been stored in trunks from one May Day to the next, chewed by mice and the smells of the tavern absorbed in the fabric.

Also bedecked in ribbons and fancy braiding, the pot-boys and serving wenches pulled carts containing barrels of beer and cider. Amongst these lords and ladies with their carts, the musicians ambled and a couple of jesters darted around, sometimes cartwheeling, sometimes dancing or juggling.

On reaching the green with the decorated maypole, the musicians gathered together and, while those who were lords and ladies for the day stepped aside, those from the New Hall and the Manor House came forward for the first dance. With backs straight and heads held high, they danced in a formal manner, holding the ribbons taut and ensuring that every step was in perfect harmony with the last.

"Look at them, all fancy." Bess pulled on Harry's arm to get his attention. "I don't know how they do a day's work with all those ribbons and frills."

"I wouldn't want to be dressed up like that," Harry commented. "I'd look a fine mess with the clay and sand all caught up in the buttons and braid!"

The ladies of the New Hall and Manor House competed with each other for whose hair was piled the highest upon their haughty heads. Ribbons and plaits of hair were entwined with tumbling curls, while the occasional ringlet hung down to caress a slender neck or tease the gentle swell of a partially exposed bosom. The necklines of their dresses were square and waists slim, while at the hips a structure of wire and hoops

142

splayed the dresses outwards. The brocades and silks opened at the front of the skirts to display layers of finely crafted French lace and, at the sleeves, the folds of lace tickled bejewelled fingers.

The daughters of these families were ornamental images of their mothers. A little less material to their dresses and fewer ribbons in the curls hanging down their backs, but clearly preparing for their place in society. The sons, in their velvets and brocades, wore sullen looks as they moved around the pole, concentrating on their step and enduring the dance with the eyes of the villagers upon them. Younger children were under the firm hold of nursemaids, not yet trusted to represent the important families at the maypole.

The bewigged men bore the dance with better humour than the young men. They knew the steps and danced in time with the ladies, while bestowing smiles on the villagers. Recognising the Leveller of the Marsh Scotts, Sir Rupert Bannerman, Harry moved slightly, slipping behind Owen.

"Don't you go worrying about him," Owen said. "You can be sure he's heard good reports of you over the past weeks and he's a fair man."

"I know," Harry conceded. "I saw that when I was in court."

They stepped graciously through three dances, while the rest of the villagers tapped feet and clapped hands to the rhythm set by the drum. Then ribbons were dropped and hung limp against the pole decorated with fresh greenery and entwined with spring blossom.

"Now it's the baliffs, jurats and landowners," Owen informed.

Harry nodded; he knew the form. It was the same

143

in Elham and throughout the country, he imagined.

They were a little less grand; the women with less ornamental hairstyles and with the folds of material hanging from natural waistline. The men still wore wigs but displayed less lace at their collars and cuffs. The vicar was more sombre in dress with a plain black neck-tie and not a layer of lace to be seen.

"Dressing up for the day, some of them are." Bess spoke with the experience of seeing these people about their daily lives. "Some of them have to work on the land with their men and you don't do that in a velvet jacket."

Harry smiled and nodded understanding that, while the bailiffs held some power, they had earned it by working rather than by privilege.

As the next trio of dances ended, the ribbons were ready for whoever reached them first. The lighthearted banter began, the pattern of the dances was less formal and the music a little quicker. Still hanging back, Harry watched with some enjoyment, gradually understanding that he was one of many villagers and no-one was taking any particular notice of him.

John Waller and his wife joined Owen, Bess and Harry. Gradually others from John's team gathered around and the group sprawled on the grass, tankards in their hands, enjoying the sunshine, the dance, and the day free of work. A couple of the younger lads got up as the music ended.

"Come on, Harry, you know the dances." One of them pulled at his arm.

Harry stood and allowed himself to be swept along with the race to catch a ribbon and managed to snatch one just before another lad, whom he recognised as a wall-worker from another team. They exchanged grins.

"I'll pass it to you for the next dance," Harry called.

The pipes played the first notes of a familiar tune before the drum joined in. Then the dancers were moving one way and then the other; the men on the outer ring and the women the inner. Harry bowed and nodded first to a young barmaid, then a stout baker's wife, then to a redhead who looked into his eyes and gave a wink with a cheeky grin. The ribbons entwined as dancers moved, and unravelled as they turned about and repeated the moves in the opposite direction.

At first, all Harry's attention was on the dance but then, as he stood while the women skipped and turned, he noticed a familiar figure. She was standing with a couple of other young women, watching the dance. Her straight dark hair was threaded with spring flowers and her dress was a lovely soft blue; she wore a pretty shawl around her shoulders. It seemed as if her gaze was on him and their eyes met for a moment before she looked away and he was occupied with the final moves of the dance. In that fleeting moment they exchanged a brief smile; at least he thought they did but couldn't be certain.

The ribbon was successfully passed onto the other young wall-worker and Harry moved, with the flow of men, towards the hog roasting since dawn.

"A slice of belly, my love?"

"Yes, please, nice and thick." Harry passed over a penny in exchange for pork and crackling encased in thick slices of bread.

He sat back with those who had become his Dymchurch family: Bess, Owen and the wall-workers. It wasn't too bad here, Harry realised. Before him the ribbons twisted and the dancers moved in time to the beat of the drum. Flutes and fiddles filled the air with perky tunes while the smell of the roasting hog kept

145

their appetites sharp.

The tune ended and yet another scramble for the ribbons began. There she was again, Phoebe; the one who caught his attention and made him wonder if... if one day he might have a chance of getting to know her a little better. Not yet, not while he served his punishment on the wall.

But what would happen after that? He'd be moving on perhaps to Sussex. Not that he had family in Sussex; it was just something he had said at the beginning, the reason he gave for passing through. No, his only family was his sister and she was settled, happily wed and probably with a family of her own before long. He'd not go back to Elham and the stepfather who had taken his father's forge for his own and sent Harry to live in the rafters. He would never go back there. Would he stay here with the best family he could hope for, in this place protected by the great wall and the secrets held fast amongst the locals? With another four months to work upon the wall, there was no need to decide yet.

Sitting there, with the sun on his body, good cider on the grass at his side and half a sandwich still in his hand, Harry's eyes followed Phoebe's slim body and noted her gentle curves through the soft blue of her dress. She had cast her shawl aside for the dance and he saw her arms reaching for the ribbon. Sometimes she moved further away but his eyes rested only on her; no other girl from the village caught his eye.

With a rush of chatter and giggles, a small group of young women passed by. One of them noticed her brother within Harry's circle of friends and another recognised a cousin. They paused to exchange banter, then one of them looked down at Harry.

"Hello there," she smiled, eyelids lowered. "You

146

must be Harry, working on the wall with my brother, Mark?"

"He didn't tell you he was so handsome," another girl butted in. "Cos, if he had we'd have heard more of him the past few weeks."

"No, he didn't," the first agreed.

Harry gave a brief smile and tried to look through the group; he had lost Phoebe within the whirl of ribbons and dancers.

"I'm not looking to see if he's handsome or not," Mark retorted. "It's nothing to me, but he's a good worker I'll tell you that, Kitty."

"A good worker and handsome," his sister replied. "Nice to meet you, Harry."

"Do you fancy a dance then, Harry?" the second girl asked.

"Excuse me, you can make do with my brother. Harry here was just about to ask *me* for a dance." Kitty flashed a bold smile at Harry, "Now finish up that pork sandwich, 'cos I'm not skipping around with that in your hand."

Harry looked at Owen with a silent plea for help, but the older man just shrugged his shoulders. "Go on, Harry lad, or we'll get no rest."

As he stood, the bold Kitty linked her arm with his and marched Harry to the maypole.

"Do you like it here in Dymchurch, Harry?" she asked. "I'm not sure my pa would be happy about me dancing with a criminal, but you were ever so insistent and my brother, well, he says you're all right."

"No need if you're worried for your good name." Harry saw a way out and clutched at it.

"I won't say no to a handsome young man and leave you to Mary. You wouldn't want her fat hands all over you," Kitty giggled. "Now you take this ribbon and

147

I'll be here next to you, and if you want to give me a kiss as we pass then I'm not shy!"

And so the dance began, with Harry's nerves rising every time Kitty neared him. She gave him a wink and occasionally a squeeze of the hand or arm, but he escaped her soft lips landing upon his own. When he passed Mary as they circled, he found her just as alarming.

Walking away from the maypole, now with Kitty's hand firmly on one arm and Mary hanging off the other, Harry noticed Phoebe standing with a group of friends. Hoping she had not noticed his time spent with these girls, he was relieved her back was turned away from him. But as the three of them strolled by, there was a scream of a child in the crowd and Phoebe turned. Their eyes met and she noted his companions. Did her lips lift and her eyebrows raise as if she saw the trouble he was in? He was sure they did.

"I won't say no to a cider, Harry love." Kitty steered them in the direction of the barrels.

"Nor me," Mary agreed.

And so their group swelled as girls joined the young men, the banter continued and they continued to feast. Women opened carefully-wrapped packets of cakes and biscuits to share and the men walked with less focus along the path between the ale and cider barrels. As the sun progressed on its westward journey, the race to the ribbons became less frantic and the dances less orderly.

It was on their third time of dragging Harry to the maypole that Kitty, Mary and the other girls were joined at the pole by Phoebe and her friend, Ellen. The dance began and Harry stepped one way, then the other, with the opposite woman; he gave a nod and they both moved on around the pole. Within moments he was looking into the brown eyes he found so mesmerising.

"How are you?" he asked.

"Very well," she replied.

They stepped away, looked back at each other and moved on. A few minutes later they met again.

"Was there any more trouble?"

"From Aunt Peggy?"

"No, from him… Aaron."

She could only shake her head as they were separated and so the conversation continued next time.

"No, he keeps his distance now… Uncle is not best pleased."

"I didn't thank you," Harry suddenly remembered.

"Thank me?"

"For the barley sugar," he grinned.

Now the men stood back, ribbons outstretched and the women danced alone. In time, Phoebe stood opposite him and their eyes met but he was too far back to speak. When they met again the final notes of the song were being played.

"I'd ask you to dance..." Harry began, "but not yet. Not until I've done my time."

"On the wall?" she asked.

"Not until I'm free of it," he confirmed.

Before the sun dipped below the horizon, the air became chilly. Women clutched shawls tight about their bodies and men put on jackets slung on the ground hours beforehand. Owen and Bess began to suggest that they would be walking home soon. Some villagers would stay until the ale and cider ran dry and then stagger to the tavern. Others would sleep off the effects of the drink, right there on the green, before wandering home in the early hours of the morning.

Harry recognised Aaron as he swaggered by, a giggling young woman on his arm, her ample breasts wobbling dangerously within a low-cut dress. The young man had a bottle of brandy in his hand and took a swig as he passed Harry. A little off-balance, Aaron staggered and the toe of his boot knocked Harry's tankard sitting on the grass. It was nearly empty and caused no harm, but led to Aaron looking down and noticing Harry there.

His eyes blazed with contempt. "Sorry Wall-Boy," he sneered, before moving on.

It was nothing. A moment which passed and no-one else noticed. But to Harry it confirmed that he still had to prove his worth in Dymchurch.

Chapter Fourteen
Phoebe

It hadn't been long after May Day, five years ago, when her father had been imprisoned. Phoebe recalled the branches and blossom had still adorned the pole; withered and discoloured where they had been hung just days. And so, much as she enjoyed the music and the dancing and the day free of work, as the day ended Phoebe thought of her much-loved papa.

"I saw you talking to that Harry who works along by the High Knocke." Ellen gave her friend a nudge. "Not taking a fancy to him, are you?"

"He's pleasant enough," Phoebe smiled. "But at this time of year I think of Papa and wonder what happened to him. I think of Ma too, lying there in the graveyard. But with Papa it's different. How can I rest when I don't know what happened to him?"

"He escaped, didn't he? From the gaol?"

"That's what they said," Phoebe scowled. "But who can say if it really happened? There's bars and bolts; did he really escape or was he taken away? Does he lie in a Marsh ditch or does he have a new life somewhere?"

"He might be back in France," Ellen suggested.

"He might be. I don't know."

At that moment Sir Rupert Bannerman and his wife

strolled by, sharing a word or two with the people of the village.

"That's who would know," Ellen looked in the direction of Sir Rupert "He'd know what happened and if your pa left dead or alive."

"Would he?"

"There's a chance he'd know and he's fair enough. He'd talk to you; I'm sure he would."

"I'll see." Before Phoebe could let her nerves take hold she approached Sir Rupert as he stopped to speak with one of the villagers. Standing to the side she waited and, when the conversation ended, she stepped forwards, raising her voice in an attempt at finding a confidence she didn't feel. "Excuse me, Sir. I'd like to speak with you."

"Of course, yes. Have you had a pleasant day?" He smiled at Phoebe as if genuinely wanting to know that all was well.

"I have, yes, it's all been very... it's been fun with the music and dancing." Phoebe's heart steadied now she was speaking and he was standing there, waiting and listening. "I wanted to talk to you Sir, in an official way. I was wanting... to come and speak to you in private about something important."

"Of course. At the New Hall?"

"If you didn't mind, Sir."

"Shall we say tomorrow? I'll be busy at my desk; so many papers to work through. Let us say eleven in the morning?"

"Thank you, yes, eleven o'clock." Phoebe bobbed a half curtsey at the gentleman and then at his wife. "Thank you. May you have a pleasant evening."

Phoebe lifted the brass knocker and let it fall once and then again on the front door of the New Hall. With her hands clutched at the folds of her shawl, she felt very small standing there. This was the first time Phoebe had ever rapped at this door. She had occasionally made deliveries to the kitchen door and it seemed only right that she go there at that time. But, no, today she had an arrangement to see Sir Rupert and of course she must present herself at the front door.

Echoes of slow, deliberate footsteps could be heard within the building. Then the smooth sound of worn metal on worn metal as the bolt slid back. Then the harsh clack of the latch being lifted and the slight creak of the door being opened inwards. Phoebe waited.

A trim servant stood at the doorway. His wig fell in neat ripples of grey hair caught back with a plain black band. His costume was a dark-green jacket with brass buttons but no braiding and his breeches were dark grey. There was no excess of material, no unnecessary ornament, yet his importance within the New Hall was clear.

"Yes, Miss? Can I assist you in any way?" His speech was slow as if he relished each and every sound coming together to make a word.

"I have arranged to see Sir Rupert Bannerman." Phoebe's words were clear, giving the impression of a confidence she did not feel.

"Very well, step inside." The servant stood aside, allowing the wide-eyed young woman to pass through into the hallway. "Follow me." He led the way past panelled walls and a wide staircase to a doorway and, having given a tap upon the door, he opened it. "Sir, a young woman, Miss Woods, to see you."

"Thank you, Brown." The Leveller of the Marsh Scotts dismissed his servant with a nod and turned to Phoebe. "Now, Miss Woods – Phoebe, is it?"

Phoebe nodded.

"Sit down here and tell me what brings you to see me."

The chair he indicated was small and upright, with carving to the legs and brocade padding to the seat. Its back cushioned Phoebe as she sank into it. He, the leveller of law and order on the Marsh, sat at a large desk, with piles of thick papers upon it, and held a quill in his hand. An open ink pot showed he had been busy working. His waistcoat was embroidered in gold thread and the buttons highly ornamental; his wig was an intricate affair of curls, held in place with a velvet bow, and the buckles on his shoes were an elaborate filigree in silver. But Sir Rupert's smile was warm and Phoebe found him less intimidating than the sombre servant.

"It's about my father, Sir. You won't recall, you being so busy, but he was French and he was sent away five years ago."

"I do remember. Jacques Bernard." He frowned a little. "My mistake, you are Phoebe Bernard – Woods is the name of your uncle."

"I am Phoebe Bernard," the young woman agreed. "But with my mother dead and my father gone, they call me Woods, it being an English name."

"How complicated to have a change of name," Sir Rupert smiled. "I wouldn't like that at all! But we digress, you came to speak about your father?"

"He was sent away," Phoebe repeated. "Ma had died and left the two of us living in our cottage on the High Street. I was fourteen and able to keep house, as well as work in my uncle's shop of a morning. My father went out to work one night and never came home again. Uncle Giles came to tell me that Papa was being held here, in the gaol, and I was to pack up

154

my belongings and go to stay with them." The words poured freely and a glance at Sir Rupert told Phoebe that his attention was fully upon her.

"There was talk, of course there was," Phoebe continued. "They said he'd done wrong, betrayed some local men. Encouraged a fight. But it wasn't true; I knew that. The riding officers, they were accusing him of bringing things into the country and not paying taxes. But it wasn't just him they caught that night; there must have been a dozen men caught in that barn out at Burmarsh. A dozen men, but when morning came it was only one of them sitting in the New Hall gaol. My papa."

"I remember it," was all the great man said. His eyes were on Phoebe, his expression thoughtful.

"He didn't hang and I'm glad of that; of course I am." Phoebe's voice rose, "but where is he? Where is Papa?"

"You know the free trade that exists between us and the French?" Sir Rupert leaned forwards and lowered his voice, "You know the things we don't speak of and we certainly never mention names."

Phoebe nodded.

"Sometimes the traders run into trouble and there is a different trade to be done. The trade of one life to save the others. Your father, he was French and wasn't to be trusted." He saw her eyes widen and a protest form on her lips, "That doesn't mean to say that he wasn't a decent and fair man, but people have prejudices. Do you understand what I mean by that?"

"Oh yes." There was a fire in Phoebe's eyes and, although she could not blame him, she scowled at the man sitting opposite her. "Dymchurch folk only trust their own type – the marsh-men and the fishermen and the wall-workers. I know it, for even though I was

155

born here to a Dymchurch woman, my French blood makes them treat me differently."

"I saved him from the gallows and the preventative officers didn't like that, not at all. But when they were merry in The Ship one evening, somehow the bolt to the cell was left undone and your father made for the beach where he happened upon a fisherman who took him back to France. He didn't want to leave you, but there was no choice."

"I didn't know that he'd returned to France. No-one told me." Even now, with just this small amount of knowledge, Phoebe felt closer to her papa. "How was I to know if he was no further away than Folkestone or Ashford, yet unable to contact me? How was I to know if he was dead or alive?"

"He was alive when he left here five years ago – you can be sure of that," the Leveller of the Marsh Scotts replied. "I really can't say much more than that. You were with your aunt and uncle; you've been well cared for."

"I'd have rather been with Papa." Phoebe reflected on what she had heard. "But if you saved him from the gallows then I'm grateful to you."

"Did I say that?" Sir Rupert frowned and yet somehow there was a twinkle to his eyes. "It was bad luck on my part that the bolt slipped. I had quite a bit to answer for, but they were soon done with me and off chasing a false trail into the depths of the Marsh."

"There's not enough riding officers to watch the whole of the Marsh and beyond," Phoebe reflected. "Not when the mists rise and there's all those hollows and reed banks, deserted churches and old farm buildings to hide away in."

"There's all manner of phantoms and witches skulking around at night. I'd not want to be a riding officer for all the gold sovereigns in Kent. No, to be a riding officer is a thankless job, drinking alone at the inn, riding alone on those twisting Marsh tracks and never quite doing your job well enough to please your superior. It's a job for a man who has no need for company nor a pride in himself."

"I thought they did well enough with a good horse and not much to do but look about and question people," Phoebe said. "But, Papa, he's in France. Wissant is his home town so perhaps he's there. That sets my mind at rest. Thank you. Thank you for seeing me and explaining some of what happened."

"I'm sorry I couldn't do more."

"Oh, Sir, I know that you did plenty." Phoebe rose from the chair. "Now I must..."

"Go along to the kitchen, my dear. There are sure to be some biscuits warm from the oven. Brown will be in the hallway, waiting you know; he'll take you along there."

"Thank you, but no, I'm needed back at the copper." Phoebe pushed on the latch and, as the door swung open, Brown sprang from his lair in order to escort her through the hallway. "It's washday, you see." Turning back towards Sir Rupert Bannerman, Phoebe bobbed a curtsey and left.

Although the sun hung radiant in the sky, Phoebe clutched her shawl tight around her as the wind was brisk, bringing with it a chill from the north. She walked along the base of the wall on the track leading towards New Romney. The fields beyond the Clobsden Sewer were bright with lush spring grass and the coats of this season's lambs were still a creamy white. In the bright sky sparse clouds raced. It had rained heavily overnight, making the track muddy underfoot, but the day promised to stay dry, albeit unseasonably chilly.

No excuse came to mind as to why she was heading to the west. If Giles or Peggy were to hear of it then she could say only that she fancied a walk and that the stiff breeze was invigorating. But she was free to do as she wished on a Wednesday afternoon and if her behaviour was ever untoward, it was easy enough to blame her unpredictable French blood. However much she found herself irritated by Peggy's constant harking back to her French roots, Phoebe found that it could be used as an excuse for numerous sins. Or those small misdemeanours that were sins in the eyes of her aunt and uncle.

The seawall ended at High Knocke and here a shingle ridge gave a natural barrier between land and sea. Half a dozen fishing boats were settled on the bank, while others were either being winched up the beach or still battling the wind as fishermen attempted to beach them in the shallows. Standing on the end of the wall, Phoebe shaded her eyes from the sun and scanned the area, looking to pick out Walter from the huddled figures in heavy coats and low-brimmed hats. One fishing boat looked much the same as the next to someone who had no particular interest in them.

There he was: Phoebe saw a curl of Walter's auburn hair and recognised the short, stocky figure tipping the catch into a crate. Stepping off the wall where it merged into shingle bank, she picked her way across it towards the boats. Her route was clumsy as Phoebe side-stepped clumps of grass and weeds with leaves ragged from being stung by the salt-water spray.

As she approached the small fishing boat, resting in a drunken lurch on the bank, Walter looked up and Phoebe gave a smile showing nothing of her apprehension about approaching him. In return, a frown spread across the fisherman's face which, although he was only just thirty, was already weathered from working on the fishing boats for the past eighteen years.

"Walter? Ellen's cousin?" Phoebe stood beside him under the shadow of the wooden-plank clinker.

"That's me." His eyes narrowed; he was not going to give any more until he knew what this young woman wanted.

"I'm Phoebe. From the village. I wanted to speak to you."

"Oh, yes, I've seen you about."

"It's about my father; he is French, you see. Perhaps you knew him, before he went away?"

"Jacques Bernard – he must have been gone two or three years." Walter gave a slow nod, as he remembered.

"It's been five."

"Five years! I wouldn't have thought it."

"You knew him then?" Phoebe questioned. "Of course you did; he fished from here."

"I knew him. Decent man."

"He was." Phoebe smiled then and the tension holding her muscles taut began to fade. "I want to find him, to go to France..."

"You do, do you?"

"I've spoken to Sir Rupert Bannerman; he told me that my papa went back to France." The words, at first seeming so awkward, flowed freely: "He did nothing wrong, I know he didn't and Ellen... Ellen said that you're a decent man and maybe you'd take me there, to Wissant; I want to find him."

"I know all about your pa," Walter paused and studied Phoebe through lowered eyelids. Then he turned and pondered over the fish in his crates, plunging his hand amongst them and removing the odd scrap of seaweed or other debris. "I knew your pa; it were me and my pa who took him back to Wissant that night."

"You took him back?"

"Just the two of us. It was just the two of us that knew of it, and him in the New Hall of course."

"So you'd take me too? You'd know the way to Wissant and you'd take me to find him?"

"There's not one fisherman here who don't know the way to Wissant and our French cousins what live there. But take you, lass? That would need some thinking about."

"But you could do it and I'd pay you." Phoebe thought of the shillings and pennies she had under her bed.

"It's not about if I can or can't and it's not about the money. There's some thinking to be done about if it's right. I'm living a simple life with my fishing and a bit of honest trading with them French. I don't want any trouble."

"Trouble?"

"With that uncle of yours and people knowing that I took a young girl across the Channel."

"I see." Phoebe's hopes began to slump a little. "I wouldn't want to make trouble for you, of course I wouldn't. But I'm determined to find my father. I want to see him again."

"I'll think about it good and proper. I can't say fairer than that." Walter began to turn away. "You know where to find me in a day or two after I've given it some proper thought."

Chapter Fifteen
Jacques Bernard
1753

"What brings him out on the boats?" Jacques inclined his head in the direction of young Aaron Chapman, who was swaggering about on the shingle bank.

"He's wanting to learn how it's done," a second fisherman, named Michael, replied. "It's only a bit of fishing. Nothing much to see."

"Nothing much," Jacques repeated in his slow drawl, a furrow deepening on his brow above his dark eyes. "I'd not want him on my boat though."

The sea was lapping up against the shingle bank at Wall End. There was hardly a breeze, but that didn't matter. It wasn't needed to fill the sails, not for this fishing trip. The sun was spilling across the sky to the west, radiating soft pinks and orange amidst the sparse streaks of low-lying clouds. It cast a warm glow on the seawall and the wooden boats, as the sea darkened to slate grey.

"He's goin' wi' Walter," thirteen-year-old Johnny piped up. He was a lanky lad from a tumbledown cottage set behind The Ocean. His pa was suffering from a twisted spine, and it was only this job Jacques gave him on the boat that saved father and son from the workhouse on the seawall road.

"Now you know to keep your mouth shut, don't you, John?" Michael said, as the three of them began to push the nose of the boat into the water.

"Course I do. I told yer that," Johnny snapped back. "I'm not going in no workhouse and I'm thankful to Jacques Frenchie for what he's done for me."

"There'll be some shillings in it for you tonight," Jacques replied. "Keep them well hidden, don't go spending more than you need to.

As the boat began to rock under the swell of the tide, Jacques and Michael scrambled aboard before Johnny gave the last push and, with the seawater soaking the bottom of his breeches, he was pulled up alongside the men. Their boat was the third of four going to sea that evening.

Jacques kept glancing back at the last boat – the one Aaron had just jumped in. He didn't like him, didn't trust him. Especially over these last few months when he saw the young man looking at his beautiful Phoebe. She had no mother to advise her against men who would be drawn to her delicate features, soft skin and deep brown eyes. Grief weighed heavy in his stomach for his pretty English wife who had been taken from him just the winter before.

In silence, Michael and Johnny dipped the oars into the water and sliced through it before swinging them upwards. The boats glided effortlessly, leaving a trail of wavelets which caught the last rays of the sinking sun. They had no distance to go, not far past the point where the tide retreated to its lowest point, before Jacques started looking for the markers. The two boats ahead of them were doing the same. One lined up against Church Knocke and the other level with Watch House.

"Steady now," he called softly as they drew level

with Spittleman's Knocke. The swollen bladder sack and gull's feathers were bobbing about to the port side of the bow. "Michael, you hold her still and Johnny, the grapple please."

Jacques took the grapple hook and swung it over the side, watching a couple of yards of rope slip into the watery depths before he put a stop to its falling any deeper. He let it move with the tide for a moment and felt the rope go taut as it caught on something.

"Pull away now," he glanced back towards Michael. "We've got them."

It was hard work, with every pull of the oars the boat stayed in place, the heavy load stopping it from slipping through the water. The grappling hook held firm and gradually Jacques eased the hidden load up through the salt-water.

"Johnny, give me a hand. We'll take them aboard." Jacques leaned over and pulled on the rope, moving one hand over the other.

Looking ahead, Jacques saw that the first boat was gliding along the coast towards the Willop, while the crew of the second were still manhandling their haul into the boat. Behind him, it took all Michael's effort to hold the boat steady as he leaned to starboard, ensuring that the vessel didn't capsize. Johnny waited at his back, knowing his time would come shortly. Then the waters broke over the first cask as it reared out of the water.

"Here we go!" Leaning forward further than before, Jacques clasped it with both hands and swung it back towards Johnny. And as he did so the second cask appeared, then the third. One by one they were stowed in the bottom of the open boat. Finally, the sack of shingle came to the surface and, as Jacques pulled it free from the water, Michael moved to a central position to keep the boat steady.

The pattern was repeated three times until six barrels lay in rows of three: one across the stern and another towards the bow. Then Jacques took the second oar and, with Michael, they set a steady pace, moving parallel with the coast in the direction of Hythe. In front of them the other two boats were now out of sight, lost in the darkening sky. Behind them, the occupants of the final boat were struggling to pull their cargo aboard.

Moving swiftly through the calm waters, they saw the dark streaks of the knocks: Watch House, Church and Palmer's. Then, as they drew close to Beacon Knocke, the outlines of the small boats could be seen, secured to posts at the base of the seawall.

"Swing her round," Jacques commanded, as he eased off his oar, holding it free of the water and letting Michael dig deep, pushing the vessel around.

Within minutes their bow was nosing against the sands and three or four hooded men were pulling at the vessel, while the three of them jumped out, landing in the shallows. It only took a few moments to remove the barrels, which Johnny had managed to free from the sodden rope and its unwieldy knots. The sacks of shingle and ropes remained in the hull.

Following a murmured exchange of words, Michael parted from Jacques and Johnny, jumping back in the boat and grasping the oars as he was pushed back out to sea. He turned about and began to glide in the direction they had come from. The other two boats were alongside him, while the fourth was beginning to unload.

Weary at being taken from their slumber, a couple of stocky ponies stood with carts on the seawall. Standing at the base of the wall, Jacques lifted the casks into willing hands stowing them in the carts. It was all going smoothly; he hoped to be back in his cottage within the hour.

"Come on, Frenchie, anyone would think you wanted the officers to catch us."

Jacques felt the rim of a barrel jabbing at his side. In return, he barely glanced in Aaron's direction. Aaron was seventeen and should know better than to speak to his elder this way; Jacques wouldn't satisfy him with a response. He swung the last cask up and scrambled to the top of the wall with the help of lowered hands from the hooded men. He wouldn't think of them as strangers, although he couldn't be sure who they were. But if he had met them in The Ocean or going about their business in the village, he would have known them as Mark the farrier and William the farmhand.

"Get a move on." It was Aaron again; who was he to start throwing orders about? Jacques shrugged; the men would have no respect for this young bully.

The carts began their trundle down the track from the seawall to the nearby road. Two horsemen rode ahead and a further two kept watch from the rear. Jacques walked alongside the second pony and cart. He wasn't expecting any trouble tonight; the riding officers had been given a false trail leading them towards Eastbridge. Some bundles of reed thatch were all they would find for their troubles if they accosted the men they followed. Perhaps he would pause at The Ocean for a tankard of ale before going home; Jacques imagined the riding officers sitting in the corner nursing drinks and their damaged pride.

The road to Burmarsh twisted one way and then another, following the line of a narrow dyke. It was before they reached the village that the small group turned onto a farm track and came to a stop by a small barn. Bolts were pulled aside and the door opened to reveal a store for grain and hay. The men formed a line to transfer the casks from the carts to their hide beneath a trapdoor in the floor. Within minutes the task was completed, it being a routine that was so well practised. The men nudged the hay back into place with the toes of their boots.

"Don't think to turn on us, we've got their backs covered!" A sudden shout came from the open doorway. It was the voice of Dymchurch's riding officer and with a bark he continued, "Tell 'em!"

The two horsemen who had been bringing up the rear were now at the doorway, with the riding officers close behind. Jacques' throat tightened as he heard the ill-concealed glee in the officers' voices. The traders would pay for tonight's run, there was no doubt about that. These riding officers were starved of success, constantly thwarted by the locals.

"They've pistols digging in our backs," one of the Dymchurch men spoke, his voice rough with nerves.

There was the glint of metal as one of the men within the barn raised his own musket. "The King's men don't get to make the rules out here on the Marsh," he roared. "Release them now and stand aside; you'll find that you'll pay with your lives if our men are harmed."

"Didn't you hear? They've pistols in our backs; will you risk our lives in order to have the glory of firing your musket?" The plea came from the doorway.

"Lower the weapon," Jacques murmured, "these good men have families to support, let's not see them die in exchange for any bullet you fire."

What had gone wrong that these two horsemen, whose sole duty was to keep watch, had become caught in this way? His whole body tensed as he waited for the next part of the scene to reveal itself.

"Lower the weapon," Jacques repeated.

"I'll not have us trapped in here, like fish in a net."

Jacques could almost feel the spittle as the words poured out. While the other traders hung back, fearing for their lives and the fate of their families, rage emanated from this burly farmer as he continued, "Not by those Redcoats who have no right to ride about watching us good men. I'll answer to the Leveller of the Marsh Scotts and his bailiffs, for those are the men who run the Marsh."

With that, there was the click of metal and, almost simultaneously, the whistle and dull thud of a bullet piercing the wooden frame of the doorway, just inches away from a riding officer. The officer's response was instant: the men in the barn heard nothing for his pistol was held up against the victim's back. The first they knew of the retaliation was when Richard Smith, farrier, husband, and father of six, fell before them.

Another shot was fired from in the barn; this time it flew wide, into the night air. The third shot from Joss Bailey punctured the barn door, as the riding officers pushed it closed. Then the sound of metal on metal sliced through the night air and into the dusty barn, as the bolt was drawn on the dozen men within it.

Now Jacques hung back, trying to retain the vomit threatening to rise within him. He watched two of the dim lamps moving toward the body lying slumped by the doorway and heard the dull thud as it was rolled over. Under the lamplight, Richard Smith's moment of death was captured, his eyes wide and mouth partly open, tongue lolling. There was nothing to be done for him. For their own peace, the men quickly ripped open some sacks and covered the body; no one wanted to see those staring eyes shining out whenever the lamplight passed near them.

"Where's John Looker?" someone called out, asking after the second man he knew had been working alongside Richard Smith

"Not here, dead or alive," was the response.

"Now don't go shouting about it," Joss Bailey's voice was low, but it commanded their attention. "They won't have left us alone, so we'll make our plans out of their hearing. Those two have had their taste of victory for tonight and, by God, I'll be damned if we'll be sitting here when they make their next move."

"A bit of brandy would steady our nerves," one of the men suggested.

"It would. We'll drink to thwarting those bloody Redcoats and have some pleasure in doing so." Joss Bailey pulled a flask from his shoulder bag, "Pass it around."

"A man is dead," Jacques said. "I'll not drink to that."

"Thanks to you," Aaron Chapman replied from behind him.

"Me?" Jacques turned. "How can that be?" He was right about this young man; all his instincts told him to be wary.

"You said to fire, Frenchie." Aaron's voice sounded brittle, as if he were mocking.

Jacques shrugged and turned away. Best to ignore him – but fear twisted his gut. There were twelve of them in the barn; Joss Bailey had already shown himself to have a temper that night and Aaron was ready to make trouble. Who else would turn on him if encouraged by these bullies? A banging on the door distracted those who had heard the exchange of words and were hanging upon them, waiting to hear what would come next.

"We'll not be leaving until you're all under the custody of the magistrates," one of the riding officers bellowed. "The doors are covered and your friend here, the one that's still alive for now, he's gone to fetch Sir Rupert."

"We've no fear of you Redcoats; you're a lily-livered duo and a pair of damned fools," Joss Bailey snarled. "Kill a defenceless man, would you? It's you who'll answer to Sir Rupert."

"He's not our superior," retorted the officer.

"He's your superior while you walk upon Romney Marsh, and a fairer man you couldn't hope to meet," Joss bellowed and, lifting his musket, he fired randomly at the barn roof. "Don't stand too close to those doors," he warned.

Jacques sat down on a grain sack, his head in his hands. This was no way to behave; they needed to work as a team, to think and plan. Tempers such as these would do no good; they could only cause harm.

"Calm yourselves," Walter Fisher spoke from the shadows. "No need for any of us to be here when Sir Rupert arrives. There's a trapdoor and a tunnel leading to the old shed standing not ten yards away."

"There'll be hell to pay when the barn's found empty," Joss Bailey replied. "They'll go through the village, taking men at random and making sure enough of us hang. As long as Marsh-men swing at the Dymchurch gallows, it won't matter to them if they're traders or not. Innocent men will die so those Redcoats can feel some pride in their miserable job."

"There's no such thing as an innocent Marsh-man!" someone sniggered.

"We've lost one man and that's victory enough for them," Aaron joined in, "but I'd say if they had another man in gaol by morning, our King's men would be happy in their work."

"What are you suggesting, Chapman?" Joss' voice was lower now, curious.

"I'm saying that there's one man here who has caused a bit of trouble this evening."

"Who would that be?" Walter asked. "If the Redcoats weren't spotted following us, I'll not be blaming John Looker or Richard Smith, God rest his soul.

"They were fools not to spot they were being followed," Aaron replied, "but I'm saying someone tipped the Redcoats off because those two were meant to be pursuing a trail to Eastbridge. And this afternoon I saw them getting friendly with a man who probably thinks he's sitting safe here."

"You're saying one of us won't swing for this?" Joss' interest was fully aroused. "One of us has a deal with them and he sits here knowing he is safe?"

Jacques shook his head; what bother was Aaron out to cause? All this talk of someone talking with the riding officers was nothing but the foolishness of a young man who enjoyed making trouble. Everyone knew he had a nasty streak to him and the riding officers were always trying to sniff out a whiff of French brandy or a flurry of lace. Why, only that afternoon they had cast their eyes over his boat, asking when he was next going fishing.

"What were you talking about with the Redcoats, Jacques Bernard?" Aaron raised his voice and his eyes searched out the Frenchman, who had thought he could stay out of this.

As his throat dried and heart thudded within a chest that felt too tight to contain it, Jacques raised his head slightly and answered in his usual manner, "They stopped by to look at the boat. Not uncommon, as any fisherman could tell you."

"Fair enough, but once we were trapped you tried to excite trouble." Joss Bailey had taken the bait and was eager to run with it.

"In what way?" Jacques response was slow, measured, spoken as if it was nothing to him.

"By suggesting that Joss fire!" This time the call came from one of the men behind him.

Aaron had succeeded in bringing suspicion and distrust into the group. Jacques knew it would spread, as fear caused the men to react without reasonable thought. He was to be the one who took the punishment for them all and the knowledge weighed heavily in his stomach.

"Fire? Why would I say that? For what reason?" Jacques tried to shrug it off.

"Why indeed? Yet a man has died for it."

Richard Smith lay on the barn floor because of Joss Bailey's temper and for no other reason. Jacques knew that and so did every other man there. But the idea of a scapegoat had given hope to each one of them and he understood that. He held no grudge against any but Aaron Chapman and Joss Bailey.

"Enough talk, do we want Sir Rupert to find a dozen of his best men waiting here for him?" Joss took charge. "We'll leave the traitor here with just Richard Smith for company. Look around for some rope or twine and bind his limbs so we can be sure he'll be waiting for them."

"And let's shift these sacks to clear the way into the tunnel." Aaron moved to the back of the barn "We'll be in our beds within the hour, knowing the Redcoats will be pleased enough with two men caught. Prize enough for an evening's work!"

171

Chapter Sixteen
Sir Rupert Bannerman
1753

Stretching his legs out, Sir Rupert basked in the gentle heat from the smouldering fire. His wife was checking that all was well with the children; supper had been eaten and the day's work was done. There had been a little trouble from a farmer who was fussing over providing his share of hawthorn for the wall, and a farmer from Eastbridge had complained that the riding officers were questioning how many wool-packs he had produced that spring. Small inconveniences which, as Leveller of the Marsh Scotts, he had to deal with. Overall, life in Dymchurch was quiet at the moment. A mild spring had meant that the lambs were flourishing in the fields of his parish and, despite the thrashing of the sea upon the seawall during the winter storms, the wall stood proud and held strong.

In the nursery upstairs his newborn baby slept. Sir Rupert's second son had been born as healthy as his other four children and was now six weeks old. His wife, Lady Charlotte, had engaged a third nursery-maid; a pleasant young woman who came from a farm in the direction of Hythe and, as the oldest sibling of twelve, had proved herself capable of helping with babies and young children. With the newly-appointed governess, that made a team of four residing over his brood of young Bannermans. Sir Rupert's days were well-ordered and quite satisfactory.

Looking up, he watched his wife enter the room. Her hips were a little fuller and breasts still pleasantly rounded since the birth. He'd chosen well: she had a pleasant manner and showed herself to be a loving mother. If she fussed a little more than necessary over her perfectly formed ringlets or the shade of her ribbons, then it didn't really matter. She was a Belsey-Knight of Sevenoaks and so was used to the better things in life.

"Baby's asleep and the wet-nurse is settled with some of cook's egg custard," she said, settling in the opposite chair and also stretching her dainty silk slipper-clad feet towards the fire.

"George and Isabella?" Sir Rupert asked after his eldest children.

"Reading with Mary-Ann." She smiled at the memory of their fair heads either side of the nursemaid's red-curls as they exclaimed over the pictures and vied to recognise words in the text.

"Eleanor and Harriet asleep, I hope?"

"Oh yes, they were asleep when I went to see baby Gabriel."

"Excellent. I'm going to have a brandy and for you, my dear, a glass of sweet wine?"

"Thank you." She picked up her tapestry frame and looked at the closely-threaded wools with little interest. "I rather tire of this, but we can't have Gabriel without," Lady Charlotte muttered, as she picked up the needle and continued with the process of creating a woven picture to commemorate the birth.

They sat in companionable silence for some time until Lady Charlotte, still weary from the birth, declared that she was going to bed. "Perhaps I'll ask Mary-Ann to complete this; she has such a neat stitch," she said, tossing the tapestry aside.

The fire was burning low and the brandy had enhanced Sir Rupert's sense of warmth and well-being. He could happily throw another log on the fire and doze in the chair for another hour, but he sensed the disapproval of Brown who, no doubt, was sitting bolt upright in the hallway or his small sitting room, waiting to do the last of his chores for the day. Easing himself out of the chair, Sir Rupert straightened his shirt and breeches and placed his empty brandy glass on the small side table.

"Goodnight, Brown."

Sir Rupert's foot was on the first stair and Brown was about to enter the room to remove the glass and make the fire safe, when the peace was assaulted by a frantic rapping on the front door. The two men turned to exchange glances of surprise as they paused in their business.

"I'll attend to this, Sir." Brown bristled with importance as he slid back the bolts.

John Looker burst in, with none of the decorum Brown had grown to expect from someone who entered the New Hall from the front door and, barely glancing at the man-servant, he addressed Sir Rupert directly. "It's been hell out there tonight, Sir. Richard Smith is dead, or as good as, I can't be sure of it. Them riding officers followed a group of us who were just going about our business on the Marsh, then before you could say Clobsden Sewer, me and Richard had pistols to our backs and the others were cornered in a barn."

Sir Rupert held up a hand to cease the flow of

174

words, "Come to my study, take a brandy to steady your nerves and let's talk this through slowly."

It wasn't unexpected; these things happened every now and then. But with only the two riding officers serving the Dymchurch area, the wily Marsh-men used their wits and had a fair amount of luck in evading them. Such was the scale of trading within the area and so many men were involved that it was becoming increasingly common for them to go about their business in full view of the riding officers. What could the two of them do to prevent two dozen men moving their goods from one place to another? Often they stood aside, knowing that if they so much as thought of raising a musket they would be overpowered and possibly not live to report the incident to their senior officers.

Sir Rupert wasn't a gambling man, but clearly the Redcoats would have their small successes as they went about trying to catch the local men, who were doing nothing more than trying to provide a little more money for their families. He saw no good reason why the men of Dymchurch shouldn't trade with those in Wissant; it was beneficial to both sides and made life a little easier all round. Only that evening he had left two of his horses tacked up ready to use and, in return, he'd receive a drop of the French brandy to which he was rather partial.

With the brandy burning his throat, John Looker began explaining, "We were following behind, on the look-out but thinking the riding officers were out at Eastbridge, when they rode out from behind some willows and had us separated from the others. There was nothing to be done, with their pistols pointing straight at us."

"Of course," Sir Rupert nodded. "And where was

this?"

"On the Burmarsh road, Sir. We rode on to Sidden's barn, just before the village and the others were in there, so they had them trapped and stood there at the entrance with pistols to our backs." John Looker took another gulp of the brandy. "They knew, those in the barn I mean, that the Redcoats were ready to fire, but they didn't listen to what they had to say and one of them fired a musket."

"Panicking no doubt," Sir Rupert muttered.

"I've no doubt of it, Sir. Well, they didn't wait for another shot to come their way. A bullet was fired into Richard Smith's back and he fell right there in the barn doorway. Another bullet went wide and the riding officers were slamming the doors leaving Richard in the barn and me on the outside with them. He's dead, I'm sure of it and a good man he was, didn't deserve it."

"True, very true." Sir Rupert was already turning to the door and he called out into the hallway, "Brown, get out to the yard and rouse one of the stable-hands; I need my Checkers tacked up at once." Then turning to John Looker, he asked, "And how did you get away?"

"They sent me, Sir. They wouldn't leave a dozen men with just one of them keeping guard, so they told me to come and get you."

"Fair enough. We'll ride out together." Sir Rupert walked into the hallway. "No, you get home to bed and stay clear. They'll have enough men heading to the courtroom; I'll keep your name out of this."

"Thank you, Sir." John Looker left through the front door, untethered his horse and disappeared into the darkness.

Walking through to the rear of the house, Sir

Rupert snatched a thick jacket from a hook and opened the back door leading to the stable block. The stable-boy was checking the stallion's girth as Sir Rupert took hold of the bridle.

"Quick work, thank you." He led Checkers out into the yard. "I'll give him a rub down when I return. No need to wait up."

With that, his foot was in the stirrup and, in one fluid movement, Sir Rupert was astride the stallion. He rode from the yard at a brisk trot and turned left onto the road leading towards Burmarsh; the night air was clear and the moon shone bright, allowing him to see the way. He passed no one else on the road. Thoughts ran in an orderly manner through his mind as he sifted through what he knew and what he expected to find on his arrival.

A man was dead; he was sure of that. Who had lost their temper and fired from within the barn? No doubt it was Joss Bailey; that man could not be trusted to keep his head steady and had a habit of running roughshod over anyone who displeased him. But would he, Sir Rupert, find a dozen Dymchurch men trapped by riding officers? He very much doubted it; these men were cunning and would not stand about waiting to be marched across to the gaol. They would find a way out of this; he was certain. And, by God, there had better not be more blood to show for their efforts.

As Sir Rupert reached the barn, one of the riding officers raised himself from the tree stump on which he had been sitting; the other was leaning against the barn wall. Both raised their pistols when they heard him approach, lowering them as he hailed a greeting.

"Blazes, I've been pulled from my fireside with tales that you have a barn full of my men! You'd better have good reason, for I'm telling you these good men have wives and families worrying over them."

"I'm sure their wives are used to such worry," the senior Redcoat replied. "They'll be feeling the shame when the Dymchurch gaol is full of the bleeding thieves."

"Your words are harsh, but I hear a man is most likely dead and that needs dealing with first," Sir Rupert replied. "And by your hand, I'm told. Show me the body."

"He's in the barn with the others." The bolts were slid back and the door opened a crack. "I'll fire if any of you rats so much as move," the riding officer snarled.

A lamp was produced and Sir Rupert knelt to pull back the sacking covering the body. A glance at the waxen face showed what he had suspected and he murmured, mostly to himself, "Not good, not good at all." Then he stood and held the lamp high. "A dozen of them, you say? Well, they're keeping themselves well hidden."

"There's sacks and bundles of hay and many a dark corner for these traitors to cower in," the senior Redcoat replied.

"Step forward and show yourselves," the second officer barked.

The lamplight rested on the figure of Jacques Bernard, bound and gagged, his back resting on a cask of brandy pulled out from the hide. His head was bowed; he didn't lift it to stare back into the light and the faces of those who stood before him.

"Untie this man," Sir Rupert ordered.

The riding officers fell to their knees and pulled at the thin twine. Sir Rupert noted that the Frenchman closed his eyes, unable to bear the humiliation. That there had been a dozen men here, there was no doubt in Sir Rupert's mind. But slippery as eels in a marsh ditch, they'd made their escape, leaving one of their own behind. Yet, he was not quite their own. The Dymchurch men showed suspicion of those who came from off the Marsh, and so their neighbour from across the Channel was never quite accepted, despite the fact that he was a hardworking man, known to be even-tempered and fair.

As the knots loosened, the senior officer began his search of the corners of the barn, behind the sacks and amongst the hay, until finally a trapdoor was discovered in the back corner. It swung open easily and the escape route was revealed.

"By God, they've scampered off down a tunnel, the bloody scoundrels!" the riding officer shouted. "But we've one of them here and he'll talk when he stands before the King's men and the Leveller of the Marsh Scotts; hell and damnation, he will."

"But he is French," Sir Rupert declared. "Are either of you practised in that tongue? My own grasp on the language is weak, I'm ashamed to admit."

There was a silence and the two riding officers exchanged glances before the senior one spoke, "Well, he's sure to be able to give some names or be of some use."

"No doubt he will," Sir Rupert spoke without conviction.

The Redcoats had been wrong-footed and Sir Rupert needed to act fast in order to save his villagers. Jacques Bernard stood, free from twine, hanging his head and unresponsive to the men who spoke. Sir Rupert preferred not to have to question the man who had clearly been left as an offering to the riding officers and the gallows. Instead he turned his attention back to the dead man.

179

"Richard Smith lies here, not yet cold and with a bullet in his back. Which one of you fired the shot? I wonder if there's a need for this man..." Sir Rupert nodded towards Jacques, "and one of you to be sharing a cell. We only have the one you know."

"When daylight comes, take a look at the door-frame," the senior riding officer replied, "The men were warned and they fired nonetheless; the bullet went into the wood here. His blood is on their hands as they knew we were bound to fire in return; we are here on behalf of the King and cannot be expected to take their shots."

"Put us in your gaol and you'll find your position as head magistrate holds little sway with the King; he'll not be pleased," the second continued.

Looking about the barn, Sir Rupert asked, "I presume there is some reason to have locked the men in here? All I see is a cask of brandy, brought here illegally I am sure, but one cask won't send a man to the gallows."

"They had two carts laden full and they'll have hidden it away somewhere. We've no doubting the evidence is here to be found."

"Let's hope they didn't take the casks with them," Sir Rupert tried to hide his snigger. "I don't want these men making fools of us."

Kicking away at the hay, the senior officer had soon found the row of trapdoors and was opening one, "Bring the lamp over." It shone upon the rounded barrels, "Well, these won't be full of ditchwater," he exclaimed.

"Now, we have a stash of barrels and no reason to think they're not full of brandy come direct from our cousins across the water, and no tax in the King's pocket," Sir Rupert summed up. There was no point in denying the presence of the brandy or they'd be suggesting he was in league with the smugglers. But it was time to get the situation under control. "We also have a man who is dead from your own pistol and another to take along to the gaol. Two men for the evening's work, I suggest there's no need to bother looking for the others. They'll be tucked up in their beds by now and it's anyone's guess as to which men they were."

"Unless he speaks..."

"And what if he tells of the bullet in this innocent man's back?" Sir Rupert reached out and took Jacques' arm. "I'll need one of you to escort me back to the New Hall, then the pair of you had better stay here for the night. Damned foolish you'll look if the brandy disappears overnight. I'll send some of my men over here in the morning to remove the casks and to take Richard Smith, God rest his soul, back to the village.

The three of them walked back to Dymchurch in silence, Sir Rupert and the riding officer leading their horses. As they turned and walked between the church and New Hall, Brown appeared at the front door.

"We'll be needing the gaol, Brown," Sir Rupert said, and if Brown felt any surprise he was too well drilled to show it.

Under the eyes of both the riding officer and his own manservant, Sir Rupert led Jacques to the gaol and, with no words exchanged, he watched as Brown slid the bolt on the heavy door of the cell. A feeling of resignation lay heavy on Sir Rupert. He had known Jacques Bernard for these past fifteen years and knew him to be a decent character. That he had been treated badly by the men of Dymchurch there was no doubt. Yet someone had to suffer for a dozen men being caught with the brandy casks or there would be more trouble from the Redcoats.

The following day, flanked by two bailiffs and with his heart still heavy, Sir Rupert Bannerman, Leveller of the Marsh Scotts, sentenced Jacques Bernard to the gallows. His crime was the smuggling of spirits into the country and therefore depriving His Majesty, King George II, of his duty tax.

Two days later Sir Rupert rode along the High Street and, on turning into the Eastbridge Road, passed the reins to a boy with the promise of a penny on his return. He went into the cottage of Walter Fisher and when he left, ten minutes after, his step was lighter and body less tense.

Chapter Seventeen
Harry
1758

"I'm going out with my brother on *Louisa-Ann* tonight," Joshua mentioned as he and Harry worked side by side, shovelling the clay that had slipped to the base of the wall. They were on the landward side and had no view of the sea but could hear the great bulk of it pounding upon the wall, just twenty feet away from them.

"He's a fisherman, isn't he?" Harry asked.

"He is, but he's not going fishing tonight and he's not going trading either. He's getting paid a few shillings to take some lass to Wissant and asked me to crew for him."

"Wissant?" Harry's interest was sparked. "Where's that, along the coast?"

"Across the Channel," Joshua paused to lean on his shovel and nodded his head in the direction of the sea.

"Across the Channel," Harry repeated. "Never heard of it. Never even been to sea."

Joshua paused as if to ponder the enormity of this statement. The grey-blue mass of water flowing towards their village twice a day was washing in with the lives of Dymchurch people. Whether they fished within its depths, protected themselves from its fury or traded upon its moonlit waters, the sea affected their daily routines. He mused that if a medicine man were to take the blood of a Dymchurch man, he'd find it laden with salt and stinking of French wines.

"It don't seem right that you've not been to sea." Joshua mused. "Get your head down after supper and have a few hours' sleep then meet up at the end of the wall, just over there." He looked over towards High Knocke. "We'll be meeting two hours before the next high tide, that's the time to pull his fishing smack into the water."

"You're going out at night?" Harry frowned. "How will you find the way?"

"Following the stars of course," Joshua grinned a partially toothless smile and ran his hand through his red hair. "They'll be as bright as anything tonight and there's a fair breeze to carry us across."

"And what's this Wissant place like?" Harry asked.

"What's it like? French of course. It's all Frenchie." Joshua shook his head.

Harry didn't quite know how to respond to this. Was it a fishing village or a town and what was their reason for going there? That's what he wanted to know, but it seemed that Joshua either didn't know or wasn't inclined to spit out his thoughts. Was this night-time adventure likely to get him into any trouble though? He didn't want to stand in front of the Leveller of the Marsh Scotts for any wrongdoing.

"I've spoken with John Waller and I'll not be here on the wall tomorrow. I'll lose a day's money but there's a shilling in it for me, Walter says. I'll speak with John; tell him you'll be with me. And you can share my shilling, if you're in need of it." Joshua turned from his digging and looked at Harry, "No need to go talking about it. Not that it's anything that those riding officers would take an interest in, but this lass, she don't want the village knowing her business."

"I won't talk," Harry replied.

"I know that. You're not one to have a beer in your belly and let your tongue flow. Keep to yourself, you do."

"And Walter, and the girl – will it be all right with them?"

"Oh, yes. He was saying that another man on board would be a help."

"It's some girl who wants to go to France; she's paying to be taken there..." Harry began to falter. "I don't know anything else, but Joshua said they could do with another man and there was no need to worry that it would cause any trouble.

"Well, there's something odd about someone who wants to be taken across the channel in the dead of night," Bess mused, while pushing the fried fish around on her plate.

"It's easier by starlight," Harry offered.

"There's more to it than that, lad," Owen said. "But if it's just the three of them and a lass too, then it seems like Harry should take a chance at having an adventure."

"I don't know that I'll enjoy it much, out in the cold at night," Harry grinned.

"Still, you can give it a try." Owen pushed his chair back. "I'll get my sheepskin jacket out for you. That'll keep out the cold and the worst of any rain that might blow over the Channel."

"And I'll pack up some food to last you a fair while," Bess added. "You'd best get some sleep now if you're leaving before midnight."

Harry crept up onto the wall at the back of the cottage. It wasn't his usual route but it seemed to match the mystery of the occasion. The moon was a radiant crescent in the inky-black sky and had mustered all its strength to throw a powerful light over land and sea. The stars, millions of sparking pinpricks, became the moon's allies and they too lit up the night-time world.

The air was fresh, but for now Harry carried the sheepskin coat. He'd appreciate it when he was out at sea, he was sure of it. Feeling exposed in the moonlight, Harry took the first opportunity to climb down the seaward slope and onto Spittleman's Knocke before jumping onto the sands. He then scurried along, not wanting to keep anyone waiting.

After a few minutes Harry stopped suddenly, for he could see another figure ahead of him. Not the stocky figure of either Walter or Joshua, but a slighter frame. Was this someone out on different night-time business, or perhaps the young woman they had spoken of? He slowed his pace, not wanting to catch up with the stranger.

On nearing the end of the wall, Harry looked across the shingle bank where the fishing smacks rested. Breaking on the bank, waves caught the moon's light-beams and threw them about. They took the stones and shells, spat them out then dragged them back into the shallows. The rhythm of the sea was restful that night as it took hold of the upper reaches of the beach.

Harry watched the newcomer of the night vanish into the cluster of fishing boats. He would learn soon enough if he or she was to be a part of this journey. Within a couple of minutes he too was stepping between the wooden-plank hulls.

A low voice hailed him.   "Harry, over here."

There they were, the two brothers and a young woman with a shawl wrapped around her head, so only her dark eyes shone out at him.

"You too?" her voice was soft.

"Phoebe?" he questioned.

"You'll need all your strength now, Harry. We've a boat to keep steady as she slides into the water and only the three of us men to do it." Walter gestured for Harry to move alongside him, "You're on this side with me. Keep her steady, she'll soon take up speed as she moves down the bank."

And so all Harry could do was fling his coat and bag into the boat and stand by with his hand on the port-side, ready to follow Walter's orders. What was all this about, taking Phoebe across to France in the still of the night? No doubt he'd find out soon enough; he had always found her to be friendly and she was sure to explain. But for that moment, Phoebe was beside Joshua and the boat between them was moving in steady jerks towards the sea already lapping at its bow.

"You jump in, Phoebe, and you, Harry." Walter called out. "Don't let yourselves get any wetter; the sea will take her soon enough. There's a ladder hanging down at the stern."

Harry held the ropes as steady as he could, while the boat still slipped away from them. "Go on, you first."

Phoebe darted up as best she could and Harry followed. He toppled into the boat and moved to the centre while Phoebe went towards the bows. Turning back, he watched the brothers, Walter and Joshua, scrambling into the *Louisa-Ann*.

"She's floating," Phoebe looked back at Harry. "We'll soon be away."

Harry, unsure of what to say in reply and aware that he was now feeling uneasy about the voyage, looked around the vessel. It felt sturdy, with the deck sunk low enough for him to feel a sense of protection from the wooden sides. The two masts held swathes of gathered canvas and ropes hanging limp against the uprights. Between the masts, a small seating area was sheltered by a three-sided cuddy. The stern area was packed with coiled rope and nets in baskets; they planned to fish on the return journey. Harry felt sure that stuck onto the tangle of fibres were the last remains of numerous sea creatures. Even with a fresh sea-breeze, the stench of raw fish wafted through the air and penetrated his nostrils.

Picking his way past coiled ropes, Harry kept a hand placed on the boom and walked between this and the bulwarks, towards the bows. Here the triangular area of deck held more baskets and yet more ropes coiled around cleats. At the point where the bows met and the gunwale rose in height, Phoebe looked out to sea. Standing beside her, Harry was going to speak, but at that moment the brothers joined them. And so the business of setting sail across the Channel began.

"Over here, Harry, heave on this with me now." Walter nodded towards a rope.

The mainsail began to unfurl and billow about. The wind was over the quarter and they were making good headway against the short choppy waves. It took all Harry's strength to hold it while Walter secured the halyard. He put his hand on the gunwale as the smack pitched and rolled, butting her way through the waves and clearing the breaker line.

No more words were passed as Walter then pushed his way past and took the tiller. Looking back across the inky water, Harry saw that they were already moving away from the beach. It wouldn't be long before Dymchurch and the wall were indistinguishable from any other part of the coastline. How deep was the water even at this short distance from the coast? What about when they were miles out to sea and neither the English nor the French coastlines could be seen? What would it be like to sink within its dark depths? Harry shook the foolish thoughts from his head. There was work to be done, even if he wasn't quite sure what it was.

"Harry, lad, I need you as lookout at the bow." Walter called. "I'll to check on the chart and Joshua can take the tiller."

"What am I looking for?" Harry asked.

"Other boats, pinpricks of light from their lamps. Them that's gone setting the nets or out for some business."

Harry shuffled along the deck to the bow, "You know I haven't been on a boat before?"

"I know that, lad, you come from inland, so I hear."

"But you're happy for me to do this?"

"There's nothing to it, Harry, you only need a good set of eyes." Walter nodded his approval. "Now I'll check the charts and if need be we'll alter the course, but this will do nicely for now."

"How long before we reach France?" Harry asked.

"With the wind in this direction and the stars as clear as we could hope for, I'd say we'll be in Wissant in six to eight hours," Walter replied. "We can't do better than that."

Harry sat at the bows for a while, grateful for Owen's sheepskin coat and with a thick woollen hat pulled low over his ears. Phoebe was there, but she seemed to be in her own private world and he was

189

reluctant to break the silence. The motion of the sea rocked him. There was a sense of rhythm about the boat going through the waves as it rose and fell. "I'll be look-out and you can sit with Joshua at the tiller; he'll explain how we find our way," Walter said, as he left the charts and the shelter of the cuddy.

Harry settled in the stern beside Joshua, amongst the ropes and baskets with nets and flags

"You just need to hold this here nice and steady." Joshua looked down at the tiller. "Now look up into the sky and there's a bright old star up there and then a row of four to the right."

Harry looked to where he pointed. "I see them."

"Keep the mizzen mast lined up with the end star of the four; that's the course we want to take. Keep her as steady as you can. You take a turn and I'm right here with you."

He kept his eyes fixed upon the mast and the row of four stars. Every now and then he turned the tiller a small amount and so the boat stayed on its course for France. It was a sort of peace out there at night with the slap of the sea upon the bow, the creaking of the hull and the fretting of the ropes.

It might have been thirty minutes or even an hour. All sense of time was lost. A sturdy figure moved along the deck towards the stern.

"You're doing a good job there," Walter said, as he rested his hand on the tiller. "I'll take a turn on this now. You can go into the cuddy or take a look from the bow."

"Am I needed at the front?" Harry asked.

"There's no danger of collision now," Walter replied. "You go where it suits you. Take a rest if you like."

"No, I'll go along to the front for a while," Harry

190

stood up and, with his hand on the side of the boat, he took a few tentative steps.

As he approached the bow, Harry could see Phoebe was still there, but she no longer looked out to sea. Instead her slight figure sat huddled up on a bench. Perhaps she didn't hear him approach or was it that she was unable to acknowledge him? He tapped her gently on her shoulder.

"Are you sick?"

Phoebe merely nodded and said nothing. Harry turned away to give her the solitude she needed. Now he was a figurehead, looking ahead from the very front of the boat.

But what was the purpose of their journey? After some time, when the exhilaration of facing out to sea had waned, Harry moved to sit on the bench beside Phoebe. Finally he took the opportunity to ask the question burning within him since he saw it was Phoebe travelling to France with them:

"Why are you going to this place, Wissant? I'm not sure if I should ask, but if I'm to be a part of it..."

She lifted her head, just a little, and was able to give the slightest of smiles, "You've come on this journey and you don't know what takes us there?"

"No, I don't." It was a foolish thing to do. To risk his life for a reason unknown to him. And if he returned unharmed, as the fishermen did day after day, then Harry risked the fury of the Leveller of the Marsh Scotts. It might be deemed that he had forsaken the rules of his confinement in Dymchurch.

"I want to find my father. My papa."

"Your father?" Was he just going to stand beside her, repeating her words and sounding as if he had no wit about him?

"Did you think I had no papa?"

"I… I thought nothing of it. You live with your aunt and uncle and I thought..."

"Ma is dead; she lies in the churchyard and has been there these past five years. But Papa, I learned that he returned to Wissant."

"Returned to Wissant? Is he French?"

"Oh yes. He left not long after Ma, but he was driven out and I didn't know… not until I spoke with Sir Rupert at the New Hall. That was when I learned that he had returned to Wissant. Until that moment I didn't know if Papa was dead or alive."

They both sat in silence for a while after that. Phoebe's head was still in her hands and her body bent double so her elbows rested on her knees. With her shawl covering her head and falling over her face, it seemed that she remained trapped within her own private misery as the waves of seasickness washed through her. Harry, although curious, didn't like to press her to tell more. He knew how debilitating nausea could be and, for Phoebe, there could be many more hours of suffering ahead.

Harry was lucky, the motion of the boat was not causing him any bother. Yes, his stomach lurched if the rhythm of the boat's pitch and roll altered and the smell of fish sometimes made him feel a little queasy but he felt at ease with the movement of the vessel beneath him. He stood again and leaned on the gunwale, not wanting to move away from Phoebe, but content to gaze out to sea. How long was it since they had left the coast? Perhaps an hour. The light from the moon and stars remained constant; dawn was still many hours away. For now he put all his trust in Walter and Joshua and wondered if the French coast would be in sight when dawn came,

The bundle of shawl moved at Harry's side and

Phoebe raised herself to an upright position. He heard her whisper his name and immediately dropped down, so he sat beside her on the bench.

"I still don't know if he lives," she said. "It's been five years since he left and anything could have overcome him in that time."

"Yes, it could," Harry admitted. Then he asked, "Will you know how to find him?"

"I'll ask. Jacques Bernard is his name and if he is no longer in Wissant then someone will know where he went."

"And will you stay there, in Wissant?" Harry pictured her future, with her father and other members of his family. Why would she return to Peggy and Giles if she could be with her family in a place called Wissant?

"Stay in Wissant?" Phoebe repeated. "No, I think I'll come home, for Dymchurch is home even without Ma and Papa."

The hours passed. Harry watched Walter as he peered at charts under the weak light of a swaying oil lamp. Sitting in the shelter of the cabin, he ate a little of the food in his bag. Later, he took another turn at the tiller and quite enjoyed feeling the wooden handle in his hand and gazing up at the stars. Then there were the moments when, with his hand on Phoebe's back, he watched her heaving over the side of the boat, before handing her a handkerchief and then a bottle of weak cider to refresh her mouth.

All this happened under the inky skies, in a world that held just the four of them and their boat. Time passed peacefully, at least for Harry. It was while he was with Joshua at the tiller for the third time he saw the light from the stars had become less vibrant and the blackness of the sky softening to a deep blue. From the east, fingers of dark red streaked across the horizon until the rim of flaming light began to show and soon the sun began its daily ascent. He watched the sunrise, mesmerised by the beauty of it, but it rose swiftly and soon the light was too much to bear.

"I'll take a turn." Walter placed his hand on the tiller. "You see if the lass needs a bit to eat."

Harry moved to the bow and stood beside Phoebe.

"Can you see the hills of France?" she asked, turning towards him.

"I'm not sure," he shielded his eyes from the light. "Yes, perhaps... yes, I see something."

Sometimes they saw France from the Dymchurch Wall, but never on a bright sunny day when the heat haze shimmered above the horizon. It was on the slightly dull days when the rolling hills stood grey across the sea. Harry had often wondered about the land the other side of the Channel. The day promised to be fair; when they landed, he wouldn't be able to look back and see the low-lying land of Romney Marsh, but surely the cliffs of Folkestone and Dover would stand clear above the Channel.

Beside him, Phoebe looked pale, her eyes dulled and body frail. She must be cold; her shawl was no match for the chilled salt-breeze. To his knowledge, she had not ventured into the cuddy all night but had sat on the bench or leaned over the bulwarks, fighting the relentless waves of nausea.

"Take my jacket," Harry began to unbutton it. "I've kept myself warm and the sun is rising."

"I don't need it."

"You're shivering." He reached out and touched her arm. "It's very warm; Owen gave it to me. I was going to take it off anyway..."

194

"Thank you," she whispered, and took the coat.

"Would you like to eat? Something plain, some bread?"

"Not yet, a little something when we come closer. As we approach the beach."

The sun continued its journey upwards. With Joshua's hand on the tiller, the small fishing smack journeyed towards the south-east. And as the sea began to absorb the azure of the sky, it shimmered under the light of the morning sun. The chalk cliffs of Cap Gris-Nez shone white and gradually buildings emerged and trees formed on the hilltop. While Harry's attention darted from one area of the coastline to the other, Phoebe's gaze was fixated on the grey stone seawall and the beach of Wissant.

Chapter Eighteen
Phoebe

How many hours had it been since the first waves of nausea had crept through her body and rendered her incapable of doing anything but huddle in her own misery? It was true that vomiting over the side of the boat had relieved some of the churning in Phoebe's stomach and the giddiness in her head. But the feeling of sickness caught in her throat and she felt that her body could barely endure lifting itself from the bench set into the bulwarks. Through her wretchedness there was an awareness that, during her worst moments, Harry had stood beside her with his hand on her back. Not intruding on her misery, but letting her know that he was there. Even offering his handkerchief as a cloth for her mouth.

Now, as the beaches of Wissant loomed closer, Phoebe stood in Harry's sheepskin coat and looked across at the long stretch of pale sand, fringed with grass-topped dunes. The cluster of village homes emerged to the right, where the dunes ended. It seemed as if the settlement sat right on the sea-front on land a little higher than the beach, not like her own Dymchurch where she lived below the level of high tide.

"Do you see, there on the beach, the fishermen working just as ours do? But look how they pull their

196

boats up the sands?" It seemed that at last the cloak of misery was lifting and as the features of Wissant became sharper, so the nausea cleared.

Still standing beside her, Harry replied, "They are using donkeys, no, horses: donkeys would be smaller."

"Yes, they are horses. I'm sure of it; that's what Papa told me."

"It looks like a nice village," Harry commented.

"Oh, it is; I am sure it is," Phoebe smiled for the first time in many hours. "Papa said it was lovely with the white sands, and the shops and houses all gathered together with a market for the fishermen to sell their catch. They are called *flobarts* – did you know that?"

"Flobarts?"

"The boats. The fishing boats." Phoebe lowered her lashes and took a sideways glance. "Do I speak too much?"

"No, I'm just pleased that you are feeling so much better. The colour is returning to your skin."

He turned away, just a little. Was he embarrassed? Did he feel he should not have mentioned the faint blush on her cheeks? Phoebe was unsure, but knew she didn't want Harry to feel uncomfortable with her. He wanted to care for her, and so she asked, "Perhaps I could eat now? Just a small amount?"

"You should," Harry looked back towards the cabin. "I'll fetch you something. Just a little at first."

By the time their own vessel was nudging the sands of Wissant, Phoebe's eyes were bright and she had eaten some bread with cold mutton. The borrowed sheepskin coat had been stowed in the cabin and the sun had thoroughly warmed the travellers. Her own body was still fragile, but she could feel strength returning to her limbs and the food had settled in her stomach.

"*Bon-joor, bon-joor.*" Walter was at the bows smiling his welcome to the two fishermen who were gesturing to the sturdy grey horses standing near the water's edge, their ropes slack.

"*Une corde.*" One of them pointed up.

"What's he saying, lass?" Walter turned to Phoebe.

"It must be that he wants a rope; the horses will pull us in." A smile stretched across Phoebe's face. "Isn't it wonderful? This is just as Papa said it would be."

For Phoebe the adventure had truly begun now. Here, before her, were two fishermen from Wissant, with their flat caps upon their heads, peaks pulled low over their foreheads. They wore shirts of rough cotton and dark blue jackets.

"*Une corde*, rope."

Walter threw a coil of rope towards the men. "*Merci, merci.*"

The rope was caught and threaded between the two horses, who proceeded to trudge up the gently sloping sands, pulling the boat until it had passed the high tide mark. The four visitors from Dymchurch leaned over the bows of their vessel and watched with enjoyment.

"I remember old Jacques saying about this," Walter said. "I didn't take much notice but it's a sight easier than all that pulling and pushing we have to do."

"Papa often spoke of Wissant," Phoebe replied, as she gazed in rapt attention at the beach, the village, the men and the horses. In the warm sunshine, with the slightest of breezes carrying the scents of the sea, this was all that Phoebe imagined it would be.

"Down you go then, lass." Walter gestured towards

the rope ladder, now flung over the edge. "It's only right that you should be the first one to step on French soil or sand, as it happens to be."

Phoebe took a couple of tentative steps on the ladder of ragged rope and uneven wood before jumping onto the soft sand. She stood before the two French fishermen and gave a slight smile, then Harry was beside her and the others were clambering down the ladder.

"*Les Anglais; vous êtes d'où*?"

"*D'où*?" Phoebe repeated. "Where? Oh, Dymchurch of course. Tell them, Walter."

"Dym-church. Dym-church. Over the sea." He waved his hand in the direction of the Channel.

"*Ah, oui. Deemchurch. Très bien – Deemchurch.*"

"We look for Jacques Bernard," Harry said. "Jacques Bernard."

"Jacques Bernard?" one of the fishermen repeated, the smile fading from his face. "*Et pourquoi lui?*"

"I don't know what he's saying," Walter turned to Phoebe. "There's a problem here. They don't like this talk of your papa."

"Why do you come here for Jacques Bernard? He is nothing to the English. Just a poor fisherman from Wissant." The second fisherman spoke now, his voice a slow drawl, his scowl evident under the peak of his cap.

It was all going wrong, Phoebe could sense the hostility from those men who had been all smiles and welcoming just minutes before. Would they be bundled into the boat and pushed back down the beach at any moment? They had come so far and she sensed that her papa was very much alive and not far from her. But these men, these Frenchmen, now stood with their legs apart and arms folded as if to make a barrier between the newcomers from Dymchurch and the man they wanted to find. They would only have to give a shout and there would be a dozen men on the beach, all glaring at her and these good men who had brought her across the Channel.

"Jacques Bernard. Papa. Phoebe," Harry was pushing her forwards towards the Frenchmen. "Phoebe. Papa." He was pointing at Phoebe and saying it again. "Papa."

The Frenchmen looked at each other, eyes widening. Then one stepped forward and, crouching down, he looked closely into the young woman's face. "*La petite Phoebe, elle est là? Elle est là?*" He reached out and touched her cheek. "*La petite Anglaise.*"

"*Elle est bien arrivée chez nous.*" The second fisherman clutched at the arm of the first. "The daughter of Jacques Bernard is here!"

"*Bienvenue. Bienvenue.*"

Walter, Joshua and Harry found that their arms were being shaken and backs slapped with an enthusiasm they had never before encountered. And Phoebe suffered her hair being taken between their fingers, her features examined and her arm stroked before one of them took her by the hand and started pulling her up the beach.

"It looks like we'll have to go with them," Joshua said. "I think young Phoebe's going to find that Papa of hers today."

"It's all changed." Walter replied. "And thanks to our Harry, no doubt about it. He sorted it out for her good and proper."

"He's a wanted man in Dymchurch," Harry strode up the beach the best he could on the soft, dry sand. "You can see why they didn't trust us."

The six of them passed through a gap, with the edge of the dunes to their left and low stone cottages to their right. They were now on a rough track, coated with a liberal amount of sand. Here, where the dunes no longer protected the land from the sea, a ribbon of boulders and wooden stakes took the brunt of the sea's fury and protected Wissant's cottages.

The track took them past ragged trees and shrubs growing from sandy soil. Small single-storey cottages, with open shutters, squatted in their own small plots. Front doors were open, clean washing hung limp in the sunshine and hens pecked around rectangles of vegetable plots. Children ran barefoot and women sat in their doorways on wooden chairs. All these things were passed by while the newcomers tried to commit fleeting images to memory.

"*C'est la belle Phoebe*," their new friends called out to the women who gazed at the strangers to Wissant and the men who paused in their work. "*C'est Phoebe*; the daughter of Jacques Bernard."

Mostly these villagers shrugged their shoulders or gave an uninterested wave. What were they shouting about, these fishermen? Had they taken too much wine already? But the children, curious to understand what all this fuss was about, began to follow at a distance along the sandy track.

One by one the adults understood the words that were being called and whispered amongst one another.

"Jacques Bernard, they say."

"What is this to do with Jacques Bernard?"

"A daughter?"

"Yes, he had a daughter left in England."

"It was Dymchurch; that was the name of the place."

"Phoebe. Was that her name?"

"Phoebe, yes, he speaks of her often."

"Could it be that she has come?"

And so they left their homes and places of work, to follow the children who had been the first to see some celebration was blossoming in Wissant that day. Phoebe, walking between the two fishermen, led the procession. It seemed almost certain that she was being taken to her father, but the words flooding from the lips of the Frenchmen came with such a speed to her unpractised ear that she could barely understand them. She tried to form questions but her words were unspoken. Such was the pace of events she couldn't place the words in any order within her head, and so there was no chance of voicing them.

Looking back, Phoebe took comfort from the sturdy forms of Walter and Joshua, and the reassuring presence of Harry, who was no longer a stranger to her. The four of them were helpless; they had no choice but to be pulled along by this current as forceful as those in the Channel. Yet she felt safe and, as her eyes met Harry's, she felt that he too was comfortable, and she drew confidence from the smile they shared.

The road ended at a market place. It was framed on one side by a plain stone church with a small belfry and a row of modest-sized windows with neatly curved tops. The roof of the church was slate and its walls were of a pale stone. Shops opened out onto the square, many with their wares displayed outside. Public house tables lay empty, awaiting the time when the sun was at its highest and the men could smoke and drink while discussing the issues of the day.

All this was just a backdrop to the true heart of the town and although Phoebe had never seen it before, it was just as she imagined it. Her papa had often spoken of his home with a longing he couldn't hide. Taking centre stage among the stalls with bread, fruit and vegetables, were the *flobarts* of the fishermen.

The boats had been pulled in from the sea and the fishermen were selling the fish directly from them. Baskets were being lowered from the sides and placed on the ground.

Women crowded around the boats, calling up to the men who were still sorting out the catch, eager to claim the best fish. Men shouted to one another from boat to boat and above the gulls screeched as they swooped, knowing that their feast would come. Somewhere a pipe was being played and close by the baker shouted his announcement that his baguettes were still warm and ready to eat.

The air was richly scented with salty fish, but other smells mingled: unfamiliar scents on the women's skin, tobacco from smouldering pipes and garlic on the breath of those who passed by.

The people in the market place didn't notice the English at first, or the fishermen who brought them to Wissant market. They were there to barter and buy, to give their attention to the goods on offer. Phoebe scanned the *flobarts*. Her father had been a fishermen; was he here, selling his catch just as he used to?

"Jacques, Jacques Bernard," Their calls went unheard amongst the shoppers and the people selling their wares.

"Jacques, *ici*. Your daughter, Phoebe, is here."

They had spotted her father; Phoebe was certain of it, for she was now being pulled to the far end of the row of four *flobarts*. Glancing back, she was reassured that Harry, Walter and Joshua were still close behind her, and so she was able to concentrate on looking

203

ahead and allowing herself to be taken.

"Jacques, Jacques Bernard!"

At last it seemed that her father heard the cries, for a man stood up in the end boat and scanned the crowd. His cap was pulled low over his forehead so Phoebe couldn't be certain. But when they called again, she was sure.

"Over here, Jacques," Phoebe's companions called.

Now they were almost at the boat and only a few village women were between Phoebe and her papa. These women were there to buy the best fish of the day and as Jacques' eyes met those of his daughter, they became the only barrier between them.

"Papa, it's me, Phoebe. *C'est moi.*"

"It's you! It is my Phoebe!" He threw his cap in the air, letting it fall among the fish, and revealing a shock of dark curls. "My Phoebe."

As he clambered over the side of the flat-bottomed *flobart*, the women began their demands.

"Two of these."

"Have you more herring?"

"The crab is good . I'll take it."

Phoebe stood helpless, not wanting her father to lose his trade. He pushed his way between the women.

"I am sorry. No, I am not sorry – my daughter is here! Marc… Marc, I am busy. Sell these good women the fish, please."

Then he was right there, standing before her. A little older; the lines around his eyes a little deeper; a few strands of silver in his dark hair. But it was her papa and he had a huge smile on his face. Phoebe hadn't known how tense she was, but now she felt her body relax and she returned the smile.

"Papa, I didn't know you were here, not until..."

Leaning forward, he scooped her into his arms, gently lifting her off her feet. She buried her face into the rough cotton of his shirt, breathing in the saltiness of his skin. They parted and he ran his roughened fingertip over her cheek. She smelt the tobacco on his hand.

"How is it that you come to be here?" Jacques took his daughter's small hand in his own. "No, wait. It is too busy; come away from the fish stalls and we can talk." Jacques led Phoebe through the crowd, pausing once to call to a woman, "Look, Marie. It is my daughter. You will meet her later, I'll bring her." Then to Phoebe, "It is my cousin, Marie. We often talk of you."

They were still behind her: Harry, Walter and Joshua. Phoebe didn't want to lose them, or for them to think that she had no care for them now she had found her papa. Walter gave her a nod and raised his hand, as if to say they would follow. They understood; she was sure of it.

"Come Phoebe; we can sit here," Jacques led his daughter to a bench outside the church. Then, for the first time he looked beyond her and at first his eyebrows knitted together in a frown before a smile spread across his face. "Of course, it is Walter and Joshua. Welcome, welcome to Wissant. It is you who brought my daughter, my beautiful Phoebe."

"Jacques, good to see you." Walter gave him a slap on the back.

"She found out you were here and came pestering us for a trip over." Joshua was pumping the hand of the Frenchman.

"Thank you. *Merci.* This is a good day. A great day for me." Jacques turned to Harry, "And you came with them? You are a fisherman?"

"No, I am... I am Harry from the village. From Dymchurch."

"'arry, I do not remember you."

"I have only just arrived, in Dymchurch, I mean."

"And you are the special friend of Phoebe?"

"Oh Papa, he came along because he hadn't been to sea before. He didn't know I was to be there." Phoebe laughed, but as she did so her cheeks burned. Would they notice? She hoped not.

"Speak with Phoebe, Jacques, and we'll wait just here," Walter said. "She'll tell you what brought her here today."

With their heads close together, father and daughter spoke of how she had only just learned that he had returned to France.

"I didn't know what had become of you. I feared you were dead," Phoebe told him.

"There was nothing to be done. I had to leave or be hanged," Jacques threw his hands out in despair. "They planned it so they could walk free."

"Who were 'they'?" Phoebe asked.

"Best not to say. You live among those people." Jacques shook his head. "But we neglect your friends, *our* good friends." He stood and stepped towards the Dymchurch men. "Come, you must be weary. We'll eat at my cottage and talk some more. Do you plan to stay? You are welcome, of course."

"Thank you, Jacques, but we must return this afternoon," Walter said. "Joshua and Harry must work upon the wall tomorrow."

"I understand," Jacques replied and he looked towards his daughter. "And you, Phoebe? Have you come to stay?"

The sun beat down on the market square, lending a warm glow to the pale stone buildings. Enraptured by the unknown words spilling from the people, the scents of this new land, and this village where there was so much more to explore, Phoebe hesitated. She looked toward Harry and saw that his confusion matched her own.

"I hadn't planned to. I hadn't thought." Phoebe tried to explain. "I didn't even say I was going, just in case they tried to stop me."

"We'll eat and drink and talk about what is to be done." Jacques took Phoebe by the arm and led her down a narrow street, away from the market square.

Chapter Nineteen
Harry

When the fishing boat came to a stop on Dymchurch sands, the sun was low in the sky to the west. It lent a warm glow to the beach, giving a rich golden colour to the sand, and highlighting the many shades of green and brown in the seaweed hanging from the knockes. The seaward side of the wall was in shadow and the sky was taking on a purple hue.

The homeward journey had been long. Not just because the wind was still pushing towards the south-east, and not because the three of them were weary from sailing through the previous night. It was laborious because for every degree the sun moved across the sky, Harry was taken further away from Phoebe. Even to stand beside her as she huddled on the bench beneath the bulwarks or to wipe the vomit from her mouth seemed better than to be without her.

Harry had busied himself with learning how to manage the sails so as to use the wind to their advantage, and spent hours at the tiller with the sun beating down upon him. With Owen's sheepskin coat beneath him, he had slept for a while in the cabin and finally, when the Dymchurch Wall was in sight, Harry had watched the fishing nets being lowered into the sea.

It took all Harry's effort to help pull the boat up onto

the shingle bank and keep her steady on the smooth planks placed beneath her keel. He didn't notice the slim figure striding out along the top of the wall, or the short dumpy woman who scurried, breathless and panting, behind him. They paused at the end of the seawall, looking out towards the cluster of fishing boats, before spotting their prey and starting their clumsy steps across the shingle.

"Where is she? Where's our Phoebe?" A long scrawny finger was pointed in the direction of Walter, who was lowering baskets of fish from the boat.

"Your Phoebe?" Walter looked about. "Does the lass have a fancy for fishing?"

"She had a fancy to be taken to France," Giles snarled. "Foolish girl that she is, but she's my niece and I've a duty to care for her."

"She left it in a note," Peggy stumbled and clutched hold of her husband's arm. "And we've been worried sick about her."

"Not to mention that she's left us in bother with the shop and deliveries to do." Giles fished the note from his jacket and brandished it before Walter. "I've seen the others and you've been gone a while with not much fish to show for it. Plenty of time to pop over to see them Frenchies she has such an interest in."

"You're right," Walter replied. "She wanted to be taken to Wissant; to see the place her father came from and she paid me to take her there. I'm just a poor fisherman and can't refuse a bag of shillings for my troubles."

"Poor fisherman?" Giles raised his eyes and spat out his response, "You're as slippery as them fish you catch, and it's not just fish a Dymchurch boatman trades in, as well you know."

"Today, it's fish," Walter stated. "Fancy some for

your supper?"

"Well, I wouldn't mind," Peggy pointed a podgy finger in the direction of the basket, "perhaps one of those..."

"We've a nice bit of mutton," Giles snapped. "Where's the girl?"

With no sign of Phoebe, and the men keeping themselves busy with unloading the fish, he moved to the other side of the boat and it was then that his eyes fell upon Harry.

"By the devil's horns, what's this young thief doing here? Do you see him, Walter, sniffing around your boat where he has no business to be?"

"He's no thief, Giles, and well you know it." Walter shrugged his shoulders, already weary of the intrusion on his patch of beach. "He came along with my brother."

"Went out to sea with my niece, did you?" Giles' voice went dangerously low.

"I went out with Joshua and Walter," Harry looked the shopkeeper in the eye for the first time since he had been released from gaol.

"And my niece?"

"And your niece was there," Harry confirmed. "But I didn't know she was going to be there."

"But she was," Giles snapped. "Blazes, you went to France with my niece!"

"And him not meant to leave the village," Peggy's eyes were agog as the drama unfolded.

"You're right about that," Giles' lips curled to show yellowed stumps of teeth. "This young troublemaker didn't just leave the village; he left the country!"

"If you don't mind, I've fish to sell and a bed to get to," Walter pushed his way between Harry and Giles. "Phoebe paid me to take her to France and I hired a crew; that's all this young lad was. He don't need no bother from you. Now I can see you're worried about the lass and she'll be back soon enough."

The colour blanched from Giles' skin. "Do you mean to say that she's not here? He craned his neck to see into the boat. "Come on, Phoebe love. You had a nice trip out and, me and Peg, we don't have any hard feelings about that. Time to come home now."

"She stayed in Wissant. Met her father there," Walter said. "It wasn't her plan but there is family for her to meet and a father she's not seen in five years. She'll be back; she was sure of that. But for now she'll spend a few weeks with her family over the Channel."

"Oh, Giles!" Peggy clutched at her husband's arm. "Tell me it's not true. Tell me that my girl isn't gone." Her eyes began to brim with tears and her lips quivered.

"She's gone, or so they say." Giles replied. "It will be more work for the pair of us if she doesn't come back. We'll get another girl, of course, but she was a willing worker was our Phoebe."

"But she was my sister's daughter and more than a niece to me." The tears began to trickle over Peggy's cheeks.

"Shush your blubbering, woman. She was a good girl, I'll say no different despite the disappointment about her not wanting to wed young Chapman. But more than likely she'll be back and we'll get some help in the meantime."

Giles turned away from the boat, his wife clinging to his arm as they took their first steps up the shingle bank. Walter and Joshua busied themselves with the fish. Harry, who had sidled along to the stern, watched them leave.

"You get yourself home, lad," Walter called. "Take

211

a fish or two for Bess."

"Thank you, I will."

Although exhausted from the journey to France and back, Harry lingered. He would wait until Giles and Peggy had reached the wall and there was some distance between the pair of them and himself. He checked through his bag, shook out the sheepskin coat and folded it, then carefully wrapped some fish to take home.

"You'll make a fisherman if you don't want to be a wall-worker," Walter grinned as Harry gave his thanks for the new experience.

"I don't know about that, but I appreciate the chance to go out to sea," Harry replied.

"You'll be hoping she comes back?" Joshua looked him in the eye.

Shrugging his shoulders and grinning, Harry turned away and began his own steady trudge up the bank. It was early evening and the wall-workers had just finished for the day. He saw them in the distance; a small group moving along the wall towards the expenditor and their day's earnings.

With the morning sun on his back, Harry hammered the clay and loose stones into the rut formed over time on the top of the seawall. Joshua shovelled in more clay and the process was repeated.

"We'll leave it a little proud." Joshua advised. "It will level out in no time."

This was one of the easiest and cleanest jobs on the wall. Harry enjoyed looking out over the Marsh one way and over the sea the other way. The day was clear, not warm enough for the heat to shimmer on the horizon. He couldn't quite see France and the beach at Wissant, but it was there, just a few hours away in a boat. It was Phoebe's second morning in France. What was she doing at this very moment and did she think of her life in Dymchurch? Harry continued to press downwards with the mallet, allowing his thoughts to wander.

"Here we go; someone's in trouble." Joshua remarked, causing Harry to look along the seawall, following Joshua's gaze.

"From the New Hall?" Harry thought he recognised the man.

"Oh yes; one of his Lordship's men."

Of course, Harry realised now the man walking at a fair pace was the same one who had taken him from the general store to the gaol on that miserable day. His throat tightened at the memory and, as the man closed in on them, Harry began to fear the reason for his coming toward them.

"Harry Farrers?" The servant looked Harry up and down.

"Yes." Harry frowned, uncertain of how else to respond.

"You're to come along to the New Hall. Tell John Waller and be quick about it."

Harry's eyes met Joshua's and he handed him the mallet. "I'm sorry."

"You've done nothing wrong. You'll be back in no time."

This time, Harry was not directed to the gaol, but followed the servant through the front door and directly into the hallway. Without pausing, they ascended a wide staircase and entered the first floor courtroom. The door was opened and Harry was directed to a bench at the side of the room. The Leveller of the Marsh Scotts glanced in his direction but continued with the matter in hand.

Harry's memories of the courtroom were hazy and muddled. Whenever he thought back on that day over two months ago, it was like recalling a dream: nothing in quite the right order and why was it that he saw the wide wooden floorboards so clearly in his mind, while the rest of the room was shrouded in mist? Of course, it was because of his headache, that horrific throbbing pain. He had sat there with his head in his hands, only focussing on the floor. He had been barely able to function as a decent human being; aware of the poor impression he was making on the men who sat at the bench.

Now he saw it all with fresh eyes: the ceiling which went into the roof space of the courtroom and the huge beam stretching across the room; the square lead-paned windows from which shafts of light shone into the room; the bench enclosed by panelling extending across the width of the room.

The three men sat, bewigged and in their braided jackets, as they had done on that other morning. Directly in front of them stood a lanky man, fidgeting as he heard his sentence; unable to make eye contact with the Leveller of the Marsh Scotts

"... And let this be the last time I see you in my courtroom. A ten shilling fine is not much to pay, but ensure your weights are in order or I'll be harsher on you next time. It is not just me you have to fear if you make a habit of cheating people out of their rightful amount of meat. Your customers will go elsewhere, to a butcher whom they trust."

"Yes, Sir. Them were old weights, like I said," The butcher nodded frantically. "I'm grateful it was found out. Don't want to be cheating customers, I don't."

"You may leave now." Sir Rupert Bannerman had

heard all the excuses a Dymchurch trader could come up with. This was nothing new to him.

The butcher scuttled off. "Thank you, thank you, Sir."

Some papers were shuffled at the bench and notes taken before one of the bailiffs called out: "John Cobb, if you would please present yourself to us."

A burly farmer stood up from his place next to Harry at the side bench and sauntered to stand in front of the magistrates. Harry watched with some interest as to what misdemeanour had been caused.

"You've stood before me on the same charge," Sir Rupert said, his tone weary. "It has come to my notice that on three occasions you have refused to cut hawthorn for use on the seawall. Does your land at Burmarsh have no need of protection from the wall?"

"I don't see that it does. It's been there for centuries."

"With a seawall or some form of natural bank protecting it."

"I'll do it; I've not had time," muttered the farmer.

"The seawall is supported by scots levied over the whole Marsh. Landowners pay their taxes to support the maintenance of the wall and provide hawthorn to be used as faggots." Sir Rupert spoke slowly and clearly, "Are you familiar with this practice?"

"Of course."

"Yet you dismiss the order to provide hawthorn?"

"I'll do it."

"You'll do it with one less hand!" Now the Leveller of the Marsh Scotts allowed his voice to rise, causing the farmer to blanch. "I've been lenient with you and I don't care for your attitude. Get yourself over to The Ship and drink as much brandy as you can take; it will help dull the pain. My bailiff here will escort you and I'll have one of my men call for the barber. Let's hope his knives are sharp."

With that the bailiff was at the elbow of the farmer and escorting the man towards the doorway. For the moment all his bluster was lost; but it would return and so, as if waiting for the moment when they would be called, two servants from the New Hall sprang into the room to assist the bailiff with his duty.

Silence fell upon the room. Dust motes danced in the shafts of sunshine and a solitary spider ambled towards a fly prone in its web. Harry shuffled a little on the smooth wooden bench and looked sideways at the boy sitting beside him. What had this boy done? He was not yet a man but he sat there with no one to act for him. They exchanged glances; Harry saw that the lad's pinched face was pale and his eyes wary.

"Harry Farrers, please stand before me," The Leveller of the Marsh Scotts spoke.

It seemed an effort to lift each foot those ten steps to stand before the magistrates. Straightening his back, Harry looked directly at Sir Rupert and tried to hold his gaze.

"When were you last here, Harry Farrers?"

"It was March, Sir; the end of March."

"And you were ordered to work on the seawall for six months." Sir Rupert picked through the papers before him and studied one.

"Yes, I work with John Waller's men."

"It says here that you are a good worker. Your time keeping is faultless and you work well within the team."

"I try my best."

"And do you frequent the inns or alehouses of an evening?"

"No, I stay at the cottage with Owen and Bess;

216

we've been making furniture."

"Yet one evening you went out overnight and did not return to Dymchurch until the following evening. You not only left the village, but the country as well."

"I went out on a boat, Sir. Joshua suggested it as I'd never been to sea." Harry's mouth dried and his stomach clenched. "John Waller said I could miss a day and I took no pay for it."

"Did you know you were going to France?"

"I… I knew we were going to Wissant; but I wasn't sure why. I didn't know Ph… Miss Woods would be there."

"One moment, please." Sir Rupert turned towards the remaining bailiff. With lowered voices they spoke for a moment.

Harry stood, his limbs now stiff. He waited.

"Mr Farrers, I do not wish a mockery to be made of this courtroom. This is the second time a complaint has been made about you and the second time I refuse to believe you acted in any way to cause distress or with any intention of malice. John Waller gave you permission to miss a day's labour and, if he wishes, you can do an extra day at the end of your six months. I bring you here today as a warning. Think of your actions and ensure that you avoid anyone who wishes to cause you harm. John Waller speaks well of you and I hold his opinion in high esteem."

"Thank you, Sir." Harry took a step back. Was he free to go?

"I'm done with you." Sir Rupert smiled. "John Waller has a need of you, I am sure."

Chapter Twenty
Harry

The sun rose as a great red ball over the horizon, then mellowed in colour as its soft light spread through the early morning mists and across the placid sea. Vibrant rays grew in strength and slipped around the edges of the curtains hung at the small bedroom window. It was still early, and his muscles had not rested enough, but it was time for Harry's day to begin.

As he picked up his breeches, clay dust fell from them and settled on the floorboards. His shirt was clean from the trunk; Harry pulled it over his head and rolled up the sleeves so his forearms were clear of material. Even this early in the morning there was no need for a jacket, but he put on a thin waistcoat and again clay dust drifted to the floor. Prodding at it with his toes, Harry vowed to sweep it up when he returned from work that evening.

It was dark in the main living room, with just the one window letting the early morning light through from the east. Embers smouldered in the fireplace; the air was pungent with woodsmoke. Harry took a knife and the loaf of bread from an earthenware pot. He hacked off a thick chunk and then took a piece of cheese from the cupboard with a slab of cooling slate at its base. The food was wrapped and placed in his drawstring bag, along with a slim flask of weak cider.

Low voices came from the main bedroom, but the front door had closed behind Harry before Owen or Bess entered the living area that morning. It was the second week of extended hours working on the seawall. Having scrambled up the track behind the cottage, Harry fell in step beside some of the team. In the distance a ribbon of workers could be seen coming into the village from the Eastbridge Road and another group from the St Mary in the Marsh area.

They met by Wall End, the regular workers and those who had joined them for six weeks of the summer.

"Good morning, lads," John Waller gave a nod. "Tide's up, so we won't go digging and making her weak, not till it's turned. In the meantime, there's plenty to do. We've that pile of old faggots that came out yesterday. You lot who are here temporary can sort through them – any wood that can be reused put to one side. The rest that's all broken up or rotting can be put in these sacks and taken home as kindling wood for your fires. Ben and David will work with you. Any questions, just ask them.

"Now you lot," John turned to his regular team. "There's all this hawthorn which came yesterday from Honeychild land. I want it cut to length the best you can, for all that it's tricky and full of thorns. And a couple of you..." he looked towards Joshua, "you, Joshua, and Harry, can work at putting eyes in the stakes."

Harry tried to keep the grin from spreading across his face. He had done this job the week before and enjoyed whittling away at the oak, working with the grain until he opened up a slit, or eye.

"We'll sit ourselves up on the wall," Joshua said, as they walked towards the cart and pulled off a dozen

219

oak stakes, which would be known as needles by the time they stopped for morning break.

They sat together on the seawall facing the open countryside, legs dangling down the side with the sun beating upon their backs. It was an odd sort of place, Harry reflected, the land so flat with the ditches cutting through it. There were not many trees of any great height or splendour, such as oaks or beeches. Just those spindly hawthorns, so favoured for their use in the wall. In a land so open you would think that no one could sneak about without being seen, he knew that the Marsh held secrets but couldn't quite fathom what they were.

"Do you miss Elham?" Joshua asked, as if reading Harry's thoughts.

"The woods and the valleys, I miss them," Harry replied. "And the folk that I've known all my life, and my sister – who may well be wed by now."

"That's a lot to miss."

"But I wouldn't go back, not even if I could. Not when my six months has passed here. Not with that stepfather of mine all comfortable in my father's forge."

"Your father's forge? I thought you were just a worker there, learning the trade."

"I was worse than that, Joshua, when my mother remarried. I'd never go back."

"Sounds like you've had a bad deal of it," Joshua concluded.

The pile of oak needles grew to one side of them as their laps and the ground around the two men became littered with wood chippings. Working with the grain, Harry used the skills Owen had taught him in order to ensure that the wood didn't split. When every stake had a neatly formed eye in it, a different process began. With a sharp knife the two friends sliced shavings from the opposite end until rough points took shape.

As the call came for early morning break, Harry took the bread and cheese from his sack. He turned to look out across the sea and noted that the tide was now a couple of feet clear of the base of the wall.

"Time to start digging," John Waller announced. He had already marked out the extent of the day's work.

The team of regular and temporary wall-workers knew what was to be done. Some tackled the clay-earth which had hardened over the first weeks of summer. Working on the landward side, they eased the tips of spades into cracks and levered out the clods of earth. Others moved the soil from the open wound in the seawall and carted it to the base of the wall to be stored in piles for reuse.

As the core of the seawall was revealed, its skeleton was unceremoniously pulled out. Decades old hawthorn branches, whose thorns no longer stabbed at the workers' hands, cracked and crumbled as they were wrenched free. These were slung aside to be sorted through during high tide the following day. By the time Harry went back home for his midday meal, an area of about ten to twelve feet had been dug away. It would need to be filled with fresh, supple hawthorn faggots before the next tide was beating against the seawall.

John Waller was standing on top of the seawall when Harry returned. The gaping hole was opened up beneath his feet but his attention was on the road to the east.

"There's no clay arrived. I would have expected two carts by now and there's not one to be seen on the road nor further along the wall."

"Why wouldn't it come?" Harry asked.

"Broken carts? Trouble on the road? Perhaps the need is greater further down the wall? I've no idea, but we need it or the wall will breach come high tide."

Running his hand through his hair, John Waller scrambled down the bank and studied the pile of dry clay-earth which had been removed. "I'll set the lads on getting this lot workable. They'll need water from the sewer to soften it.

"David, we'll need those buckets from the cart and set up a chain of men filling the buckets from Clobsden Sewer to give this clay a good old soaking.

"Joshua, you and Harry go along towards Burmarsh and find out where those carts are. We'll need at least six loads within the next few hours and I won't lie easy unless we have eight."

The two friends set off along the seawall. "We'll meet up with the other teams and see if they've had their clay." Joshua said. "But we need to keep an eye on the road as well."

It was the same as they neared Marshlands Gut; the team had done their best to prepare for the clay but it was slow in coming. "They've only just had their first lot along at Watch Knocke," the workers complained.

They dropped down from the wall to the village road and followed it past the Ocean Inn and the village shops and stayed on this track rather than follow the road running alongside the seawall. When they reached the orange-brick vicarage, the young vicar appeared, looking rather bothered and being trailed by a boy in ragged clothes and bare feet. The vicar didn't seem to notice the two wall-workers, but kept turning back to the young urchin, questioning him before hurrying on.

Curious as to what had got the vicar moving at such a pace, Harry and Joshua matched his speed. As the road turned inland to Burmarsh, Sir Rupert Bannerman passed them on horseback, before slowing to speak with the vicar.

"The doctor is there," Sir Rupert was saying as they drew close to him. "It's a nasty business, there's no denying it. Make speed and put him at ease before he passes, for I fear that there will be no reprieve."

The vicar broke into a run, with the urchin still bobbing along at his side. Sir Rupert reached into his pocket and, without checking their value, he tossed a few coins in the direction of the boy. Leaving the vicar to find his own way, the boy scrambled about on the ground for his reward before scampering on. There might be more coins to come; the Leveller of the Marsh Scotts was known for his generosity.

The scene at the Burmarsh Road was one of confusion. Five or six clay carts were abandoned at the roadside. Their boys, hanging back behind the carts, were clearly eager to look on from a distance. The ponies, though unrestrained, were disinclined to wander from the lush roadside grass.

On the opposite side of the road, looking as if he had been dragged from the dyke, was a man lying on his back. One of his boots was missing; his breeches were sodden and beribboned with duckweed. An open jacket showed a dishevelled white shirt. The village doctor was kneeling at his side, a hand on his chest and his ear at the man's mouth.

"There's nothing to be done for him," the doctor called out as the vicar neared. "All we can do is pray that he passes with comfort to the next life. I've sent a boy for opium; it will numb the pain."

"Was it a fall?" the vicar reached in his capacious

223

pocket for a slim Bible.

"No, not a fall." The doctor rolled the body onto its side, revealing a slowly spreading stain of dark blood on the riding officer's back. The tattered grass beneath him was drawing the blood into its sinuous leaves and the dry earth took on a reddish hue.

"Was he alone?" the vicar questioned. It was rare for the riding officers to ride the Marsh roads without company. To be in a pair was dangerous enough, but there was no choice. Just the two of them were assigned to patrol the coastline and Marsh from West Hythe to Wall End, a distance of four miles.

"His companion rode off as if the devil was behind him," the doctor informed. "Or so those cart boys told me."

The vicar reached out for the riding officer's clammy hand and looked into his face. His complexion was taking on a greyish hue. He was probably past hearing the words of God through His vessel on earth, but the words continued to flow from the vicar's lips.

"Almighty God, look on this your servant and comfort him with the promise of life everlasting, given in the resurrection of Your Son, Jesus Christ our Lord. Amen.

Sir Rupert stood looking down upon the dying man with the vicar and doctor at his side. Harry and Joshua gazed upon the scene for a moment before turning their attention to the cart boys.

"What's going on here? There's been no clay delivered to Marshlands Gut or Wall End," Joshua spoke sharply to the cart boys.

"It were the carts, mister, they were taken for other business."

"What can be of more importance than carting clay to the wall?"

"Nothin', mister, but it weren't for us to say. Not to them who wanted the carts."

"The carts were used for something else?" Joshua frowned. "And I'll wager those poor ponies were already worn out before they started their day's work."

"They were." The boy looked subdued.

At that moment Sir Rupert Bannerman, Leveller of the Marsh Scotts, approached Joshua and Harry. "It's a damned nasty business. He's slipped away as peacefully as we could hope for, but an officer of the King is dead on my land and there will be trouble. You can be sure of it."

"He's dead then!" the boy exclaimed. "I knew it were bad when he fell in the dyke."

"You saw it happen?" Sir Rupert asked.

"I saw nothing, I had my back turned at that very moment."

The other urchins, who had sidled closer, stared with wide eyes at this man of great importance who was interested in whatever they had to say.

"And the rest of you. What did you see?" bellowed Sir Bannerman.

"Nothing, I were lookin' after the pony."

"There were a bang. A big one, but we didn't see who fired."

"Must have been hiding."

"We didn't see. We didn't see who shot him."

"We was just with the ponies. They took fright."

A man had died and a killer running free on Romney Marsh. Harry understood the serious nature of the matter, so why was it these lads had nothing to tell – or chose to have nothing to tell?

Sir Rupert paced up and down then barked at the boys, "What are you doing, just standing about with these carts? Are they not needed? Clay is wanted on the seawall before the next high tide."

"That's why we are here, Sir," Joshua ventured to say. "We've no clay at Wall End nor Marshlands Gut."

"Get on with it then!" Sir Rupert roared. "We can do nothing for this unfortunate man, but we can do our best to ensure the wall is ready to hold back the next tide."

"Thank you, Sir," Joshua turned away. "We need this clay or there'll be trouble later."

"I'll make it my business to check that you have enough and keep the carts moving beyond six o'clock if that is what's needed."

"Thank you. We'll get back to Wall End now." Harry replied.

The two young men walked on in silence. Harry's thoughts moved from the body of the riding officer to the odd business of the ponies and their carts being prevented from carrying the clay. There were mysteries to be solved in Dymchurch, that was clear enough. Ponies and carts. He recalled the day when a procession had moved along the seawall and yet no comment had been made. He'd not seen it before nor since, but the unusual moment was stored away as something that made him feel uncomfortable. Then there were the preventative officers, riding about the area on their horses. What exactly were they looking for? Always asking questions, yet they only received a shrug or a display of innocence from those whom they accosted on a daily basis. It seemed to Harry that the dead officer had seen something he shouldn't have noticed or questioned too much for someone's liking.

"What did they need the carts for, Joshua?" Harry blurted out.

"They shouldn't have used them," Joshua replied.

"Used them for what? The same as when they were on the seawall a few weeks back?"

"It's just trading," Joshua shrugged as if it were nothing at all, hardly worth talking about. "But we needed those carts for the wall, and they should have shown respect for that if nothing else."

"Trading? Well surely it didn't have to be done at that very moment when the carts were needed for clay?"

"It's not as easy as that. When the goods need moving, that's what they do and we say nothing about it," Joshua explained. "If the King didn't charge such high taxes there would be no need for it at all."

"It's coming in from abroad then? The King's not getting his taxes and so it has to be kept hidden?"

"Something like that," Joshua agreed. "It carries on, all along the coast. But we don't talk about it. We say nothing and we see nothing. That's the way of the Marsh."

"But I saw it. In the middle of the day. Bold as anything they were."

"True, but I didn't see it. I looked the other way."

"Why move the goods around, in the middle of the day? A huge gang of them, there was." Harry frowned. It made no sense at all.

"They've lost all fear." Joshua said. "With only two riding officers to patrol from west of Hythe to Wall End, what chance is there of them getting caught?"

"But they got caught today." Realisation hit Harry. "That's why a man is dead,"

Joshua gave no reply.

Chapter Twenty-One
Harry

By mid-afternoon, the whispers had flowed along the length of the wall and reached Wall End. A body was laid out in the vicarage opposite the church. Not any body, but that of a riding officer and his death couldn't be passed off as an accident, not with a shot wound in his back. His fellow officer had fled to Hythe, fearing for his own life, no doubt. Trouble had come to Dymchurch; everyone who heard the news feared that the peaceful nature of the village was about to be upturned. Questions would be asked and those who raised them would be searching everywhere for answers.

Early the next morning, Harry heard the news that a band of the King's men had arrived in Dymchurch the previous evening. The captain and four of his dragoons came with the riding officer, John Clements, who had fled at the time of the murder. Captain Charles Amherst had rapped on the door of the New Hall just as the family sat down to supper.

"He insisted on eating first, invited the captain to join him at his table and refused to speak of the nasty business until the women had left," John Waller informed his team. "The dragoons and riding officer were fed in the kitchens of course. Sir Rupert

Bannerman gave them all beds for the night, and they say that John Clements wouldn't return to his own lodgings but slept with the dragoons above the stables of the New Hall, with his musket at the ready."

"How do you know?" Harry asked.

"It was the talk of The Ship."

"And The Ocean, and every tavern in between," David added.

"They were seen arriving of course." Joshua added to the story. "It was one of the clay-cart lads who first spread the news. There was no mistaking them – they were riding their horses three abreast and wearing red jackets with brass buttons and those tricorne hats.

"They were closeted away with Sir Rupert for at least an hour," David said, "Then they paid a visit to The Ship and went along the road to the tavern on the seawall."

"Asking questions, were they?" Harry still stayed at home of an evening, keeping away from trouble.

"Wanting to know who was about at the time of the shooting. Buying drinks for everyone and thinking to get their tongues wagging."

"And did they wag?" Harry asked. "It was only the young lads with the clay carts when we got to the Burmarsh road and saw him lying there."

"They didn't say anything much at all. They've no fear of the King's men," Joshua replied. "But they fear those who took a man's life and will think nothing of silencing another."

"And the one who is the officer for Dymchurch, not the murdered one, God rest his soul, but the other riding officer, John Clements, he kept quiet," David added. "Didn't want to be back on the Marsh, anyone could see that."

"I'll bet he didn't," Harry agreed.

"Sir Rupert will personally escort them around the village today and for however many days they plan to be here," Joshua informed. "They've questions to ask and he'll not allow them to go snooping about unattended, you can be sure of that."

"We could talk of this all day, but you can work at the same time." John brought the team to order. "Now I've marked out the area to be dug out today and you all know what you're doing. We've been promised extra clay today and some of you will be packing extra on yesterday's patch as well."

They came not long after the mid-morning break. Having just tied a bundle of hawthorn, Harry passed it on to be stacked in a pile and straightened his back for a moment. He was used to seeing the seawall swarming with labourers during these weeks of intensive work, but it was the red jackets of the dragoons that caught his attention.

With backs straight and three-cornered hats on their heads, the King's men trotted at a brisk pace along the top of the seawall. They made way for no one and, even from a distance, Harry saw the labourers scatter rather than run the risk of being trampled. Sir Rupert took the lead with the captain beside him; the four dragoons were two abreast and the riding officer brought up the rear.

"He'd feel safer amongst them," Joshua reasoned.

Harry nodded. If the riding officer feared for his life, he'd make an easy target at the rear. This was Dymchurch, and although it seemed that there was trading going on, and not the type to line the King's pockets with taxes, there was no reason to believe that this man's life was at risk. Yet one man was dead and for no good reason Harry knew of. It made no sense to him and, as a newcomer, he knew it could be sometime before he understood the people who lived within the shadows of the seawall.

As reins were tightened, the horses stopped abruptly at Wall End. Sir Rupert scanned the group of Dymchurch men and seasonal wall-workers.

John Waller stepped forward. "Can I help, Sir Rupert?" He nodded, to show his respect to the visiting officers.

"We need a word with young Harry and Joshua," Sir Rupert replied, as he swung down from his horse. "Their labours here are of utmost importance and so I'll take as little of their time as necessary."

"But while we speak with them, my dragoons will talk amongst your men." The captain looked down through his pale blue eyes and his moustache quivered below ruddy cheeks. "My officer is dead and we'll speak with every man in this village until one of them tells me who saw fit to take his life."

The large man dismounted from his sleek chestnut stallion and stood beside Sir Rupert. "Captain Amherst," he announced, offering his hand to John.

Harry and Joshua approached the two men. Feeling rather small and insignificant beside the imposing figure of the captain, Harry waited for John to make the introductions.

But it was the Leveller of the Marsh Scotts who spoke first: "Harry Farrers and Joshua Clayton. You'll hear the truth from these two, Captain, and make no mistake about it. Young Harry has been working in the village for the past three months and I've had very good reports of his conduct from John Waller. He lives a sober life and keeps away from any trouble.

"Joshua here is a true Dymchurch man and I can't say better than that. He works hard on maintaining the

231

seawall and is well-liked. I've heard talk of him running his own patch of wall and there's proof of his good character."

"I'm pleased to hear it; now…," Captain Amherst stepped towards them and lowered his voice, encouraging Harry and Joshua to also move closer.

Sir Rupert Bannerman stood just behind the captain, ensuring that he heard every word.

"You were there, I hear. At the scene of the crime." The captain's tone was friendly, as if to wheedle confidences.

"We arrived after it happened," Joshua began. "We'd had no delivery of clay and set off to find where the carts were. When we reached the vicarage, the vicar came out, in a hurry, and set off at such a pace with some boy. We followed and it was when we reached the Burmarsh road we saw the riding officer lying there."

"We arrived shortly after Sir Rupert," Harry added. "He passed us on the road and caught up with the vicar."

"And you came to take a look?" the captain asked.

"We came to look for the clay carts and there they were, six of them," Joshua informed. "The riding officer was there with the doctor; but we were in need of the carts and that was our concern."

"And can you tell me why the carts were there?" Captain Amherst asked.

"The boys said they had been asked to use them for something else, but they were empty by the time we came across them," Joshua replied.

"What else would they be used for?"

"I didn't ask. I was that angry for them not being used for the clay. We had to fill the wall and whoever took them away from that duty should be standing before the Leveller of the Marsh Scotts." Joshua looked at Sir Rupert. "Isn't that right? We all have a duty to maintain the wall and to prevent it is wrong."

"That is the way of Romney Marsh," Sir Rupert agreed. "But I have to admit that as a man was dying I took my eye off the business of the carts. Especially as he was one of your men, Captain, and his death was clearly suspicious."

"Did the boys give any explanation as to what the carts had been used for?"

"They scampered off as fast as they could manage," Joshua said.

"But you would recognise these boys?"

"I can't say that I would," Joshua frowned as if trying to think. "There's so many of them, young lads from big families who send them out to earn a few pennies whenever there's work to be had."

"And you, Harry? What can you tell me about those boys?"

"I'm sorry, Captain; I'm new to the area and I couldn't say who they were."

"But if one came along with a clay cart now, you'd recognise him?"

"Maybe," Harry said with reluctance. "But they all look the same to me, ragged and desperate."

"You walked from here until the road turned to Burmarsh, and back again; did you see anyone acting in a suspicious way?"

"Nothing at all," Joshua stated. "Just the women shopping and the young ones running about."

While they spoke, Harry saw that the captain's men were moving amongst the other wall-workers. Pausing in their work, each resting on a shovel for a moment, they shook their heads and shrugged their shoulders. No one had seen anything. Of course they hadn't; they had been here, working on the wall. And in the evening, when they could have been listening to gossip in the taverns, they were resting at their own firesides. It was a long day labouring on the seawall.

Captain Amherst gave the call and his men turned away from the workers. They were done with them for now. With ease, they swung themselves onto their horses and, having turned to face the east, the King's men trotted back towards the village. The next Harry knew of them that day was when he saw their horses tethered outside The Ocean. He was returning home for his midday meal and spotted the dragoons' red coats through the open doorway of the inn. They were clearly still busy questioning the men of Dymchurch.

That afternoon, the men worked swiftly in order to fill the wall. It had been opened from the top to its base, exposing the ancient structure. They had been labouring together for four weeks now and each one of them knew the role he had within the team. The faggots had been prepared throughout the morning, using mostly fresh hawthorn cut from the local farmland, and some old pieces of wood pulled from the wall that morning and still strong enough to be reused. The first layer of neatly-tied faggots had been pushed into place and Harry stood within the wall, a wooden mallet in his hand, driving the oak stakes with their needle heads amongst the hawthorn faggots. And so the needles began the job of holding the faggots in place.

"Pass the edders, Joshua," John called.

"Right away."

"Now, through the eyes."

Harry and John worked the flexible rods, or edders, through the eyes of the needles and the

234

faggots were secured within a framework of wooden stakes, driven into the earth, and edders that wove across the top. Putting his hand into a bag, John produced some short wooden keys.

"Use a smaller hammer for these," he reminded Harry. "I'll leave you to finish off."

Harry drove the keys into the eyes and the edders were kept in place with no room to move. Joshua moved in beside him and together, with mallets, they pushed the needles further into the earth, causing the faggots to compress. As soon as they stood aside, the other men were there, ready to press clay amongst the faggots. The process of rebuilding this small part of the seawall had begun and it was repeated throughout the afternoon.

"We went along to pay our respects," Bess told Harry on his return from work. It was the fourth day since the murder of the riding officer. "Not that we knew him, or thought much of him. But it seemed like the right thing to do."

"Did many go to the funeral?" Harry asked.

"Them who could spare the time. There was all those from the New Hall and the Manor House of course, looking smart as usual. Captain Amherst and the dragoons put on quite a show with their red jackets. The women from the New Hall and the Manor were in more sombre dress than the usual fancy stuff they have a liking for, as you'd expect."

"So, he was buried here in the churchyard? He didn't return to wherever he came from?" Harry asked.

"There's a fresh grave waiting to settle before it has its stone. He's stayed right here in Dymchurch. I reckon this is the last place he'd want to be."

"Probably," Harry agreed.

Captain Charles Amherst and his men stayed in Dymchurch for ten days. On some days they were seen heading out along the Marsh lanes towards Eastbridge or Burmarsh or St Mary in the Marsh. On other days they remained within Dymchurch, questioning every villager they saw. The young lads who worked with the clay carts were among those who were most often accosted by the King's men. These boys tried to pass by them, with their heads bowed, but they couldn't hide away. Not when they travelled the length of the village with a pony and cart, hour after hour throughout the day.

It was said that Captain Amherst was becoming increasingly frustrated with the lack of information coming from these boys. Wide-eyed and seemingly with very little wit, they just stared at the men, shaking their heads, denying that they had witnessed the shooting. There must have been a hundred of these boys, all of a similar age, each one pale and scruffy. The King's men had no idea which had already been questioned, and none of them admitted being among the six who had possibly witnessed the crime.

The Leveller of the Marsh Scotts was equally unable to suggest which boys had been there at the time of the murder. "There are so many urchins who appear for a penny or two at this time of year, I couldn't tell those from Burmarsh or West Hythe or somewhere else altogether," he said, or so it was reported in the bars, on the streets and on the seawall.

The reward on the posters was doubled to twenty pounds: an enormous amount of money and equivalent to a year's wage for a labourer on the land or the seawall. But still no one came forward with any information.

In the New Hall, Captain Amherst met daily with Sir

Rupert Bannerman and, as they spoke, the footman or the serving girl stood at the door, ready to repeat their words to the curious villagers. The frustrations Captain Amherst suffered were well reported within the cottages huddled under the wall and those beside the reed-lined ditches on the lanes winding out into the Marsh.

On the day the King's men left, the news travelled swiftly along the seawall. It was carried as shouts and calls from one man to another. It was estimated that news conveyed in this way could move from one end to the other in less than ten minutes. No man was held within the damp walls of the Dymchurch gaol and no man swung from the gallows. Captain Amherst and his dragoons had left without picking up any hint of who the murderer was.

A few days' later, Dymchurch's riding officer returned to continue his duties. He brought with him not one man to replace his murdered colleague, but three.

"That Captain Amherst is not a happy man," John commented, as his team sat on top of the wall during their mid-morning break. "Not happy at all. He'll be wanting to make trouble for Dymchurch folk."

"There's not much trouble to be had from four riding officers," Joshua replied. "Not when they have to cover four miles of coastline and the Marsh beyond it, with all our hidey holes, and traders as wily as any you'd find on Romney Marsh."

Chapter Twenty-Two
Harry

"You've done your time now, lad." Owen gave a pat on the arm. "Six months labouring on the wall and you're free."

"I am, and it feels good," Harry grinned.

"Sit yourself down on the bench and let's have a cider while the sun still blesses us with her warmth."

It was the end of September and the sun had shone constantly on the village of Dymchurch over the last weeks. While the sea sparkled and the sands dried to a golden brown, the wall-workers enjoyed her soft rays but were also relieved that the intense heat radiating from the blazing sun throughout July and August was now lessening.

Stretching his legs out, Harry sat on the bench outside the front of the cottage. The sun was on the last stretch of its journey that day and cast a mellow light on the front of the wooden cottage and the faded reed-thatch. The grass at their feet was still vigorous, although well-worn in the places where Owen's boots had trampled upon it as he moved from cottage to workshop and back again.

"Here you are." Owen offered a tankard of cider and sat next to Harry, cradling his own drink in rough hands. "Now, has John Waller offered you a permanent place on his team?"

"In the early summer, June it must have been, he said I could stay on if I wanted," Harry replied. "And he said the same as I left just now."

"You've worked hard and set people straight on a point or two," Owen reflected. "They thought you were simple. I thought so myself and I'm not ashamed to say it. But it was that bump on the head making you all of a muddle and I thank the Lord that the confusion has passed."

"The head's been all right," Harry said. "And it's been good on the wall. Hard work, but John's got a good team."

"And have you decided whether to stay on or take up my offer?"

Harry paused before replying. Owen and Bess had been kind to him, even building him his own room on their cottage and he got a lot of pleasure from working with wood. He was skilled as a blacksmith of course and could have enquired at one of the two forges in the village, but cutting and carving wood was more tempting. Owen was well-respected in Dymchurch and Harry was sure there would soon be enough work for the pair of them.

"I'll stay on the wall for now. John will need all the help he can get come November. I know the conditions will be harsh, but I don't want to leave the team." Harry took a sip of cider and continued, "I've got some thinking to do. Last March I was planning to move along the coast further away from Elham and that stepfather of mine. But he would never come this far and he has no interest in me. He's got my father's forge, which is enough for him. I'll work the winter on the wall and if Dymchurch still suits me and I'm accepted here then I'd gladly join you. Is that fair enough?"

"Of course, lad. You want to find your own way here and now your penance is over, you'll have your chance." Owen started to fish around in the deep pocket of his jacket. "I've got this for you and it's yours whether you stay or move on. I wanted to give you something to remember us by and to show you how fond we are of you."

Owen passed Harry a small cloth pouch and watched as he loosened the string ties. Harry's fingers held onto a smooth object and he withdrew it, carefully easing it past the folds of cloth and out of the opening. Then he put the silver-coloured disk into his hand and turned it over to reveal the intricate design of a clock face.

"A pocket watch," Harry whispered. "Owen, this is really special. It's too much."

"No, lad, you've brought such pleasure to me and Bess. It's something to remember us by. Now when you go out tonight, you can fix it to your belt and be as good as anyone in Dymchurch." Owen stood up. "This wind is getting brisk, let's settle down by the fire."

The Ship was popular in the evenings. Quite a crowd of wall-workers gathered around the bar and tables. It was Joshua's birthday and that made it as good an excuse as any to down a few pints of beer or cider after work. The evenings were drawing in now and, as the sun slipped below the horizon, oil lamps shed their soft light on the rough table tops and the bar, stained with layer upon layer of spills. Bottles of wine, brandy and other spirits were clustered behind the bar, glass gleaming where the light fell upon it.

As he entered, a rush of cold wind came in with Harry, pushing the sawdust across the floor in the direction of the bar. Closing the door behind him,

Harry paused. It was the first time he had gone into a Dymchurch tavern. Staying true to his earlier resolve, he had spent all his free time at home during the six months he paid his penance on the wall.

A haze of tobacco smoke hung in the air, causing Harry's eyes to smart. It mingled with the woodsmoke from the log fire belching outwards as the wind blew down the chimney. After the fresh salt-breeze sweeping through the village, the stench of stale ale, body odour and tobacco was an assault to the senses.

"Over here, Harry," Joshua beckoned from the bar.

With a nod of recognition, Harry walked over to him. Farm labourers and wall-workers moved aside to allow him to pass by.

"Can I buy you a drink on your birthday?" Harry asked.

"I'll not say 'no'." Joshua lifted his tankard and let the dregs of his ale flow down his throat.

The barmaid was not much older than fifteen years of age; her skin was fair and wisps of blonde tendrils escaped from her hair, which was tied back with ribbons and covered with a cap. A huge apron covered her dress and protected it from splashes of drink falling in her direction no matter how hard she tried to stay clean and respectable in appearance.

"What can I get you? A tankard of ale?" she smiled at Harry.

"No thanks, cider please. And an ale for Joshua, too."

"Not seen you here before." She gave a warm smile. "I've seen you about, but not in here."

"I've not been in," Harry replied, not wanting to explain any further.

"Got money to spare, have you?" Harry didn't recognise the voice of the person who had stepped up close behind him. Turning slightly, he recognised him as Aaron Chapman and his spirits sank. He was looking to enjoy an hour with his companions, having seen nothing but friendship from his fellow workers on the wall.

"It's my friend's birthday, so I'll buy him a drink, that's all." Harry picked up his tankard and went to turn away, but found Aaron blocking his way.

"Not been here before? Keeping away were you?"

"I'm here now," Harry replied.

"Come on, Harry, over here," Joshua called.

Aaron stepped back, allowing Harry to join Joshua, his brother Walter and other men from the village. His friends soon moved to make space for him on a bench. It was mostly the young wall-workers and fishermen in their corner of the tavern; a couple of farm labourers joined them. Through the murky atmosphere, John Waller nodded and raised his hand in a greeting to Harry.

They all chatted about local news from the farms and villages. Fishermen and farm labourers were exchanging gossip with those who worked on the seawall. After an hour or so, their eyes wandered toward the pretty barmaid and they spoke of other local girls. Aaron Chapman moved towards the group. Although talking to the people either side of him, he kept looking towards Harry. He carried a smirk on his face. Harry shifted his position a little so as not to be able to make eye contact. It was time to leave, he was sure of it.

Finally Aaron called across the table, "Harry, where is it you come from?"

"Dymchurch," was the brief reply.

"You are no more from Dymchurch than the brandy hidden in the cellar."

"It's where I live and work for now." Harry wasn't going to respond to the bully.

"You're no Marsh-man and it's only Marsh people who should work on our wall. You've done your time, so move on."

"I'll do that when John Waller says, or when I decide to," Harry replied.

At that moment two of the Dymchurch riding officers swaggered into the bar. They looked about as if expecting the wool-packs to be sitting right there, ready for a trip across the Channel.

"It's all ship-shape and orderly in here, officers," one of Aaron's companions called out. "But I hear at The Ocean, they're supping brandy that were ballast in a boat only last night."

"Oh, are they? Well, we'll stop for a drink here before moving on up the road." The officer stepped up to the bar. "A glass of your finest French brandy, if you please."

"I've none of that here," she replied. "Just some English brandy from the Weald."

"Ale then," the officer snapped.

"That Aaron's taken a dislike to you." Walter muttered to Harry. "And he's not one to forget about it."

"I've done nothing to him."

"It's a bit of a mystery where you came from and he doesn't like strangers around here," Walter said. "He doesn't like anyone much. Keep away from him if you can. His family have a bit of power around here."

"I have a feeling that when he's done with the riding officers, Aaron will turn his attention back to me," Harry murmured. "I'll slip out now and if you could say goodnight to Joshua for me there will be no fuss over my going."

Walter nodded his agreement.

243

Harry turned towards the seawall when he left The Ship. He passed some cottages and found the ribbon of a track snaking along the base of the wall. The sky was vast, with a crescent moon high amidst the pinprick stars. Pausing for a moment, he gazed up at the bright lights and wondered at how far away they were. Then, pulling his jacket tight about him, Harry walked on.

The sea-breeze was brisk, carrying with it the scents of salt and seaweed. Flurries of woodsmoke were caught up and briefly mingled within it before moving on, adding another scent to the wind. It pressed on spindly tree branches, and crept into crevices, causing rustles, creaks and whistling sounds. On the beach, it whipped the sea into small waves frothing upon damp sands.

It would only take a couple of minutes to reach home; Harry picked up his pace. He was eager for the fire, perhaps a chunk of fruit loaf or pie and then his own bed. There was a rustle from behind a tree and a twig snapped – perhaps a fox? Then a footstep and Harry was sure he wasn't alone; turning around he saw a figure stepping out from the shadows.

Aaron was a little shorter than Harry, just a little. His figure was wiry and his step light as he approached. He stood before Harry and, for a moment, neither said a word. Aaron's hair was a glossy black in the moonlight, his eyes narrowed and his arms folded across his body. As he took a step closer, Harry's body tensed. This is what he had to avoid. He wanted no more trouble.

Shrugging his shoulders, Harry turned and walked away. One step at a time, that was all he had to do. No need to stand there and wait for the confrontation. He wouldn't run: of course he wouldn't. But he could walk and hope by behaving in a calm manner he could get home safely. The tug on his shoulder told Harry differently and he swung back round to face Aaron Chapman.

"It's just us now, Wall-Boy," Aaron snarled. "You've done your time for thieving, so move on." Reaching out, he pushed at Harry's shoulder, "You don't fit in around here. Damn you and your bad blood."

"I've done my time on the wall. What does it matter to you if I'm here or not?" Harry kept his voice steady.

"It matters because I don't take to outsiders butting in." Aaron jabbed at Harry's chest.

There was no pain; it hadn't been that forceful, but the sensation of Aaron's finger on Harry's chest stayed with him.

"Perhaps I'll save a bit of money and move on in a few months. I'm on full pay now." He was trying to give himself time. Make it seem like he wouldn't cause any more bother.

"You're waiting for my girl. Hoping she'll come back soon." Aaron spat on the ground at Harry's feet. "She'll not be back for the likes of you, but she's missing me. I'll tell you that." A wide grin flashed across his fox-like face. A couple of broken teeth showed in the moonlight. "She's been in touch, you know. Begging me to take her back. I'd only have to give the word and she'd leave the French and be back in my arms. But, I don't know. She's pretty enough, I'll give you that." He paused for a moment, as if to reflect on Phoebe's attractions, "Perhaps I'll see how willing she is before I decide."

Harry's throat tightened. Attempting a shrug of indifference he forced out the words, "I'm not waiting for anyone's girl. She said she was coming back and maybe she will."

"Got all cosy, did you? The two of you on the boat?"

"She was very sick on the boat; then she was taken to meet her father." Harry thought of the hours spent at Phoebe's side and the whispered confidences. "I barely spoke to her," he lied. "Walter kept me at the tiller. She went with her father and we returned to the boat."

"What was she thinking of, going over there? I'd have told her not to bother. Kept her dancing to my tune."

"She wanted to see her father. She didn't know if he was dead or alive,"

"Dead or alive? He went off with Walter one night; I could have told her that. He was alive when he slipped out of the cell and got on that same boat as the one you took."

"But you didn't tell her," Harry pointed out.

"I'll set her straight on a thing or two when she comes back. It will be soon, I'm telling you, Wall-Boy. She'll be back soon, before the weather turns." Taking a step closer, Aaron took a grip on Harry's collar, "And you'll be keeping away from her."

Harry pulled away. Turning from Aaron he took a couple of steps along the muddy track.

But Aaron wasn't done with him. "And when my girl comes back, you'll be gone, you son of a whore. You'll be gone from the wall and that cosy cottage you've made your home."

Harry felt the push of the palm of a hand on his back, his boots slipped and he lurched. Feeling foolish, he swung around in time to see Aaron's fist swing towards his jaw. He moved aside, but not in time to avoid a glancing blow. Why would she do it? Why would a lovely girl like Phoebe give herself to this

246

bully? Pain seared through his jaw, but it was the hurt in his heart causing more anguish. He faltered, not wanting the confrontation. Thinking of his home in the cottage under the wall, he wanted to be there, to feel the warmth wrapping itself around him. But in a flash, he saw himself leaving Dymchurch and walking on along the wall, beyond High Knocke and to an unknown future. He wouldn't stay to watch Phoebe wed this man.

It only took those moments of indecision for Aaron to take his chance with his fist again. This time he hit his target and Harry took a blow to the side of his face. A vision of the cell at the New Hall flashed before Harry; he was scared. Not wanting to be unjustly imprisoned there but understanding the laws of Dymchurch and knowing no matter who started the confrontation and no matter who came out the worst, it would be Harry who suffered the loss of freedom and a third time in front of Sir Rupert Bannerman and the bailiffs.

Harry's face throbbed and finally he let his rage flow. What was it that gave Aaron Chapman the claim on a lovely young woman and the right to tell law-abiding people where to live their lives?

""Get the hell out of my face, Chapman." Harry, lean but strong from six months' labouring on the wall, jabbed at Aaron's shoulder, then gave a punch in the bully's stomach.

No one had ever pushed Aaron Chapman, except his own father who beat his son regularly during his years of growing up. It was part of his upbringing, his education as a man. It formed him into the young man he had become and his father was proud.

Grabbing Harry by the front of his tunic, Aaron pulled him forwards and then pushed him back so he fell hard on the ground. The kicks came swiftly, three of them before Harry could grab at the ankle of his attacker. It was not enough, Aaron faltered and broke free before placing his booted foot on Harry's chest.

"You'll not last around here," The boot pressed down further on Harry's ribcage.

Harry's jacket was damp from the wet grass and clay-soil. Stones and twigs dug into muscular shoulders. He lay prone for a moment, not wanting the humiliation of being seen to struggle.

"I don't forget that you were in jail for stealing and you got away with it. I don't forget that you've had an eye on my woman." Harry received a final kick in the chest before Aaron swung away. "I'll be watching and you won't get away with anything else, damn you, Farrers."

Rolling onto his side, Harry drew his knees up to his chest before slowly shifting into a sitting position. Running fingers over his misshapen jaw, he felt an oozing stickiness amongst the swollen bruises. Then, with a hand clasped tight over his ribs, Harry moved forwards onto his knees and, with his spare arm, he pushed himself upwards. With his figure hunched and arms still held fast across his chest, Harry took those first slow steps towards to safety of his home.

Chapter Twenty-Three
Harry

There was no avoiding Bess when Harry slunk into the living room the next morning. Sitting at the table with his hand covering the swollen jaw, his chest hurt as he tried to breathe slow, shallow breaths in and out. Bess was busy stirring the porridge and her reaction to his injuries came as she placed the steaming bowl in front of him.

"Oh, Harry, love! What the blazes has happened to you?" Stepping closer she pulled his hand away from the injured face. "My Lord, it's all swollen up." Then raising her voice she called, "Owen, come along here. Harry's been and got himself into some trouble."

Owen ambled in, then his usual placid expression changed as his brows furrowed. "By the devil's blood, what... who did this to you? Was there trouble at The Ship?"

"Not at The Ship. Well, that's where it started."

"But not where it finished?"

"I was followed," Harry admitted. "I left early; I could see there were trouble-makers around and I tried to avoid them the best I could, but I was followed."

"Why would anyone want to make trouble for you?" Bess asked, while wiping the dried blood with a cloth soaked in one of her lotions.

"There's some people who just seem not to want

me around," Harry said.

"Not Giles Wood?" Bess' face showed her surprise.

"Not him. Although he'd see me back in gaol if he could."

"Who was it then, lad?" Owen asked.

"Aaron Chapman."

"Oh, he's taken a dislike to you for no good reason. Still sore about young Phoebe leaving I suppose."

"It seems as if I got mixed up with it without meaning to." Harry winced as the lotion seeped into the cut on his jaw, "Sorry, Bess, I know you mean to help. She's a nice girl, Phoebe I mean, but he's no need to worry about me. She's coming back to him, so I don't know what all the trouble is about."

"Coming back is she?" Bess queried.

"To marry him."

"I thought she had more sense than that," Owen mused.

Bess applied some more lotion to Harry's wounds while he ate his porridge with no interest. When he got up from the table, Bess looked at her husband with wide eyes. Harry was clutching at his side and had clearly taken a beating there. Owen shook his head slightly. "Don't fuss any more over the lad," were his unspoken words. "He'll come to us if he needs help." Bess turned away, suffering her own pain at the sight of Harry's injuries.

"I won't go to church this morning," Harry said. "I'll go this evening and hopefully the bruising will be fading by then."

"That's fine. You have a rest this morning," Owen replied. "And just remember this, Harry: you live with us as one of our family, and that makes you a

Dymchurch man. You've done nothing wrong; you work hard and live decently."

"You need to keep your distance from him though," said Bess, as she dished up the breakfast. "His father was a troublemaker when he was a young man."

"He still is," muttered Owen. "Keep away and let us know if he causes you any problems. You'll find most of Dymchurch will treat you with the respect you deserve. We have a duty to maintain the wall and that is what you are doing."

Back in his room, Harry lay on his bed pondering the possible arrival of Phoebe. It was something he had hoped for, especially now his penance on the wall was over. He still had little to offer her, but he had a feeling that she liked him and they had shared a couple of adventures. But with her Uncle Giles and Aaron Chapman ready to cause trouble, if he wished to spend time with her, it wouldn't be easy. He was being foolish even thinking of it now. Sometimes he wondered if she would ever return and now it seemed that she would, and it was to be the wife of another man.

Feeling irritable and wanting to divert his thoughts, Harry swung his legs off the bed and reached for his jacket. Damn, it was caked in mud after he'd ended up on the ground the evening before. Reaching in the pocket he felt for his watch; then he felt in the second pocket. As his chest tightened, he pulled the jacket closer and checked again. He shook it upside down then looked through the muddy breeches he had worn the evening before, and on the wooden floor of his bedroom.

With more speed than he would have thought possible, Harry pulled on the jacket and tied the laces in his boots. With a call to Bess and Owen to say that he was going for a walk, Harry left the cottage and followed the track he had taken home from The Ship. Skirting the edge of cottage gardens, the track stayed close to the base of the wall and so Harry walked in its shadow until he reached the place where Aaron had confronted him.

Scuffs on the track and some flattened grass confirmed that Harry was in the right place and, before the search had begun, a dull rim of metal could be seen, partially embedded in the earth. His fingers grasped it and a shilling slid out. He hadn't thought of that, about the money which had been in his pockets. There must have been two days' pay. It was good to have it back, but the shilling was worthless compared to the pocket watch.

He continued to look around the same spot, pulling back clumps of grass and stones. It didn't take long to find a penny, and then a halfpenny nestled amongst the grass. He kept hunting, widening the search area, pulling dock leaves, dandelions and arching strands of bramble aside. As his fingers closed on the dulled silver disc, Harry felt the tension ease from his body.

"Thank God for that," he muttered. Now to check that its face was intact.

Time stood still, but the clock face was undamaged. With fingers rough from manipulating hawthorn, packing clay and shovelling sand, Harry carefully twisted the crown and felt the tension as it wound the mechanism. He let go and placed the timepiece to his ear. It sprang into life, sending out rhythmic clicks. After watching it for a moment and satisfying himself that the slender hand was moving, Harry rubbed the clock with his jacket sleeve and placed it in his pocket.

With three coins also safe in his care, it was worth spending a few minutes searching for others that may have been lost. Harry made a fingertip search of the area and soon retrieved another penny and a sixpence.

"That was worth doing," he murmured, as the coins were pocketed and he slowly raised himself from a crouching position until he stood, albeit rather hunched up due to the pain in his ribs.

Moving away, Harry kicked at loose stones and pushed ragged weeds away with his feet. A clump of earth shifted slightly and a hint of something interesting was exposed. It wouldn't be his money as it was too well buried, but perhaps still a coin as the colour was a dull gold. Quite likely a coin more valuable than those he had in his pocket. Pushing the damp soil away with the toe of his boot, Harry frowned and crouched down to examine what was possibly the edge of a gold coin. Yes, there was definitely something worth digging for.

A small, but strong twig made a useful tool for digging around the presumed coin and he could soon make out its battered shape. It was quite small, maybe too small to be a coin and certainly not a modern one. As digging progressed Harry saw that it had small holes on each side and oval links through the holes. He pulled slightly on the object but it was stuck and he didn't want to be the cause of any damage. Absorbed in his task, Harry soon uncovered two more battered discs attached to the first one by the small links. He rubbed at one and saw that it seemed to be embossed or engraved with some pattern or mark. Then he worked a stone loose and uncovered another four in no time at all. All thoughts of his aching ribs were forgotten as Harry continued to dig and push the earth away. When he lifted the bracelet from the ground, it had nine discs all linked together and a curved clasp.

Having looked around to check that no one was watching, Harry held the bracelet up to the light and, although it was still dirty, it seemed to be complete. He examined what he had first thought were discs and realised that they were heart shaped and patterned, although he could not quite see what the design represented. Placing the bracelet in his pocket, Harry retraced his steps along the track to the cottage.

Owen and Bess had gone to church; Harry sat at the table with a dish of warm water, a small brush and a cloth. Dipping the brush into the water, he worked away at the golden ovals linking the heart shapes. Tiny ridges emerged around the edges of the hearts and gradually the patterns on them were clear of dirt. The clasp was totally filled with earth and he pushed some out with a tiny stick before finishing the process with his brush. Harry was drying the bracelet with a soft cloth when Owen and Bess returned from church.

"You look a lot happier," Bess commented.

"I went back to where I had that trouble with Aaron last night," Harry said. "I'd dropped my money and can't afford to do that. I found it all though and I've got my keep." He handed four shillings to Bess. "Look at this thing I found. Could it be gold?"

Harry passed the bracelet to Bess, who gave it a rub with her apron and held it up to the light at the window. "Well, I'd say it must be. It's dark in colour though and that means quality. It looks old. What do you think, Owen?"

Owen looked at it for a couple of minutes before he replied, "It looks like gold to me and it's well made. I think you've found something of value there. I'll get my magnifying lens and we'll take a closer look."

Mesmerised by the delicate bracelet, the three of them took it in turns to examine it.

"I can't believe how it could be there at the base of the wall, with all that work going on year after year, and not a crack or bit of damage to be seen," Owen handed it back to Bess.

"I'd say they were flowers on the hearts," Bess concluded. "They're so delicate it's hard to be sure."

"It's old, despite it being undamaged," Owen continued. "Probably worth something."

"How would we know?" asked Harry.

"I think..." Owen pondered on the matter, "I think we had best ask the Leveller of the Marsh Scotts and perhaps he can advise us. What do you think, Harry? We'll take it with us to evening church and I'll have a word with him afterwards."

"You keep it for the time being," Harry suggested, "and see what he says."

"I think you've got something quite special here, lad," Owen said, as he wrapped the bracelet in a clean cloth.

Harry sat between Owen and Bess in the candlelit church that evening. He gazed at the backs of Sir Rupert Bannerman and his family who sat in the front pews. The jewels threaded through the hair of Lady Bannerman glittered in the candlelight and, as she moved within her seat, the gold thread in her dress shimmered. The whole family stood tall for the hymns and their voices rang clear for the responses.

Singing with gusto, despite the pain in his ribs, and noticing Aaron flashing menacing glances at him, Harry looked away and tried to concentrate on the service. He wore his collar high, hoping to conceal the bruised jaw, but saw some enquiring looks in his direction.

The service ended and the congregation began to make their way out into the chilled evening air, blinking as their eyes became accustomed to the darkness. When Owen approached Sir Rupert, Harry held back, still uncertain of his place within the community. He watched as the two men walked side by side towards the New Hall and Sir Rupert shooed his daughters away as he concentrated on Owen's words.

From a distance, Harry watched as the cloth with the gold bracelet folded within it was taken from Owen's pocket and passed to Sir Rupert. The two men shook hands and Owen turned away. He joined Harry and Bess in the churchyard.

"He's interested in taking a look," Owen announced. "No point in trying without a light and a magnifying lens. He'll send a message with his thoughts in a day or two."

It was four days later when, having just pocketed his day's earnings, Harry heard the expenditor call him back.

"Harry, Harry Farrers, isn't it?"

"Yes, sir."

"I've a message for you from Sir Rupert Bannerman. You're to step along to the New Hall immediately."

"Now?" Harry looked down at his muddy breeches and stained tunic.

"That was the message." The expenditor turned away and was passing coins into the next outstretched hand.

Harry looked towards John Waller. "Would you mind calling in to tell Bess I won't be home for a while?

256

I've been asked to go along to the New Hall."

"Not in trouble again?" John grinned.

"I hope not," Harry attempted a smile in return.

At the end of the day, the wall-workers collected their money from the expenditor, who stood near Church Knocke. It was only a matter of minutes before Harry walked down the slope of the seawall, past The Ship Inn and was approaching the New Hall. All the time he walked, his hands were brushing at the dirt on his clothes with little effect.

Slowing his pace, Harry walked towards the front door, his eyes darting towards the path leading to the gaol. Should he look for a kitchen door, or the servants' entrance? He hadn't been told and so he found himself at the panelled front door, with his hand on the knocker. The sound of metal on wood could be heard echoing within the entrance hall and then the ponderous footsteps approaching the door.

The footman, standing there in all his neat splendour, paused to look Harry up and down from his scuffed boots to his grubby shirt collar.

"I was told to come here to see Sir Rupert Bannerman."

"He is expecting you," the footman's tone was weary. He need make no effort with this young man who had spent the night in a cell just six months beforehand. "Wait here a moment."

Harry stood and looked about the panelled hallway; a coat of arms hung in its newly gilded frame and a couple of paintings showed countryside views. He gazed up the staircase leading to the courtroom; the upper floor of the house was shrouded in shadows. "This way." The footman returned and beckoned Harry towards the rear of the house. He held a door open and announced: "Harry Farrers, Sir."

"Come in, come in." Sir Rupert was all smiles.

"My apologies, Sir," Harry waved his hands in dismay towards his working clothes. "My clothes, I..."

"Not at all. Sit down, a little dust can soon be brushed away," Sir Rupert gestured towards a chair to one side of the desk. "We have a saying here in Dymchurch, no doubt you have heard it before: Serve God, Honour the King, but first maintain the wall. You serve this community well and I have no gripe with a man dressed as a labourer on our seawall."

"Thank you, Sir."

"Will you take tea with me?" Looking towards the footman who hovered in the doorway, Sir Rupert gave his orders: "Ask Molly to bring us a tray of tea, please, Brown."

"I've been away, you know," Harry's companion informed. "To Canterbury, where I had some business. I took your bracelet to a friend of mine and he confirmed that you found something very old and valuable. In fact he is certain that it is Roman, which places it at about one and a half thousand years' old. You may have noticed the Roman remains on the hillside below Lympne?"

Harry nodded. "Just a few months ago, when I went to see where the clay came from, I saw the stone walls and Owen told me about the Roman port."

"Portus Lemanis. Quite substantial, from all accounts," Sir Rupert continued. "Ah here's Molly; she must have had the tray prepared. Thank you, Molly, if you would just place it here and I'll pour in a moment.

"I have a particular interest in those ruins and that time in history. Romney Marsh was a very different place then, you know. There was quite a wide tidal inlet there and a shingle spit stretching across, not far from where our own seawall is today. They've slipped on the hillside, the ruins I mean – impossible to see how they would have been. Quite impossible. The fort was substantial though, we can see that."

"You think the bracelet came from people living in the Roman villa?" Harry asked.

"It seems likely." Sir Rupert picked up the teapot. "Do you take sugar?"

"One, please."

"The road to Canterbury is a fine example of Roman engineering and there is another from Canterbury to Dover and, of course, to London. What a pleasure to ride upon it after our winding lanes.

"But I digress, we are here to talk about your bracelet, although I just wanted to share a little of the Roman influence here on Romney Marsh. They used the Marsh for salt pans, you know. The low-lying land had water flowing over it which lay in pools and dried leaving the precious salt behind."

Harry frowned, struggling to keep up. "But, it's not my bracelet, Sir. I merely found it."

"It was found on common land, so I feel you have a claim on it."

Harry took a sip of tea, uncertain of how to respond.

"It's particularly interesting that the whole bracelet has survived. Very rare, usually only a fraction of an item like this would be found and that is why it is so valuable."

"Valuable?"

"Several guineas. More than you'd earn working on the seawall in a year!" Sir Rupert took a sip of tea before continuing, "Riches enough to buy a plot of land and build a cottage, start your own business or whatever you cared for. You could be a wealthy young man!"

"But the money, it's not mine?" Harry's eyes widened.

"If you want to sell the bracelet,it is. Just give the word and my manservant will travel to Canterbury with your instructions. I hope you don't mind, I took the liberty of leaving it in the care of my friend. It's not really safe to travel around with such treasures."

"Of course, I understand."

"You've some thinking to do, young man. I assume you'll want to sell the bracelet and no doubt you will be in need of some advice. You won't go wrong in talking to Owen Bates or John Waller, but you may also call on me if needed.

Reflecting on all the things the money could buy, Harry spent a moment deep in thought. It didn't seem quite right that the money should go to him to spend as he wished, or even take from the village if he chose to leave.

"I think that the right thing is to spend the money on something to benefit the people of Dymchurch. I'd like to help the village in some way." Harry frowned a little, "I can't say how but I'd like to think about it."

"Of course. Your generosity shows what a fine young man you have become. Talk to people and see what is needed, then we can meet again to speak of your plans. Shall I send a message giving the order to sell the bracelet?"

"Yes. It's no use to me but the money can do some good."

"What do you think to us keeping the money here in safety and you and I will meet again soon with some of my jurats to make plans?"

"I'd like that." Harry stood up. "Thank you for your time. I had better get home now and share the good news."

Chapter Twenty-Four
Phoebe

Her hands sticky with bread-dough and face slightly moist from perspiration, Phoebe paused in her labours when the bell tolled for the third time. Straightening her back a little, she lifted her hands from the dough and rubbed off the pieces clinging to her fingers. The bells continued in their doleful rhythm. What could be the meaning of this on a Monday morning?

Curious, Phoebe moved from the scullery, through the dark living area with its shuttered windows and huge scrubbed table where the family sat, talking and eating until late at night. Her grandmother rested on a wooden chair at the doorway of the cottage, a shawl wrapped firmly around her shoulders, despite the warmth coming from the September sun.

"Grand-mère. The bells, why do they toll?"

The old woman merely put her finger to her lips. Her wizened forehead was creased in a frown and her lips moved, at one with the bell. The sound of the hammer upon brass resonated throughout Wissant and still it continued.

Just as Phoebe began to think that the ringing would never stop, silence came.

"Seventy-three," Grand-mère said, partly to herself. Her forehead remained crimped in a frown and she held the palm of her hand up. Say nothing, I am thinking, the gesture told her granddaughter. "Seventy-three," she repeated. "Ah."

She sat in the same position for a minute or two. Phoebe stood waiting, peeling the last of the dough from her fingers and letting it drop on the hard mud and thin grass framing the pathway leading to the cottage. The chickens ran, necks erect and eyes alert, then bent to clear the specks of dough.

Grand-mère hadn't said – it wasn't her way – but her heart was filled with love for her English granddaughter. And if the bells had been tolling for the end of her life, then she would have died happy, having been united with Phoebe for these past four months. Her hair was now a steely grey, tied firmly in a small bun at the nape of her neck and her skin was like that of a small brown monkey. But she saw in Phoebe the young woman she had once been. She liked her gentle manner, her long, silky, brown hair and the fact that she worked hard for the good of the family.

In the evenings, granddaughter and grandmother sometimes studied notebooks of poetry written by the old woman herself when she had been Phoebe's age. With her finger running along the spidery words, Phoebe learned to read unfamiliar French words. Together they tried to form new poems, using words to express the new sights, sounds and scents Phoebe had been experiencing.

As Grand-mère raised herself from the chair, her neighbour of sixty-seven years reached the wooden fence between the gardens. They had lived side by side all their lives and now each was as frail and hunched as the other.

"Seventy-three, did you hear it, Esther? Seventy-three." Grand-mère's eyes sparkled as the news was shared.

"I heard it, Jeanne. It is a good age."

"It is and not many of us live to see it."

"Seventy-three." Esther repeated, "It must be Annette."

"I was thinking that too. Annette, she knew her time was near."

"I pray she passed peacefully."

"We can only hope. God bless her," Grand-mère nodded.

"And did the girl know her?" Esther's beady eyes fell on Phoebe.

"The girl, Phoebe?" Grand-mère turned to look at Phoebe who stood listening, trying to understand. "Of course. We drank coffee at her home only last week." She looked down at Phoebe's hands, remembering the scraps of dough. "Phoebe, the bread. The oven will be warm."

"Of course, Grand-mère."

Phoebe returned to the scullery and to the bread dough in the lead-lined kneading trough. With a sigh, she plunged her hands back in and tried to engage in the rhythmic stretching and pounding needed to make the dough. Allowing it to form in a rounded shape, Phoebe placed the dough in a cloth-lined basket before taking a knife and marking a cross on the top. Then, holding the basket in her arms, she left the cottage by the back door. She walked to the front of the house and noted that the two old women were still gossiping over the fence.

The communal baking house was not far from the market square and, as she walked there, Phoebe passed her aunt.

"Is this the first time you've heard the bells toll for a death?"

"Yes, I didn't know and Grand-mère wouldn't say, not while she was counting."

"We have to count," Marie smiled at her niece. "Otherwise, how would we know?"

"I understand," Phoebe said. "I listened to Grand-mère and Esther; they are still there, talking about it."

"It is the favourite thing to speak of when you reach the age of those two old women!" Marie informed. She looked into the basket, "The bread looks good, now run along and bake it. I've cheese and salad to eat with it at lunch-time."

"Are the boats in yet?" Phoebe asked.

"Not yet, but soon. Your papa is probably on the beach by now."

Phoebe reached the baking house just as the oven was being opened. Her bread was placed on a long-handled shovel and sat beside the others prepared that morning. Not feeling comfortable with staying to talk amongst the women, she decided to walk to the seafront while the bread baked.

The first of the *flobarts* was being pulled, as if it were a cart, up the track from the beach to the market place. Phoebe stood aside to watch the fishermen who trudged beside it, shouting an order every now and then. Every day ragged boys awaited the fishing boats and ran to the beach, ready to take over once the horses had pulled them up the sandy bank. For a coin they helped haul the boats to the market place. Then they loitered, waiting for scraps of fish to take home to their mothers. It was a thankless task; too many boys and too few *flobarts*. Those who got to the beach early enough and laboured without complaint gained the most coins.

Running down the sandy beach track, Phoebe saw

her father, Jacques Bernard, jumping from the boat he shared with his sister's husband. He helped fasten ropes to the horses' harnesses and, looking up, he saw his daughter.

"*Bonjour, ma chérie.*"

"*Bonjour, Papa.* You have plenty of fish?"

"Of course! Plenty of fish."

"I must run… the bread is in the oven."

"I will see you in the market place?"

"You will, Papa."

Turning back to the town, Phoebe retraced her steps. As she passed cottages, she noted that the men and women of her grandmother's age were gathering in small groups. The bells must have drawn them together, Phoebe thought. They were discussing the passing of Annette, she was sure of it.

That evening they sat around the huge wooden table. The fire smouldered in the grate and the remains of their supper was pushed aside. Phoebe warmed a glass of red wine in her hand and listened to Grandmère's tales.

"She was six years older than me, Annette was. I remember her and the others, they've all gone now; I remember them looking after us little ones when our mothers were busy baking or with the babies. Esther remembers it too; we would play in water meadows or on the dunes. And Annette was there with her sister, watching over us.

"The sister… do you recall her name, Marie? Of course – it was Eveline. She was older than Annette, four years at least, and she left the village to work at the château. She barely returned after that but I recall her passing at least ten years ago.

"Seventy-three, a fine age. Annette did well. It was

only last week I took coffee with her…"

Tante Marie, Oncle Marc and Papa listened to Grand-mère's tales, often raising their eyebrows and gently correcting her. Phoebe's attention was more rapt: for her these stories were new and they told of a lifetime she knew little about. Her three younger cousins were all asleep in bed. Two boys and a little girl; they had become the siblings she never had.

Reaching across to the supper dishes, Phoebe pulled some plates towards her. It was time to take them to the sink in the scullery before she became too weary. Marie took the pan of hot water from its hook above the fire and followed Phoebe. Respectful of Grand-mère, who was still reminiscing, the two women worked in silence scrubbing, rinsing and drying the dishes.

Later, Phoebe lay in bed listening to Grand-mère's gentle snores. She no longer slept in a corner of a storeroom, but had a space under the eaves within the old woman's room. There was a chest for her clothes and a wash-stand behind a curtain. Due to her advancing years, Grand-mère often lit a small fire in the grate during the early evening. As Phoebe settled into bed, the room was warm with the comforting aroma of woodsmoke.

This was the time when she thought of her family in Dymchurch and, as the months passed, she even felt some affection for Aunt Peggy, her mother's sister. As for Aaron, to be away from him still gave her a feeling of relief. He would have shifted his affections, if he had truly had any, onto some other young woman. Hopefully someone more suitable, someone used to living in a fine house with a cook and a maid. Aaron would marry soon, she was sure of it and, no doubt, continue to dally with the tavern wenches.

Was it time to return to Dymchurch? Phoebe had never planned to stay in Wissant. Of course she had arrived not knowing if she would find her papa. Then she thought to stay for a week or two. How long had she been here now? It had been the second week of May when Walter had brought her across the Channel; Phoebe counted the months on her fingers. Four and a half!

What was it Harry said when they had met at the Maypole and exchanged some words? He would have asked her to dance, had he been free. The freedom he spoke of was about the seawall. He was bound to labour on the wall for six months and perhaps he felt he needed to prove his worth. Phoebe would have danced with him that day and been glad to do so. Harry had arrived in March... the end of March when the seawall had breached. Again Phoebe counted the months on her fingers. He would be free now.

By the end of the week Phoebe was trailing behind the horse-drawn cart carrying Annette's body. She had a curiosity to follow the body of this dear old friend of her grandmother until this life was finally buried. Most of the village were there and the walk between the church and the cemetery gave the opportunity to catch up with family news.

"Jacques, is this your daughter? *La belle Phoebe*?"

"It is. She has been with us since May. It is a miracle!"

"We thought we would never see her."

"I thought I would never see her again."

They came to the cemetery gates and silence fell upon the group as, in twos and threes, the mourners stepped through and into the town of the dead. Neatly regimented lines of tombs stretched across the area, regular of shape, their stone clear of any dirt or debris. Memorial stones stood to attention, with names and dates adding to the story of each tomb. The coarse sand paths between them were narrow, often too narrow for someone to walk between the tombs. Placed amongst the plain stone boxes were their more extravagant neighbours, those which had the vault stone topped with a small decorative chapel.

Along the paths they trailed, hemmed in by the vaults jostling for space and overshadowed by imposing chapels. Finally the funeral party came to a stop by the open vault to be Annette's final resting place.

How different it was, how grand compared to the lopsided headstones surrounding the church back home in Dymchurch. Her mother lay beneath a small grey stone with clumps of ragged grass at its base. Her maternal grandparents were nearby, not precisely to the right, just roughly in that direction. Phoebe would regularly wipe the moss from the stone, but it lay under the sweeping branches of a horse chestnut and the moss clung on with defiance, loving the moist shade.

Her attention returned to the present time, as Phoebe stood back from the coffin lying across trestles on the pathway. Close friends and family gathered close and took first turns at sprinkling the holy water. Watching carefully, Phoebe realised that she would have to take her place in the line, and so she must learn the ritual from others who went before her. Her father gestured for Phoebe to follow him. He followed the pattern familiar to him and stepped aside.

Now Phoebe took the jug of holy water with its brass sprinkler and carefully swung it north, south, east, west and then over the coffin. As she did so, she whispered a prayer, uncertain of how to phrase it:

"Lord, take care of Grand-mère's friend, Annette. May she rest in eternal peace."

Listening to the rise and fall of the priest's voice, Phoebe attempted to join in with the communal prayer, but found the words unfamiliar. Her lips moved soundlessly as she watched Annette's body being lowered into the cavernous vault.

"Phoebe, let me take you to meet the family." Grand-mère slipped her small brown hand onto Phoebe's arm and tugged gently.

"The family, are there more to meet?" Phoebe's eyes widened in surprise.

"There are stories to tell of those who are no longer with us."

"Of course." Phoebe allowed herself to be led away from her family group. Others were now dispersing throughout the graveyard, no doubt thinking of their own dead.

Not far from the low boundary wall, there was a low grey stone tomb.

"My mother and my father," Grand-mère announced. "*Ma mère* lived to a good age; the women in our family do. *Mon père*, he went eighteen years before her. They are together again now, with his family."

Phoebe gazed at the lines of names on the headstone and, leaning forward, she traced the fourth name on the stone with her forefinger. "Henri Morel, 1670 to 1719; it was a long time ago. Jeanne Morel, 1672 to 1737." Turning to Grand-mère she said, "Your mother, she gave you her name and she died two years before I was born."

"Your papa was in England when she passed," Grand-mère replied.

Phoebe continued to trace the names on the stone, looking at those engraved at a time before her own life began.

"Here is my sister; she died young. And my brother, Michel." Grand-mère showed Phoebe two of the names below. "Now come this way and you'll meet your grand-père; he passed shortly after Jacques returned."

"Papa told me," Phoebe replied. "He was pleased to return in time."

What was it like for this family when their son, their only son, went to live across the Channel, she wondered.

"Did you ever hear from Papa?"

"He sent a message." Grand-mère looked into the distance as if she were seeing the Channel and the distant shore. "He told us that he had married and we heard when you were born. We knew Jacques was well and happy."

"He missed you all; he often spoke of you." Phoebe saw that Grand-mère gave a slight nod before turning from the grave.

They reached the large upright stone before the family vault. It showed the names of the dead contained there.

"He was pleased to see his son return, but greatly saddened to hear of the loss of your mother and grieved that he never met his first granddaughter."

"Edouard Bernard," Phoebe read. "1690 to 1754. I'm sorry I never met him."

"He was a good man. Gentle and fair."

"A fisherman?"

"Of course, and a trader too. He did business with

the men of Kent, just as we do today."

"But we don't meet with the Dymchurch fishermen anymore; not since Papa came home."

"Not with the Dymchurch men," Grand-mère scowled. "Not since they betrayed Jacques. We have no need of them; our English friends are now from Lydd and Dungeness."

Phoebe nodded her understanding. Dungeness and Lydd, these were places as foreign to her as Wissant had been. She knew Dungeness was the shingle headland to the west and could be seen from the Dymchurch Wall. It was said that the stones extended far back from the beach and that it was a barren place with little vegetation, and a small population of hardy fishermen and their families.

New Romney was the furthest point to the west that Phoebe had travelled and Lydd was beyond it. Midway between New Romney and Dungeness, it was another town, a small one she believed but she knew nothing more about it, other than it was said to have a large area of open common land, an unusual feature in those parts. Lydd was not on the coast but the trading with the French was as prolific there as it was in any coastal village or town. Perhaps the instinct to trade had been born into the men of Lydd from the times when salt-water creeks had extended to the town?

Phoebe was still gazing at her grandfather's headstone when Jacques joined them.

"She is meeting the family," Grand-mère informed. "It will be my time soon."

"The bells won't toll for you yet," Jacques put his arms around his mother's shoulders and gave her a gentle squeeze.

"I'll not complain when they do," the old woman

replied. "I've had a good life and now I have met my eldest granddaughter I'll have no gripe when it's time to join Edouard."

"They are looking for you. The women you like to gossip with." Jacques looked towards the group of elderly women clad in black.

Raising her eyes, Jeanne Bernard gave a sigh and took a step away from the grave. "Your papa can tell you about the family; he will have different tales to tell."

"You seem a little thoughtful today," Jacques turned from the grave and gazed across the cemetery and to the countryside beyond. "I don't believe you are thinking of the old woman, Annette. Do you think of *Maman*? Or your life back in Dymchurch?"

Phoebe frowned as she visualised the long snake of a seawall with the sands to one side and the cluster of cottages to the other. She saw the reed-lined ditches winding their way out into the countryside, the stunted willows and the twisted hawthorns. Giles' gaunt profile, and the long fingers jabbing at the air as he made his demands, flashed into her mind. And Peggy, her mother's plump, dissatisfied sister, who had shown a softening of her character in the weeks before Phoebe left.

"I think of Dymchurch, but mostly with no great longing," Phoebe admitted. "I should be grateful to Aunt Peggy and Uncle Giles, and I feel bad for Walter who had to tell them that I was staying here for a while."

"Do you feel you should be there with them? We try to bring you into our French family but I do not forget that you were raised in England."

"But you make me so welcome here, Papa," the

272

words flowed fast from Phoebe's lips. "Here, in Wissant, I have my little cousins and all the family around me. Tante Marie is like a mother to me and I am learning the French ways. Yet, I think… I think of my home in Dymchurch and it confuses me as to where I should be."

"You are loved very much by your family here in Wissant, but your Tante Marie worries that you are missing the friends you have in Dymchurch. The girls of your own age who grew up alongside you."

"I do miss them," Phoebe admitted.

"I want you to know that I didn't expect you to stay for the summer. If you had stayed a week I would have been content, and this time with you has brought warmth to my heart – to all our hearts."

"It has made me so happy to be here."

"Soon the mists will come and the cold winds. You know you can call Wissant your home for as long as you wish to. But if your heart is in England then you need to return soon."

Phoebe nodded her understanding as she stood beside her father and followed his gaze across the softly undulating countryside.

Chapter Twenty-Five
Harry

The Leveller of the Marsh Scotts stood on a platform outside The Ship and banged a spoon on a tin plate. The late afternoon glow from the sun cast a warm light on the old church and the orange brick of the vicarage and manor house, giving an impression of a summer's evening, yet it was now almost the end of October. Trestle tables were set up and casks of ale had been rolled outside; a huge fire burned bright and a roasting pig was tended by the landlord. Serving girls, in vast aprons and floppy white caps, bustled around offering drinks and then gently chided those who had partaken of too much thirst-quenching liquor. The air was rich with the scents of woodsmoke and pork, combined with the salt rolling off the sea.

Sir Rupert Bannerman knocked the wooden spoon on the plate again, and this time the murmurs of the crowd ceased.

"Good people of Dymchurch, let us all pause for a moment amidst our revelries and think, for a moment, about what, or who, has brought us together today.

"A month ago a young man of Dymchurch came to me. Now there may be some of you who take offence to this term, a young man of Dymchurch. As you know I speak of Harry Farrers, whom we all know came from Elham. And in fact, he has only been in our

274

community for seven months. But he has earned the honour of being called a Dymchurch man and let no one dispute it."

Grunts, whispers and nods of approval rippled through the crowd. Harry, flanked by Owen, John Waller and Joshua, stood to one side of the wooden platform. It hadn't been so long ago that he had feared he would stand on another platform, not far from where they gathered now. He only had to glance to his right, to see the gallows rising between the church and New Hall. Within the village, Harry still had his enemies, those who had taken a dislike to him for no good reason, but he now felt less fear of them. The approval of Sir Rupert Bannerman had been gained and that held great sway within the community.

"I first met a confused young man just a day after he arrived in Dymchurch," Sir Rupert continued. "He had done wrong in intending to buy from the general store on God's own day. I thought him a simple lad, ignorant and unaware; I'll admit that now. And I'll admit to being wrong; his befuddled manner was born of a day's travel and some injury caused to his head. There are those who would have sent him to the gallows, but luck came to young Harry in the form of Owen Bates, who offered him a home.

"Under the guidance of John Waller, Harry proved himself a good worker on the seawall. There is no more worthwhile job on the whole of Romney Marsh and Harry does his duty in learning the methods needed to maintain the wall. I could say that, between them, Owen Bates and John Waller have shaped young Harry into the man who stands here today, but Harry made his own choices to live a sober life and work hard at learning new skills."

Whispers began to flow amongst the people. This

speech had gone on long enough, the pork smelt good and their bellies were hollow. It had been said that a haul of brandy had been stored nearby overnight and Sir Rupert had handed over a guinea or two to bring a couple of barrels to The Ship and ensure a good supply for the evening.

Uneasy with all the attention upon him, Harry looked down at the sandy ground and rubbed the toe of his new leather boot on the dry earth. This was the first the villagers knew of the gold bracelet and its value. At least, it would be the first they knew of it when Sir Rupert told them why the gathering was taking place.

Noting the confusion and frustration within the crowd, Lady Bannerman, who stood at her husband's side, whispered to him.

"My apologies." The Lord of the Marsh Scotts stood a little higher and straightened his green jacket, the brass buttons shining as they caught the sun's rays as it began to slump beyond the roof tops and willow trees.

"I forget you don't know why we are here in celebration today, so I will make haste to tell you all."

The murmurs in the crowd subsided.

"Come and stand beside me, Harry."

Looking towards Owen, Harry's eyes pleaded with him. Did he really have to stand before the village? He hadn't thought he would and it seemed that his limbs had stiffened, not allowing him the ability to take those few steps.

"Come on, lad. We'll stand with you." Owen placed a hand on Harry's forearm and tugged a little.

"You're not alone," John Waller gave his support and the three of them stepped up together.

"Now, as I was saying, a month ago this young

man of Dymchurch came to me. He had found a gold bracelet in the earth at the base of the seawall and, having cleaned it up, he realised that it could have some value. I took it to Canterbury and left it with a friend who is somewhat an expert in antiquities and I felt sure he could put an age and a value on the piece.

"Without doubt he told me that it was Roman, which puts it at one and a half thousand years old and of no small value. I spoke with Harry to inform him that, if he chose to sell it, then he would be a wealthy young man. Now, people of Dymchurch, this is when Harry Farrers showed the extent of his true character and the goodness of his heart. Without thought of his own fortunes, he pledged to spend the money on the good of the village."

Approval was shown in the whistles and calls ringing out from the crowd. Forcing himself to look towards the villagers, Harry attempted a smile. Sir Rupert patted his shoulder and said in a low voice, "You have to know how to work these people. A cup of brandy and some good being done for the village and all this other business is forgotten." Harry nodded his understanding.

"What is it, I hear you ask? What is it that young Farrers pledges to spend his money on?" Sir Rupert's smile was broad. "I admit to feeling shame that I had not thought of this myself. He suggests that we build a school for the children of the village. We have, as you know, the room beside the workhouse. But is it right that our children are educated in such a place? I've a plot of land in Mill Road, close to the village centre and big enough to build a decent building, along with space for them to exercise."

Cheers rang out from the crowd.

"I'll drink to that," someone shouted.

"And why not?"

"Good fellow!"

"A true man of Dymchurch!"

Finding the enthusiasm infectious, Harry allowed a broad smile to spread across his face. "Thank you for your advice," he said to Sir Rupert, "and for taking the bracelet to Canterbury."

"Now we eat and drink by the light of the fire while the sun bids us farewell for the day." Sir Rupert held out his hand. "A brandy...?" he looked at Harry, who shook his head a little. "No, a cider for this young man, I was forgetting he is of sober habits! A brandy for myself though and make it a big one. The torches will be lit and we'll celebrate for as long as we can stand!"

It seemed as if Harry had been given leave to step off the stage and, having looked at Owen for his approval, he rejoined Bess and Joshua. He felt the tension ease from his body; there had been no heckling or animosity from the crowd. Just an acceptance and gratitude for Harry's gesture of helping to provide a schoolroom for the village children.

"There you are." Walter joined them and pushed some bread and pork into his hand. "A new school then. I can't say I'm sorry about that! With three boys of my own, I'll be pleased to know they are getting some decent teaching. They say that Sir Rupert and the vicar are looking out for a new schoolmaster. Someone with some learning, mayhap from out of the village."

"And I was talking with Fred Woodman yesterday evening," Owen said. "The bailiffs have approached the pair of us and we're to make some sets of new desks and benches. That'll keep us busy through the winter."

"I'm pleased you are to be a part of it," Harry grinned. "Sir Rupert tells me the land has been cleared and the stone base of the wall will be going down within a week or so. They plan to have the timbers in place before the first frosts."

"And they're cutting the reeds from the edges of the dykes; good and dry this year they are," John Waller commented. "Be a fair lot of them if you choose to thatch the roof, or maybe there'll be enough money to have tiles."

"I don't know about that," Harry frowned. "What experience do I have of building?" I'll leave it to those who know and Anthony Richards, the bailiff, he's going to oversee the build for me."

"You'll be surprised what you do know," John pointed out. "Didn't you build your room with Owen? And even working on the wall, well, it makes you think about how to put something together and make it good and strong."

"I'm certainly interested in seeing it all come together."

Through the crowds the first long whines of a bow on a fiddle reached Harry's ears. Then the merry sound of a pipe joined in. With feet dangling off the side of the stage and a collection of cups and tankards beside them, five villagers began a jaunty tune, enticing the merry-makers to dance.

Less orderly than those steps around the maypole, the villagers danced together. Harry, who usually shied away from these events, found himself with one village maiden and then the next, vying for his attention. He laughed and spoke a little with them, but there was not one of them whose smile he sought, or whose hand he regretted releasing when the notes of a song faded

279

away.

The cider flowed from Harry's tankard with ease, but his first cup of brandy came from the most unexpected source.

"Time to make amends if we're all to be living side by side in this village." Giles Woods offered the small metal cup in his scrawny hand.

"I... I don't really..." Harry took the cup.

"Don't take a bit of the good stuff from France? Of course you do, lad, when there's celebrating to do." Giles turned to his wife who hovered behind him, "Do you hear that, Peg? The lad's not had a tipple of brandy tonight."

Peggy stepped forwards, bestowing a wide smile. "It won't do you no harm, not a bit o' brandy. The skies are darkening and there's quite a chill in the air; it's just what you need to warm you through."

"Be like liquid fire going through your veins," Giles agreed.

Harry took a sip, allowing the brandy to coat his tongue. Stronger than anything he had tasted before, it caught him by surprise. What enticed people to drink something that scorched them in this way? Made bold by the cider already travelling through his body, Harry took another sip, this time allowing it to flow down his throat, licking at the sides and burning him. He paused to consider, while Peggy and Giles looked on, their faces in the shadows of a torch flaming not far behind them.

"It's only right that you learn a taste for these things, now that you're a wealthy man." Giles took a sip of his own cup of brandy. "A new school building for the children, now that's a fine thing to do for Dymchurch."

"Thank you." Harry looked to the side, planning his

280

escape.

"I've a mind to put that other business behind us, now that you're settling here. It must have been a mistake; you're no thief. Must have been in a muddle, what with that knock on the head the good doctor spoke of."

"I don't know that I am, settling I mean. I'll stay a while longer though."

"Not settling?" Giles clawed at Harry's arm in a gesture of friendliness. "What better place to be than in our little village snug under the wall and all the good things that come to us from our friends across the Channel?"

"I... I don't know. Well, I'll see the school built of course."

"Oh, you'll stay. I feel sure of it, don't you, Peggy?"

Now Peggy had her chance to voice what had been at the forefront of her mind all the while she had stood listening. "Have you heard from our Phoebe? Any message from France? Because we wouldn't mind if you had. We'd just be happy to have word of her."

"Me? No, I wouldn't expect..."

"I was hoping she'd come back to me." Peggy's body slumped a little.

"When we were in Wissant, she was planning to come back to Dymchurch. But I've heard nothing and wouldn't expect to."

"I think she's lost to us," Peggy turned to her husband.

"What about Aaron Chapman?" Harry asked, with a sickening feeling. "He was talking about her, saying she'd be back."

"You never know, Peg. Might be worth a word with him."

"You could, Giles. I just had a hope that Harry here might know."

Harry scanned the crowds as best he could; darkness was now settled on the village and only the fire and torches lit the area by The Ship. "I've not seen him, but it wouldn't hurt to take a look around."

With this Harry gave a brief smile and turned away. The brandy had brought warmth to his body and the aftertaste was not unfavourable; he would get his cup topped up before rejoining his friends.

Now the sky was an inky black and, hanging just above the seawall, there was a huge harvest moon, immense in comparison to the usual silver sliver or full moon of its second self. It was perfectly round and, even from this vast distance, the mountain ridges and craters were clear to see. Its golden surface gave no heat, yet Harry felt warmth exuding from its very presence. Feeling in awe of its beauty, and with his limbs on fire from the brandy coursing through his veins, he was drawn to view the moon from the seawall and see its light cast across the sea.

The path to the wall was uneven and, with his sense of balance disturbed by the alcohol, it took some time for Harry to negotiate the potholes and clumps of ragged weeds. His head was doing strange things: thoughts were spinning around and not fitting into an orderly pattern. On hands and knees, he crawled to the summit of the seawall and there it was, the harvest moon in all her amber-coloured glory, casting her reflected light in a shimmering banner across the sea. The sea was calm and the tide was high, gently slapping against the base of the wall. Harry found the movement mesmerising after the chaos of the celebration.

Not taking his eyes from the moon and her trail of light, Harry crossed the top of the wall and sat himself down, finding it took more time than usual to settle with his legs dangling over the edge. Now he could sit and admire the scene before him. Yet despite the harmony around him, the sounds of the pipe and fiddle still hammered in his head and the thrill of swinging through the dances still flowed through his limbs. His body was not at peace, it was screaming out with the exhilaration brought on by the celebration and the brandy.

While the cacophony within his head became a muddle of all the tunes played that evening and the brandy refused to allow any sensible thoughts to take hold, Harry stared at the golden moon. Swaying gently with the tide he allowed the memories of the music, the cheering and the dancing stay to with him until after some time he became aware that his body was cold and stiff. His seat on the seawall was now damp and uncomfortable, he shifted a little and resigned himself to having to leave the wall and return to the celebrations.

Turning to look towards Wall End, Harry frowned. A lone figure was walking from the west. Not more trouble from Aaron Chapman? Harry had noted his absence that evening. Knowing he could easily slip back down the track to the safety of the crowds, Harry paused and watched the approaching figure.

Chapter Twenty-Six
Phoebe

"We turn inland now, Miss," the old man muttered.

Phoebe felt her stomach lurch as the cart jolted on a slight dip and came to a halt along the Romney to Dymchurch road. The barrels behind her shifted a little, gently clunking one against another. Throwing her bag to the ground, Phoebe jumped from her precarious seat at the front of the cart and managed to retain her balance as she landed.

"Thank you." No more words were needed. They had not spoken since he had picked her up from the shingle beach near Lydd.

She stepped away from the cart and it continued on its journey, now turning into the track to St Mary in the Marsh, rather than following the coast road. It was one of several carts heading in the same direction, accompanied by a dozen men on horseback, some leading pack-horses. Lowering her head, Phoebe turned her back on them as soon as she had steadied herself and picked up her bag. They had helped her on this journey, but she respected the need to keep their identities unknown.

Remaining where she had first set herself down, she listened to them moving away and allowed her body to adjust to standing on English ground. The sea journey had been a seemingly unending time of misery as her body shifted up and down with the rolling waves and she had only moved from her huddled-up position at the bow in order to be relieved of the nausea building up inside her.

Then, no sooner had she staggered up the shingle beach, she had been told to sit at the front of a cart. And, as the last rays of the sun's light disappeared beneath the Marsh, the misery of feeling so sick was exacerbated by the constant and erratic lurching of the cart through potholes and over loose stones.

All this she could have endured if she had been sure of a welcome back home in Dymchurch. If she had been certain that to leave the warmth of her French family was the right thing to do. How could it be right to part from her much-loved Papa and Grand-mère and Tante Marie and the precious children? But there was something or – and she felt foolish for even thinking it – someone who compelled her return to the village of her birth. Weak from the hours at sea and fearful of what the next few hours would bring, Phoebe could only hope that she still had a bed in the storeroom for the night.

With her bag clutched before her and body hunched, Phoebe trudged along the coast road towards Dymchurch. On reaching Wall End she almost crawled up the bank and onto the top of the seawall. Now she saw the golden harvest moon to its best advantage, hanging low in the clear night sky above the sea. Casting a pathway of light across the gently undulating waters lapping at the base of the wall, the moon was truly beautiful. The gentle curve of the seawall stretched out before Phoebe, its features gradually softening and disappearing into the night.

It only took ten minutes or so before the terraced shops and cottages of the High Street began to take shape. Nearby the clusters of low cottages and outbuildings crouched. Flickering light showed at some of the windows, but most were in darkness. On reaching Marshlands Gut, Phoebe walked down the track from the wall and, with nerves twitching in her stomach, she walked towards the general store.

"You won't find them in," a voice came from behind her.

Phoebe jumped; she had thought herself alone in this night-time world. "Not in?" she repeated.

"Saw 'em myself goin' off to The Ship. For the celebrations."

"Celebrations?"

"That's what they were doin'. Best get along there; they'll be pleased to see you."

With those words said, the figure was gone, leaving Phoebe unsure of exactly who it was, she was so covered up in a voluminous shawl. What should she do, find her way along the passageway and into the kitchen, or seek out Giles and Peggy at The Ship? She was loathe just to sit there, awaiting their dubious pleasure at seeing her again. If there were a celebration of some form at The Ship, then perhaps a brandy had passed their lips and in turn her uncle and aunt might be more welcoming, maybe even accepting of her time away.

The gentle swell of the sea and the soft moonlight had calmed Phoebe's churning stomach over the time she walked on the seawall. Retracing her steps, she soon returned to its summit and continued on her journey. As she walked, she looked down upon the roofs of the cottages, seeing the texture of their reed thatch under the moonlight and spiralling trails of smoke from the chimneys soon becoming lost in the night sky.

Then she came to an area of seawall where the main road ran alongside it, making it so wide that a tavern and a few of the cottages were built high upon the ancient structure. It was here that Harry had saved her from having to return to the general store with a muddied apron and damaged packets. Very few sounds of merriment came from the tavern, which seemed odd; surely every drinking house in the village was the haunt of the men-folk in the evenings? As she passed the workhouse, with the school building attached, the first sounds of a celebration came to her ears. A distant whistle and the haunting whine of a bow on a fiddle, mingled with the occasional shout or call. Through gaps between the rooftops and stunted trees, the glow of torches and licking flames of a fire shone bright.

As she neared the point where the road separated from the wall and led down to The Ship, Phoebe's eyes were drawn back to the lights indicating that the celebration was of a great scale. And so, when she spotted the lone person on the wall, it took a moment for her eyes to adjust to the darkness and gentle glow of the moon.

Who was it, sitting with shoulders rounded and head resting in their hands, legs swinging over the edge of the wall? It could be any one of the wall-workers or villagers, yet her heart gave an irrational leap and her throat tightened. It was hardly possible, but could it be the one whom she missed the most of all the Dymchurch people? The young man who would shy away from a village event?

He straightened his back and turned towards her, and Phoebe imagined him to be frowning, staring through the darkness. Perhaps he was as surprised as she was to see the lone stranger on the seawall. She

287

hadn't yet reached the track down to The Ship when he began to pull himself upright, and stood, albeit a little unsteadily.

Feeling no fear of this person, Phoebe continued and, as she neared him, the moonlight showed his hair to be a light brown in colour. It outlined a young and lean figure, and she felt drawn to this person. There were still about five yards between them when her hopes became a reality.

"It can't be," were the first words he spoke. "It must be the brandy; the damned brandy."

"The brandy?" she repeated, with a slight accent to her voice which had not been there before the summer spent with her family.

"Phoebe, how…? You're back!" He ran his hands through his hair as he took a couple of steps and stood before her, looking down into her face, and now she could see the frown of disbelief.

"I had to come back before the seas became too rough."

"You came by boat?"

"It's the only way," she smiled at his confusion.

"Not Walter, he's here. I mean… not here. At The Ship. Who brought you?"

"The Wissant fishermen, they took me to the beach near Lydd and we met up with some Romney Marsh men there. Then I came by cart part-way and walked the rest."

He reached his hand out and placed it on her arm, "You must be exhausted."

"The journey… it wasn't good and…" She shrugged her shoulders. "You know…"

"He said you'd be back, but I wasn't sure. It must be true then." Harry took a step back and looked out to sea.

"He?" How could it hurt so much to have him move apart from her in this way? The pull on her heart was immense.

"Aaron. He said you were coming back."

"He didn't know; why would he?"

Again he ran his hands through his hair and, even in the darkness, she saw him frown. "The damned brandy," he repeated. "It was… it must have been a month ago, before all this started." He waved his hand in the direction of The Ship and the sounds of merriment. "He… Aaron I mean, he was causing trouble… no, no, I didn't mean… he was saying, just saying…"

"Saying what?" she asked.

"Saying that you'd be back. To be with him."

"He knows nothing of my return; it's nothing to him." Had she come back to more bother from Aaron? Phoebe hoped not, hoped that he'd found himself a more amenable girl to centre his desires upon.

"Oh, I shouldn't have said." Harry rubbed his forehead with his fist, "Damned brandy!"

Phoebe began to smile as she realised. The brandy. This newcomer didn't frequent the taverns of Dymchurch; he was a young man trying to prove himself as decent and law-abiding. What had led him to have his mind befuddled by brandy? She felt sure that his character could not be that much changed in the last few months, but his next words led her to believe that the Dymchurch she had returned to had indeed changed.

"It was your uncle who insisted I took some…"

"My uncle?"

"He's got my head spinning; I should have refused, but he… well, never mind."

"My uncle has been drinking brandy with you?"

289

"Not drinking with me." Harry gave an apologetic grin. "He offered me one and I didn't think much of it, but I took another and found it quite pleasant." He turned away to face the sea and Phoebe saw his body slump a little as he continued, "But now you're here and I find my head is muddled. I wish I'd never taken it; you must think me a fool."

"I don't think it at all." She reached out, placing her slender hand on the rough material of his jacket sleeve. "I know nothing of Aaron expecting me back; I've not thought of him the past five months. I came because I wanted to return home."

"I was hoping you would." Harry faced her once more and stepped closer, "Do you remember… when we met at Mayday and I said I would ask you to dance?"

"When your time on the wall was done?"

"It's done now. I'm not here for the penance; I'm here because I choose to be. So if… if I asked you to dance? At The Ship, with the others… Did you hear the music?"

"I heard the music."

"Would you dance with me, Phoebe?"

"Of course."

"Perhaps not yet, it's beautiful right here, just the two of us."

They stood, with the sea breaking on the seawall, the sounds of merriment drifting through the night air and the harvest moon casting its warm light upon them. Her body taut with expectation, Phoebe held his gaze and longed to feel his lips on her own. Yet she was nervous of it too; used to Aaron's rough ways and her own lack of feeling toward him. She knew that when Harry held her in his arms the moment would be very special. He reached out and her breath quickened as he lifted her chin with his forefinger and leaned down to brush his lips upon her own.

Breaking away, she saw him check her response and she smiled, just a little, to show that this was what she wanted. The reason why she had come home. As he lowered his lips towards hers again, Phoebe let her bag fall to her feet and she linked her hands behind his neck, drawing him closer. She tasted the brandy as they kissed gently, slowly, easing away, then compelled to explore these new sensations for just a moment longer.

When they parted and she lowered her arms, their eyes still held each other's gaze and, with rough fingertips, he stroked her neck and jawline.

"I'm sorry, my head isn't quite where it should be. I've thought of this… wanted, for so long and now the damned brandy leaves me not quite knowing whether I'm coming or going."

"You'll sleep it off," Phoebe shrugged her shoulders. "And tomorrow, we could take a walk or… that is if you'd like to?"

"I'd more than like to," Harry grinned. "I'll come and collect you at… at say two o'clock?"

"Oh no, I wouldn't expect," she frowned, recalling one of the problems which lay before them. "I could meet you, perhaps at Wall End? Or by the church?"

"Of course, you don't know," his smile spread and she noted how he caught his lips on this lower teeth, as if to prevent it from spreading any further. "It's all changed, just this very evening. Remember how it was your uncle who gave me my first taste of brandy? He'll be happy enough for me to call for you, strange as it may seem, and I hardly believe it myself. I'll tell you about it, as we walk to The Ship. You said you wanted to dance and we shall, and soon."

291

Harry bent down to pick up her bag and swung it as if its weight was nothing. "They'll be pleased to see you, I'm sure of it." And taking Phoebe's hand in his own, he led the way down the rampart of clay and hawthorn, towards the dancing lights and the sounds of music and laughter.

The End

About the Author

Romney Marsh writer, Emma Batten, loves to combine her interest in local history with creative writing. It's important to her that historical details are accurate in order to give readers an authentic insight into life on Romney Marsh as well as creating engaging stories.
She is actively involved in Marsh Ink Writers' Group as well as writing articles for local magazines.

But First Maintain the Wall is Emma's fourth Romney Marsh novel.

Her first, *A Place Called Hope*, is set in the 16th century and tells the story of the lives of three young women living through the decline of the remote settlement of Hope on Romney Marsh.

Her second novel, *Secrets of the Shingle*, is a mystery set on the wild, windswept wastes of the Dungeness peninsula in the 19th century and seen through the eyes of a naive young school teacher.

Her third, *What The Monk Didn't See,* is the story of New Romney and the 1287 storm which changed the fortunes of the town forever.

For more details take a look at Emma's website:
www.emmabattenauthor.com

712
78
185
40.
75.
20.
₃200
_____
1308
− 355
_____
953
− 111
35
10
25
198
279
150
_____
429

953
429
_____
524
− 40.
− 34
_____
450.
− 60
20
(330)
50.
_____
300.